# TRESPASSES

# TRESPASSES

*Louise Kennedy*

RIVERHEAD BOOKS

NEW YORK

2022

RIVERHEAD BOOKS
An imprint of Penguin Random House LLC
penguinrandomhouse.com

First published in hardcover in Great Britain by Bloomsbury Publishing, London, 2022
First North American edition published by Riverhead, 2022

Grateful acknowledgment is made for permission to reprint lines from "The Irish for No"
by Ciaran Carson from *The Irish for No* (1987). Reproduced by kind permission of
the author's estate and the Gallery Press, www.gallerypress.com.

Library of Congress Cataloging-in-Publication Data
Names: Kennedy, Louise (Ph. D.), author.
Title: Trespasses / Louise Kennedy.
Description: New York : Riverhead Books, 2022.
Identifiers: LCCN 2022005718 (print) | LCCN 2022005719 (ebook) |
ISBN 9780593540893 (hardcover) | ISBN 9780593540916 (ebook)
Subjects: LCSH: Northern Ireland—History—1968–1998—Fiction. | LCGFT: Historical fiction.
Classification: LCC PR6111.E553 T74 2022  (print) |
LCC PR6111.E553 (ebook) | DDC 823/.92—dc23/eng/20220307
LC record available at https://lccn.loc.gov/2022005718
LC ebook record available at https://lccn.loc.gov/2022005719

Printed in the United States of America
1st Printing

BOOK DESIGN BY LUCIA BERNARD

*For Stephen, Tom and Anna*

There is a melancholy blast of diesel, a puff of smoke which
  might be black or white.
So the harbour slips away to perilous seas as things remain
  unsolved; we listen
To the *ex cathedra* of the fog-horn, and *drink and leave the
  world unseen*—

CIARAN CARSON, "THE IRISH FOR NO"

Ah! That first affair, how well one remembers it!

STANLEY KUBRICK, *BARRY LYNDON*

# TRESPASSES

# 2015

They follow the guide, a thin, pale girl. She's wearing a linen sheath dress in moss green, and there's a fine spiky tattoo wound around her right arm that looks like barbed wire. Cushla moves to the edge of the crowd, away from the French and Italian tourists in expensive rain gear; her own age, which still surprises her. Away from the man on her left, pushing fifty, with steel-gray hair that's greased back, small glasses, and a soft wool jacket.

The guide stands slightly to the side of the next exhibit, a couple feet from Cushla. This close, she can see the barbed pattern on the girl's skin. It's gorse, spiky tendrils of stems and golden flowers. Cushla likes her for it, for choosing the shrub that chokes the hills here, not roses or butterflies or stars.

It's a piece of sculpture, made of resin, fabric, glass fiber. A white figure on a plinth, chalky, sarcophagal, a shrouded look about the face, features indistinct. The body is oddly sexless, though it is male; there is breadth in the torso, bulk at the chest. From the waist up he looks peaceful, sleeping head resting near the bend of an arm. There is something not right about the pose, though; his limbs are splayed awkwardly, have not been arranged.

The girl begins to speak. This work is from the seventies, she says. The artist was moved to make it when her friend was murdered. While the almost classical composition is a familiar representation of death, the disordered configuration is shocking, hinting at the violence of the moment of the subject's murder and the chaos of the hours that followed. She gives us her friend as Everyman, yet his rather untidy bearing makes him human.

The others move toward the next piece, a structure like a TARDIS fashioned out of six doors taken from Armagh Prison. Cushla hangs back and steps toward the sculpture. The girl with the gorse tattoo was wrong. The artist hasn't shown Everyman. The detail is intimate, accurate even, almost as if the cast had been molded over his body. The neat ball of fat at his middle. The slight raise of his right shoulder. A doughiness about the jaw. She looks at his face, afraid she will see fear or pain, but he looks just as he did when he was sleeping.

Someone touches her arm. It's the man with the small glasses.

Miss Lavery, he says. Do you remember me?

# The Irish for No

# 1

Cushla wrapped her handbag in her coat and pushed it into the gap between the beer fridge and the till. Her brother, Eamonn, was bent over the counter with a stock list. He looked up at her and his eyes narrowed. He inclined his head at the mirror that ran the length of the bar. Cushla leaned in to check her reflection. Father Slattery had marked her with a thick cross an inch wide and two inches long. The rub of her finger raised the piney, resinous scent of whatever blessed unguent the ashes were mixed with and blurred the cruciate shape to a sooty smudge.

Eamonn slapped a wet serviette into her hand. Hurry up, he hissed.

Most of the men who drank in the pub did not get ashes on Ash Wednesday or do the Stations of the Cross on Good Friday or go to Mass on Sunday. It was one thing to drink in a Catholic-owned bar; quite another to have your pint pulled by a woman smeared in papish war paint. Cushla buffed until the skin on her forehead was pink, the serviette blackened, flittered. She tossed it in the bin.

Eamonn muttered something under his breath. The only word she could make out was *eejit*.

The regulars were lined along the counter. Jimmy O'Kane, the single egg he bought for his tea bulging in his breast pocket. Minty, the school caretaker, who got through so much Carlsberg Special Brew the pub won an award for having the highest sales in Northern Ireland, even though he was the only customer who drank the stuff. Fidel, in his khaki cap and tinted glasses. By day he measured mint imperials and clove rock in his mother's sweetshop; by night he was brigadier of the local branch of the Ulster Defence Association. A fitter from the ship-yard called Leslie, who didn't speak until he was drunk and one night told Cushla he'd love to bathe her. Another man. Middle-aged, with a whiskey in front of him. Dark-eyed, faintly jowly. He was wearing a black suit and a stiff white shirt from which the collar had been de-tached, clothes that were conspicuous among the overalls and drip-dry fabric. His hair was flat to the ears then wavy at the nape of his neck, as if it had been sweating under a hat. Or a wig.

Cushla climbed onto a stool to turn up the volume on the television. When she climbed down, the man with the whiskey was flicking at the filter of his cigarette with his thumb, as if he had just looked away.

The news started the way it always did, with a montage of short scenes. A riot. A boy of six or seven climbing up the side of a Saracen personnel carrier to poke a stone into one of the slits from which the soldiers pointed their guns. A march on Stormont, thousands moving up the long avenue to the parliament building. They had added a new one. A single parked car on an empty street. It looked like a photograph until the car bulged and exploded into a great ball of smoke and fire and its doors somersaulted away from it, glass from the surrounding buildings falling like hail onto the tarmac. The segment finished where it always did, on an image of Mary Peters holding up her Olympic medal.

She won that three years ago, Eamonn said.

It's the last thing that happened here we can be proud of, said the man. His voice was deep, almost rough, despite his refined accent.

Right enough, Michael, said Eamonn.

How did Eamonn know his name?

Fidel inclined his head at the newsreader. Barry's had the beard trimmed, he said, looping his own brush around his thumb and teasing it into a long, tapered point.

The news. A country road; a police Land Rover parked sideways across its white lines, a pair of legs draped in cloth protruding from a bald whitethorn hedge. Men in balaclavas behind a Formica table, woolly faces pressed to a row of microphones, lit sporadically by camera flashes. A pub with no windows, damp smoke wheezing from a crater in the roof.

The last item on the news was a human interest story. Everyone liked this part because it was usually something nonpartisan they could comment on. A reporter had been sent into the city center to ask people what they thought of streaking. It's ridiculous, said a woman in a knitted hat, sure it's far too cold. There were sniggers around the bar. A tiny man slick with Brylcreem said he'd do it if somebody paid him enough. The next man barked "it's obscene" and walked off. Then they stopped a girl with long dark hair and big eyes. She was wearing an Afghan coat, the collar fluffed up around her face. I think it's fantastic, she said, something different. She seemed stoned.

She has the look of you about her, Cushla, said Minty. Would you be up for a bit of streaking yourself?

Leave my sister alone, you pervert, said Eamonn, smirking. Normally she would have had a reply that would shut them all up, but she was aware of the man with the neat whiskey and tidy nails.

Eamonn told Cushla to do a sweep for empties. She went onto the floor. Three men with crew cuts were at a corner table cluttered with soapy-looking tankards. As she reached for the last, one of them placed it on the carpet. You forgot one, he said, his Adam's apple bobbing in his neck. She bent to pick it up and he laid his hands on her hips, just above her arse. She eased herself free of him and went back to the bar to the sound of their laughter.

Did you see what that soldier did? Cushla asked Eamonn as she dumped their glasses in the sink.

No. He said it without looking at her and she knew he had.

He frigging groped me.

What do you want me to do about it? he said, only it wasn't a question. He couldn't do anything.

They lived in a garrison town, although it had not felt like one until 1969, when the troops were sent in; not that the soldiers ever patrolled the streets there. The Laverys met them across the bar, when they were out of uniform. The first few regiments were all right. Then the Paras arrived. They liked to leave reminders. Cigarettes ground out on the carpet, tiles they had peeled from the wall lying broken on the floor of the gents'. The day after Bloody Sunday, a group of them came into the bar. Even Fidel and the boys were uneasy in their company and soon there was just Gina and Cushla and the soldiers; her father was too sick to work. Gina sat on the stool, pushing her glass under the optics, watching them. She managed to ignore them until one took a bite from his beer glass, the others egging him on, and spat splinters and blood into the ashtray. Cushla had watched as if it was a horror film as her mother strode across the floor. What English jail vomited you lot up? Gina said, before phoning the barracks; she had rung to complain so often she knew the commanding officer by name. She told him in her telephone voice to remove his men, that they weren't welcome anymore. The military police took them away, but the sight of squaddies in the pub still made Cushla uneasy. Gina had shown her hand.

When she could bear to raise her head, the man gave her a smile. His eyes were kind. He had heard everything, and she was ashamed, more for Eamonn than herself, and set about tidying the shelves of bottled beer.

Nice view, an English voice said. She glanced in the mirror. The groper was standing at the counter, a banknote in his hand. Behind her, the beer tap gasped as Eamonn pulled pints for him.

She's pretending she can't hear me, the groper said.

Perhaps because you are humiliating her, said Michael. Cushla felt herself turn. He had swiveled on his stool and was facing the soldier, the whiskey resting on his left palm.

Come on, mate. I'm having a laugh, the soldier said, so shrilly he sounded like a whining child.

Humor is most effective when it's mutual, Michael said.

The groper leaned forward, paused, then drew his neck back in, as if he'd thought better of it. He picked up the three glasses awkwardly and went back to the table, beer dribbling across the floor. Eamonn was staring implacably at the television, but she knew by the set of his chin he felt emasculated. Fidel and the others too looked as if nothing had happened. Who was this man?

She busied herself, wiping, tidying, trying not to look at him. The door banged. The soldiers' table was empty, a couple of inches of lager left in the bottom of each glass.

The regulars began to slope home. You should get out of here for an hour, Cushla told Eamonn. See the kids before they go to bed.

I don't want to leave you on your own.

I'll be fine now.

OK then. Give me a ring if you've a problem, he said, and then he was gone.

Michael lit a cigarette and blew the smoke down his nose. Throw another in there, please, he said, sliding his glass at her.

She glanced in the mirror as she was pouring his drink. He was watching her. She was emboldened by having her back to him and didn't look away.

She put the whiskey on the counter. Cushla, isn't it? I'm Michael. Would you like one yourself? he said, closing his fingers around the tumbler. The room looked better with him in it. Behind him, the shabby lanterns that were fixed to the walls were casting circles of warm light on the teak tables, and there was a squalid opulence about the jade-green tweed that upholstered the banquettes and stools.

I'm teaching in the morning. Thanks, but, she said.

Where do you teach? he said. It was one of those questions that people asked when they wanted to know what foot you kicked with. What's your name? What's your surname? Where did you go to school? Where do you live?

I teach P3s in St. Dallan's.

So the children are seven or eight? That's a nice age.

It is, she said. I had P1s for the first two years. Spent most of my time bringing them in and out to the toilet.

You brought the children to get ashes this morning, he said.

He must have seen her removing them. Eamonn's irritation with her. Yeah, she said.

I lived in Dublin in my youth, he told her. It's wall-to-wall Catholics down there, you know. It was said lightly, but he was looking at her so keenly it was a relief when he took his eyes from hers and drank.

I got ashes this morning myself, said Jimmy O'Kane in a loud whisper.

You made a better job of getting rid of them than I did, said Cushla.

A wee taste of Lifebuoy on a dishcloth, said the old man.

Cushla glanced at Michael. His eyes were creased in amusement.

She made a cup of tea and pulled the stool around to face the tele-

vision. A drama had come on. Helen Mirren was lying on a settee stroking a white cat, while her husband was confronting Malcolm McDowell
about sleeping with her. Cushla didn't know why she would go next to
or near McDowell, who was skinny and cruel looking and wearing a
prissy blue jumper, when she was married to Alan Bates, who was thick-
set and brooding. Helen Mirren got up and walked around the room.
She was wearing a white shirtwaister. She looked classy. Cushla had on
a pink cheesecloth shirt and jeans with a patch that said "Push My Panic
Button" sewn on one of the back pockets.

Jimmy finished his pint, bottom lip working at the rim to catch every drop, and patting his breast pocket gently, shuffled out the door.

Michael ordered another drink. He told her the drama was Play of
the Year in 1960. He thought Mirren was put to poor use and that Mc-
Dowell had been pigeonholed by doing *A Clockwork Orange.* Cushla
told him she couldn't finish the book, never mind watch the film. Oh,
but the film was beautiful, he said, even its violence is exquisite. He said
he knew the man from Armagh who played the cripple. He wrote a bit
himself. A couple of documentaries, short plays. Barristers are frus-
trated actors, he said. He talked as though he was used to being listened to.

When Eamonn came back he pinched Cushla's cheeks as if she was
a toddler. Thanks for babysitting, he said to Michael.

I'm twenty-four, Cushla said. Eamonn regarded her with his usual
blend of disdain and indulgence; Michael with an expression she
couldn't read.

He left when she did, holding the door to let her walk out ahead of
him. Her arm brushed his as she passed. He felt solid, substantial.

The pub was down a slip road at the end of the main street, overlooked from behind by the clock tower that stood in the grounds of the
ruined priory and, from the front, a low-rise block of council flats. She

crossed the dim car park to where she'd left her little red Renault, near the underpass that ran beneath the new dual carriageway to the lough shore. There were voices bouncing in the concrete tunnel, cigarettes sparking in the dark. An acrid smell from the water, the hum that came before the tide rose, oily and muddy.

Good night, Cushla, called Michael. He was beside a big brown car near the entrance to the pub.

Cheerio, she said. When she turned on her headlights he was still standing there, a heaviness about his shoulders that made him look older than when he was sitting at the counter.

The police had made a Control Zone of High Street and it was desolate. As she approached the bank, three men spilled onto the pavement from another bar. The soldiers from earlier. The groper stumbled in front of her car and Cushla had to press the brake to the floor to avoid hitting him. He clapped his hands on her bonnet and peered through the windscreen. When he saw it was her, he flicked his tongue out and wiggled it, an obscene gesture made ludicrous by the youth of him. Headlights lit up her car from behind and she checked her rearview mirror. It was Michael. He raised a couple of fingers at her and waited, engine idling, until the boy's friends pulled him away. Cushla set off slowly, leaving them laughing on the curbside. Michael trailed her home and, flashing his lamps once, continued out the road toward the hills.

The bay window on the ground floor of the Laverys' house was indecently bright among the dark facades of the other houses. Inside, Cushla drew the gold velvet curtains in the front room. The embers had sunk low in the grate, a fur of white ash that collapsed to dust when she emptied the tall brass ashtray that was standing by her mother's armchair.

She put the fireguard in place, switched off the lights, and climbed the stairs.

Is that you? said her mother.

Who else would it be? said Cushla, pushing open her door. Gina Lavery was reclined against three pillows, a pair of knickers over her rollers. The radio was on low. She always left it on all night, said it was company. Some mornings she told Cushla things she had dreamed, about George Best and round-the-world yacht races and the US space program, only to find out they were true when the newspaper was delivered. All that subliminal information she was taking in.

You left the curtains open again, said Cushla.

Who'd waste a bullet on me? said Gina. She was trying to sound imperious, but there was a cloy in her voice from the sleeping tablet. Were youse busy?

The usual. And three soldiers as well.

Scum.

I let Eamonn go home for a wee while.

I don't like you standing behind that bar by yourself.

It was OK. A man called Michael kept me company. About forty-five. Dark. Awfully-awfully. Said he's a barrister.

Michael Agnew. And he's fifty-odd, said Gina.

He looks younger, said Cushla.

Is he still gorgeous? said Gina. He was a lady-killer in his day. God, I haven't seen him for donkey's years. He got on great with your daddy.

Eamonn was thirty-two, and had worked in the bar since he was fifteen. He must have remembered Michael from then. Where does he live? Cushla asked.

In a big house out the hill road. Has a flat in town as well. The wife wouldn't be great, said Gina. Then she did that thing that all the women in her family did when they felt sorry for someone: crumpled one cheek and mouthed the word *help* out of the side of her face. It was short for "God help her."

What's wrong with his wife?

Gina tilted her hand to her mouth as if she was throwing a drink into it. She's from Dublin, she said, as if that explained it.

Oh? Is she a Catholic?

No, she's from some posh Protestant family.

Do they have kids?

A son. He must be seventeen or eighteen now.

Cushla leaned over her mother and kissed her cheek, taking in her sad scents. Je Reviens and cigarettes. Setting lotion and gin. Michael Agnew's wife was not the only woman who was fond of the drink.

In her room, Cushla laid out clothes to wear to work in the morning. A-line plaid skirt, navy lambswool jumper, gray blouse. Like a school uniform. She had never given much thought to how she looked behind the bar, throwing on clothes she didn't mind spattering with bleach, tying her hair up to keep it from her eyes. Not until now.

# 2

Her mother's cough woke her, a treacly hack that made Cushla feel sick. She got out of bed and opened the curtains an inch. Morning was struggling through a seam of low, gray cloud. A figure came out of the house across the road and dropped to the ground as if he was about to do push-ups. It was Alistair Patterson, a prison officer who claimed to be a civil servant, checking under his car for a bomb. His wife was watching from the doorstep in a turquoise nightgown, holding their dog.

The storage heater under the window hadn't taken the chill from the room, and Cushla dressed quickly. Her breath fogged the bathroom mirror as she washed and applied a cursory amount of makeup. Downstairs, she put the kettle on and slotted a slice of bread in the toaster. She went to the back door and opened it, fanning it back and forward to expel the stale smoke and cooking smells. Rain began to fall, slow, heavy drops that clattered on the lid of the bin. Soon it was coming so fast it splashed on the black and white tiles. She closed the door again and made breakfast for her mother, carrying it upstairs on a tray.

Gina was as Cushla had left her the night before, with the addition of a lit cigarette. The knickers had slid down her forehead.

Someday I'll come home and find you burned to a crisp, said

Cushla, confiscating the cigarette and stabbing it into the cut-glass ashtray on the bedside table.

Gina lugged herself upright and took the tray from Cushla. She picked up a piece of toast and bit the center, her mouth contorting in disgust as she chewed. It could do with more butter, she said.

Butter's bad for you, said Cushla.

It's so dry I'm more likely to choke to death than have a stroke, she said, tossing the slice back onto the plate. And you needn't think of giving me margarine. She pronounced it with a hard *g*, as if she had been about to say *Margaret* but changed her mind at the last minute. Gina would not have baked beans or corned beef or beetroot in the house. She had an aversion to relishes because she had worked in a piccalilli factory during the war and had to wear gloves to dances so the GIs couldn't see the yellow staining on her fingers. Cushla's father had tolerated her snobberies. Gina grew up hungry, he said, so it makes her feel good to be picky.

Cushla went downstairs, grabbing her basket from the hall table, and set off for school. The Laverys lived in a row of redbrick Edwardian houses. Opposite were homes from the same period clad in white stucco. The dwellings got smaller and more modest as the road neared town, and the final stretch was lined by plain terraces that had been built in the fifties. In summer, Union Jacks flapped from their windows, and without them the houses looked boxy and spartan. A small figure was rounding the corner toward the narrow street that led to the school. It was Davy McGeown, a child in her class. He had no coat on. She tried to avoid the puddle that formed outside the chippy on rainy days, but another car was coming toward her. The water made a whooshing sound as Cushla's tires displaced it. She glanced back to see Davy, arms out, looking along the drenched length of himself.

She drove through the gates at the rear of the school, parking quickly.

Inside, she walked against the arriving children along the corridor that led to the main entrance. Davy came dripping through the doors, his skin ruddy with cold.

I soaked you, she said.

He shook his head like a puppy, showering her with drops of rain. I'm all right, he said through chattering teeth. She brought him to the staff toilet and went at his face and hair with a series of paper towels. He winced at their roughness.

The bell rang. That'll have to do, she said.

Mr. Bradley, the headmaster, was in the corridor when they came out. He loomed over Davy and said, Where's your coat?

I forgot, sir.

Right, he said, as if he was trying to think of an appropriate punishment. Davy's name sometimes came up at staff meetings. His father was a roofer who rarely seemed to have work, his mother a Protestant, and though the children were being brought up Catholic, she had not turned. For Bradley, they might as well have been members of the Manson family.

It was just a mistake, said Cushla, placing her hands on Davy's shoulders and steering him away.

Some of the other teachers expected the children to stand when they entered, but Cushla liked to slip in and hear the chatter. Davy went to his seat in the front row, under Cushla's nose: not because he was naughty but because the others tormented him. Cushla emptied her basket, hanging her coat on the back of her chair. The children fell quiet and posed the way they had been practicing for their First Holy Communion. Hands touching, fingers pointing toward heaven. She led them in a Hail Mary, their mouths so accustomed to reciting it the words were slurred, just sounds and intonations, like an anthem sung at a football match.

Before lessons they did The News. Cushla hated doing The News, but the headmaster insisted. He said it encouraged the children to be aware of the world around them. Cushla thought they already knew too much about the world around them. Davy stood up, always the first to volunteer. His red jumper was dark with damp at the shoulders and neckline.

There was a bomb in Belfast, he said.

He says that every day, said Jonathan, who sat beside him.

Well, today he's right. Thank you, Davy, said Cushla.

Jonathan got to his feet. It wasn't in Belfast, he said. A booby-trap bomb that was intended for a British Army foot patrol exploded prematurely, killing two boys near the border. They died instantly.

Booby trap. Incendiary device. Gelignite. Nitroglycerine. Petrol bomb. Rubber bullets. Saracen. Internment. The Special Powers Act. Vanguard. The vocabulary of a seven-year-old child now.

Well done, Jonathan, said Cushla.

Another boy stood up. There was a thing about streaking on *Scene Around Six*.

Cushla thought of the previous evening in the bar, Michael Agnew swirling his whiskey while Eamonn and the others teased her. And that smile. She felt her face redden.

Enough of that, now. Does anyone have any happy news?

Davy rose again. My da got a job, he said. He looked about him for approval, but the others weren't listening. Running about with no clothes on, one of the boys was saying. In the nude.

Cushla pulled their exercise books toward her and called the children up alphabetically by first name. She had asked them to write a poem inspired by Wordsworth's "Daffodils." Davy had written, "Daffodils are like spears, swiftly swaying to and fro," the words curving into the stem of the single flower he had drawn on the right-hand side of the page. It's brilliant, Davy, Cushla said quietly. He tilted his head as if he was considering his work's merit and went back to his seat.

The last was Zoe Francetti, one of the children from the army barracks. There was a primary school in the compound but sometimes the Catholic ones were sent here. Zoe was from London and had lived in Germany and Hong Kong. It made her seem worldly and exotic, and the other children didn't appear to mind that her father was a British soldier. She had drawn Sindy in a long pink evening gown. It's not what I asked for, said Cushla, but it's really good.

A scrape of a chair. She raised her eyes in time to see Davy close his fist and bury it in Jonathan's upper arm. What's going on? she said.

He said I stink, said Davy.

He didn't stink, but his clothes reeked of cooking. You should have told me, Davy, not hit him, said Cushla.

I'm no tout, he said, holding out a red palm. She was supposed to cane him. If that didn't work, she was supposed to send for the headmaster.

Stand up, Jonathan, she said. The child got to his feet with dignity, as though he was about to make a speech. That was a hurtful thing to say. Tell Davy you're sorry.

Jonathan opened his mouth and closed it. I didn't hear you, she said. Sorry, he said.

Davy, tell Jonathan you're sorry for hitting him.

I'm very sorry, he said, offering his hand to the other boy, who barely touched it, the gesture more punishment than peace offering. She ordered them into opposite corners of the room. They were still there when the headmaster came in with the parish priest.

Father Slattery was wearing a black velvet jacket over his vest and collar, his long face ghoulishly pale, as though all the blood had been drained from him. The school was built on parish land it shared with the church and parochial house. Slattery was wont to roam the playground and school corridors, entering the classrooms unannounced to deliver his frightful catechism. Cushla had complained to Bradley that the visits were unsettling. He's the priest, she was told. She had another reason for disliking him. When her father was in the hospital, delirious with morphine, Slattery had prayed with him and then persuaded him to write a check for a color television.

Two bad boys, said Slattery, taking in the disgraced figures in the corners.

Davy glanced at Cushla, eyes pleading with her. Jonathan was staring at the loop of the leather strap that was sticking out of Bradley's pocket. Cushla turned to him, to appeal to him to stop this, but he was backing out the door.

Slattery crossed the classroom with silent steps. He paused behind Davy, then turned and moved on, coming to stand in front of Cushla's desk. She snapped her fingers at the boys and they scuttled to their seats. Slattery began to recite the Act of Contrition. The children did not join in, afraid, she suspected, of making a mistake.

They don't know their prayers, he said, eyeing Cushla slyly. What else do they not know? An involuntary tut came out of her, and she sat in her chair, folding her arms.

What's the first line of the Confiteor? said Slattery. No one answered. The Mysteries of the Rosary? Still no hand flew up. He began reciting them in his slow, mournful voice. Joyful. Sorrowful. Glorious. Beautiful words intended to terrify them. He stepped toward Davy and pointed a slender finger into his face. What age are you? he said. Davy looked confused, as if it was a trick question. Surely to God you know what age you are, said Slattery.

Seven, said Davy.

Seven. I want to tell you a story about a wee girl not much older than yourself, he said, hands clasped lightly at his chest. She was sent out for a message by her mother, he went on, raising his hands, turning them palms up for emphasis, like he did at Mass. Have any of you been sent out on a wee message by your mother? Some of the children nodded. A gang of men followed her home, he said. They pulled her into an entry. Grown men. They did what they wanted with her, and when they were finished they carved *UVF* onto her chest with a broken bottle.

Was the wee girl seven? Davy said. He was working at his pencil, flaking paint from its chewed end.

It doesn't matter what age she was. What matters is that the Protestants hate us, said Slattery, landing his hands flat on Davy's desk. The thud made the child jump. You're one of the McGeowns, aren't you?

Yes.

You'd need to be listening more than anyone, living in that estate.

The bell rang for break. Its bleat normally made the children push their chairs back and take out their snacks, but they sat on. Laughter and shouts were coming from outside as the other pupils streamed into the playground. A football bounced on the tarmac near the window, momentarily distracting Slattery.

Cushla went to the door and flung it open. OK, class, out you go, she said, but they didn't move. Go! she said, and they rushed past her.

How's your mother? said Slattery.

Fine, said Cushla. She stalked out and along the dim corridor, leaving the priest alone in the empty room.

Gerry Devlin, who taught the other P3 class, was by the kettle. He had only joined the staff in September and had already taken over training the school choir, writing lyrical poems for peace that he set to music, showing Cushla up with his enthusiasm. A watched kettle, he said.

Ha, said Cushla.

How's your morning going? he asked, running a finger around the neck of his shirt, which was purple, with a big rounded collar.

Slattery was in. He grilled the kids on catechism and told them a horrific story.

I get the guitar when I see him coming. Drowns the bastard out.

She couldn't help laughing. Even he doesn't deserve that, she said.

He looked around him wildly, as if he had forgotten something. I'm going to a party, he said eventually. His leg was jiggling, making his trousers ripple like a sail.

That's nice.

Do you want to come?

Cushla hadn't been out since the staff drinks at Christmas. Her social life was limited to driving her mother to Mass and working the odd shift for Eamonn. It would be nice to go out. Even with Gerry Devlin. OK, she said.

What?

I'll go to the party with you.

Great. The bell rang, and he sloshed the rest of his coffee down the sink.

When is it on?

Oh. Saturday night.

The two P4 teachers were sitting near the door. One of them winked at Cushla as she left the room. She would have to suffer sidelong looks in the staffroom until the end of the week. Gerry Devlin lurking by the kettle, asking her questions he'd clearly prepared earlier, the leg going. She should have told him she was busy.

In the classroom, Cushla doled out squat bottles of milk from the crate Paddy the caretaker left—bizarrely—by the radiator every morning and told the children to take a few extra minutes. They lingered by her desk, ripping off the foil caps and stabbing their tongues into the inch of cream that had settled on top.

What's the UVF, miss? said Zoe.

Ulster Volunteer Force, said Jonathan.

Jonathan, you could go on *Mastermind*. Chosen subject "Acronyms of the Troubles," said Cushla.

But was that story true, miss? asked Lucia, when the empty bottles were back in the crate.

Father Slattery is very old, said Cushla—a lie, as the man was scarcely sixty—sometimes he gets mixed up.

Lucia and Zoe looked unconvinced, as if they had understood in some way what had happened to the girl. Children here knew too much.

For the rest of the day, the children were skittish. She allowed them to pack their satchels a few minutes early and they skipped from the classroom before the bell sounded.

The sky was heavy with the threat of rain. By the time she passed the main entrance it had begun to lash down, and dozens of mothers were waiting, umbrellas touching like a badly made quilt. On the other side of the road was the secondary school, where Minty was caretaker. It was attended by Protestants who had not passed the eleven-plus. Bradley's opposite number had agreed to different start, finish, and lunch times because his pupils liked to express anti-Catholic sentiment through song and verse and the throwing of missiles.

Davy was a hundred yards down the road. Cushla braked and pressed the horn, throwing open the passenger door. Do you want a lift? she said.

I'm not allowed to get into cars with strangers.

I'm hardly a stranger. I'll explain to your mummy.

He hopped into the passenger seat. His jumper smelled of steak sausages, but she refrained from reaching for the handle of the window, remembering how hurt he had been that morning. The Laverys' house was on the way to the council estate where Davy lived. Eamonn was rarely at home when the girls were awake and Cushla had said she would come early. She could change now and go straight to the pub after dropping Davy off. She began to tell him to wait in the car, but he was halfway out the door.

Gina was at the kitchen table in her dressing gown, a quilted monstrosity with a purple and orange paisley pattern. There was a bottle of Gordon's gin in front of her, its green glass unseasonably festive. She blinked slowly, like a porcelain doll. I'm not long up, she said, her voice thick.

Cushla leaned into her ear. Please. Just get up.

Gina put her hands flat on the wood and pushed herself upright. She took a step toward the door but her foot caught on the leg of the table. She sat down again.

Jesus, Cushla said, hooking her arm under Gina's and pulling her to her feet.

Davy stood aside to let them pass. Is your mummy all right? he said.

She's just tired. Take a biscuit from that tin by the kettle and I'll be down in a minute.

Cushla hauled her mother up each stair until they were on the landing. She brought her into the bathroom and left her looking at her reflection in the mirror. Cushla went to her bedroom to change for work, reaching for the old clothes she normally wore. She hesitated. Michael Agnew might come in again. She pulled on jeans—a newish pair without patches—and her most grown-up top, black velour with a scoop neckline. It made her breasts look huge, which was not necessarily a good thing; she couldn't picture Michael slobbering over page 3 the way Minty did.

Mummy? she called as she crossed the landing, aware as the word came out of her mouth that it was a ridiculous way for a grown woman to address her drunk mother. There was no reply, so she pushed the bathroom door open. Gina was on the toilet, head lolling gently. Cushla shook her shoulder and her mother tilted toward the wash basin, her cheek sliding down the porcelain. She jolted upright, regarding Cushla suspiciously. Sort yourself out, said Cushla, looking away as her mother groped for her drawers.

Cushla propelled her across the landing and onto her bed. You're awful cross with me, Gina said.

Stop feeling sorry for yourself, said Cushla. She took the cigarettes and lighter from the bedside locker and ran downstairs to Davy.

He had split a custard cream and was gouging the filling from it with his bottom teeth. Is your mummy sick? he said.

Something like that, said Cushla.

He crammed a rectangle of dry biscuit into his mouth. Cushla poured him a glass of milk and he dunked the remaining piece. How the other half live, he said. He said it a second time because he made her laugh.

A hundred yards from Cushla's house was a bend—around which Michael Agnew had disappeared the previous night—that led to a road that ran above the town. For half a mile there were grander houses amidst grounds like parkland and then fields that sloped up to the left, the fairways of the golf club. The carry-on with Gina had taken so long there were teenagers standing at the entrance to the estate Davy lived in, dressed in the uniform of the high school. Boys, their trousers at half-mast, denim jackets over regulation jumpers; girls, who looked years older, lids bruised with blue eyeshadow, strips of blusher on their pallid cheeks. Cushla indicated and waited for a line of armored cars to pass on its way to the British Army barracks farther out the road. A boy was approaching from the opposite direction, in the black blazer of the Catholic grammar school on the outskirts of Belfast. He was neat in himself, hair brushed, shoes polished. There's our Tommy, said Davy. As he spoke, the others began closing in on his older brother. Tommy took a step away from them, but one boy raised his hands and pushed them into Tommy's chest. He stumbled off the pavement and onto the road. Cushla turned the corner and slowed beside him, opening her window.

Do you want a lift? she said.

His face was flushed crimson—with shame, she thought at first—but he said no. He was glowering with rage.

Davy was almost on top of her. Water off a duck's back, he said.

She pretended to adjust her wing mirror to get a look at Tommy. He was walking along the pavement slowly, his head high.

Davy directed her through the grid of beige houses, past curbstones still smudged with the previous summer's red, white, and blue paint. The McGeowns' house was at the very back, a field of gorse rising behind it. Three coal bags were slung by the front door, net curtains shrouding all the windows. The words *taigs out* were dribbling down the low wall that contained their front garden.

Davy insisted she come in. They waited on the doorstep while a series of locks turned. A slim, peroxide-blond woman answered and bent to plant a kiss on Davy's forehead. She was younger than Cushla expected, still in her thirties, but the blue and orange nylon tabard she wore over her clothes gave her the look of someone older. What did I tell you about wearing a coat? she said.

My head's like a sieve, said Davy. Miss Lavery gave me a lift, but.

Betty, said his mother, by way of introduction.

He would have been quicker walking, said Cushla, but he never fully dried out from the drenching he got this morning. I had to call in home and it took longer than I thought it would.

Her mummy's not a bit well, said Davy.

Oh? said Betty.

She could hardly walk.

Betty's eyes widened. Away on, Davy, she said, scanning the street. Her face softened into a smile as Tommy came up the path.

How was your day, love? Betty said.

Grand, said Tommy, raising his chin briefly in Cushla's direction.

Betty began rummaging in the wide pocket of her tabard. You're wheezing, she said.

Tommy had grabbed Davy and was jabbing his fingers between his ribs. How's Wee Man No Height? he said.

Davy wriggled and cried out. Father Slattery was in, he said.

Father Slaughter, said Tommy.

Watch it, you, said Betty, handing him an inhaler.

He gave a small laugh and sprayed it into his mouth, closing his eyes and holding his breath until his hands began to tremble. The rest of his body was still, almost serene. He exhaled slowly. Let me guess, he said. "You're going to hell for being half heathen and living in that estate." He was watching Cushla as he imitated the priest's voice.

Good impersonation, said Cushla, struggling to hold his gaze.

He told us a story, didn't he, miss? said Davy. About a wee girl who got cut with a bottle..

Oh yeah? said Tommy. There was such scorn in his tone she felt she had to get away from him.

I'd better head on, she said, hating the squeak that had come into her voice. I'm late for work.

She walked down the path, the locks turning behind her. In her car, she glanced at the house. The net curtain on the downstairs window had been drawn aside and Tommy was watching her leave, the letters on the garden wall deepening her sense of disquiet. He hadn't told his mother what happened on his way home. Davy hadn't mentioned it either. Tommy was right to have laughed at her. She had sat on her arse and let Slattery terrorize his little brother with jibes he had been subjected to himself at that age.

Eamonn had been expecting her at four. It was a quarter past. As she rounded the bend before home she thought of her mother, slack-jawed on the toilet. She parked across the driveway and ran indoors and up the stairs. Gina was unconscious, right arm flung dramatically across the pillows on Cushla's father's side, the thinness of the limb a worrying contrast with the boozy bloat of her face. Her breath was coming in raspy, irregular sighs. Cushla would have to stay with her. She went downstairs and dialed the number of the pub.

Eamonn was livid. I didn't ask you to work, you offered, he said. I have Leonardo here ready to cover for you. I'm going to have to keep him, for all the use he'll be.

Leonardo's real name was Terry. He was an out-of-work painter and decorator. The only aspect of the job for which he showed any enthusiasm was bringing in the stock, because he could help himself to bottles of cider when no one was looking.

Cushla normally played down Gina's drinking, not to shield Eamonn—for as far back as she could remember their mother had been prone to bouts of drunken melancholy—but out of a sense of failure; she was supposed to be looking after Gina yet was unable to keep her sober. She found herself telling him everything. Gina had been necking from the bottle. The overflowing ashtray was surrounded by cylinders of burned-out Silk Cuts. The lipstick she had at some point attempted to apply adhered mostly to her teeth. Cushla remembered Betty's face when Davy said Gina could hardly walk. She had not looked particularly surprised. For all Gina's efforts at hiding her drinking, trying to stay out of the bar, never leaving the house without her makeup and fur coat, people knew. There must have been a whiff off her in the hairdresser's, in the butcher's. At the altar when she opened her mouth for Communion.

You're exaggerating, said Eamonn.

She's a mess, said Cushla, and I can't leave her.

Look, I need to go. There's a few in already.

Who's there?

Minty's here. And Jimmy. And your babysitter from last night.

Cushla replaced the receiver and looked in the hall mirror. The woman she was willing to be for Michael Agnew was looking back at her. Raging.

# 3

Gerry arrived at the door in a three-quarter-length leather coat in an orangy shade of tan and a manufactured musk so thick Cushla could almost see it.

You've the place nice, he said, taking in the heavy furniture, the flock wallpaper. It was so obvious it was an older person's house that Cushla laughed.

It's my mother's house.

I see. Is she here?

The sitting-room door flew open. Gina came out and gripped Gerry Devlin's hands in hers. Cushla watched, horrified, as her mother turned the smile on him, her back stiffening to show off her bust, one leg slightly forward. She began asking him questions. Where he was from, his mother's maiden name.

My mother died when I was fourteen, said Gerry.

Ach, dear.

She kept at him until she found a connection—his aunt was a neighbor of Gina's sister—and winked at Cushla as they left.

By the car he took off his coat and laid it carefully across the back ledge. She watched him and felt pity. There was a bag of eight-track cartridges on the passenger seat. He murmured apologies and selected one, slotting it into the player. Soft Celtic rock filled the car as he drove off. He whistled along and turned down the road toward Belfast.

What kind of music do you like? he said.

Jazz. She didn't know why she was trying to make him feel inferior.

On the bypass, a fleet of gray Land Rovers was on the inside lane, bombproof maxiskirts skimming the tarmac. He glanced at her and saw she was still holding the bag. Shite, he said, and took it from her, sending the car briefly across the white lines. Cushla snatched it back and placed it at her feet. For a few hundred yards the last vehicle drove alongside them, the armed police it carried alert to erratic driving. Even in the darkness she could see Gerry was flushed.

The city at night. A ferry at the docks, blue-white lights glaring over its bulk. The amber reflection of streetlamps flickering on the black river as they crossed the bridge. Along High Street, past the Northern Whig building, the electricity showrooms, the cathedral. Slowly around Carlisle Circus and the severed plinth that had once held a marble statue of Roaring Hanna, a Catholic-hating pastor. The IRA had blown him up; even dead historical figures were legitimate targets.

It looks funny without your man, said Cushla.

It was the one bomb I had no problem with.

Bottom of the Antrim Road, still scarred by the Blitz, dim gaping spaces where streets had been. Ahead an army checkpoint. Gerry stopped and opened his window. A soldier approached the car, a rifle swinging at his waist. He leaned in. The music sounded like a provocation, the traditional air overlaid with drums and electric guitar. Where are you going, mate? he said.

A party, Gerry said.

I want an address, mate.

Why, do you want to come? said Gerry.

It was meant to be a joke, but the soldier wasn't smiling. He looked over his shoulder and said, We've got a comedian here. A second soldier stepped forward.

Look, we're going to Fitzwilliam Park, Gerry said.

The first soldier opened the driver's door. Step out, he said.

What?

Step out.

Gerry hauled up the hand brake and wiped his hands on his trousers. He got out and stood in front of his car, one button too many open on his shirt, a silver Celtic cross glinting on his chest. The soldiers were bulked out by flak jackets, and between them he looked flimsy; hideous as it was, Cushla wished he was wearing the leather coat. The first soldier swung his rifle to the left, landing it in the center of Gerry's back, and prodded him toward the footpath. The other had walked around the back of the car and was searching the boot. He closed it so hard Cushla jumped. Then he opened a rear passenger door and began rummaging. The coat landed on the hand brake.

He slammed the door shut and tapped his gun against her window. She rolled it down.

You've got the war paint on, sweetheart, he said, his face fully in the car. His complexion was cratered with acne scars and his mouth smelled of Juicy Fruit.

Her hem had ridden halfway up her thighs. She pulled it down over her knees, but the fabric snapped back up when she let go.

Did you hear me? I said you've got the war paint on.

We're on our way to a party.

Is your boyfriend on a promise?

No.

A few feet away, Gerry was facing a brick wall, his hands behind his ears, the scene lit by a streetlamp and the wink of his hazard lights. To his right and left, premises on the row were closed and caged by metal, apart from a chip shop a few doors up, THE RITZ in large red letters on its cracked sign. A length of loose guttering was drooling thick, rusty liquid onto his forehead. He lifted a hand to wipe it away and the soldier tapped his elbow with the butt of the gun.

You're teasing him, then.

No.

You're a prick-tease.

She remembered a recruitment advertisement she had seen in a magazine. *If you've got it in you, the army will bring it out.*

On the footpath, the first soldier nudged Gerry with the butt of the gun again and Cushla opened her mouth to object, but Gerry was walking toward the car, his gait jerky, mechanical, blinking rapidly. He sat in the driver's seat, wiping his forehead with the back of his hand. Cushla took a tissue from her handbag and passed it to him. He blotted his face, hand trembling, and drove off slowly. What did he say to you? he said.

Nothing much. Shite talk.

The road climbed up toward the Cave Hill. He turned left and eventually parked outside a semidetached house with a bay window. Music and laughter were coming from inside. A woman answered the door. She was pregnant, full milky breasts swelling from a lilac empire-line dress. There was a tray of sandwiches in her hand that were curled at the edges. What in God's name happened you? she said.

Don't ask.

She told Gerry to clean himself up and sent Cushla to the sitting room. There was a lava lamp on in a corner, red candles burning in the sort of brass candlesticks old people used when someone died. Carly Simon was playing on the stereo. There were girls draped over the arms of chairs, men standing about holding bottles of beer. A couple of people smiled at her. She stood at the edge of them, wishing Gerry would hurry up. After what felt like an hour, he reappeared, hair wet and combed forward. His attempt at removing the stain from his shirt had left an apricot-colored blot. He looked as though he was coming toward her but made a detour to two men who were by the fireplace. He began talking animatedly, lifting the shirt off his skin with his thumbs and index fingers, looking down at himself. Cushla crossed the room to them.

Oh, he said, as if he had forgotten he had brought her. This is Cushla.

His friends were called Harry and Joe.

Youse got pulled over, Joe said.

Bastards, Harry said, in a Derry accent.

I teach in St. Finbar's, said Joe. The soldiers lie in front gardens training guns on the boys when they're going home from school.

Thirty thousand troops, said Harry, in a place this size. That's not counting the police.

An argument had started by the stereo. A man with a furry black beard was holding a record high in the air and a girl was reaching up, giggling, trying to take it from him. We're having a fucken singsong, and that's the end of it, he was shouting.

Get the guitar, Devlin, said Harry, and Gerry went to his car.

Joe stood looking at his feet. You wouldn't see many soldiers over your way, he said, glancing slantways at Cushla.

Only when I'm pulling pints for them, she thought, and said nothing.

"Give Peace a Chance!" somebody shouted when Gerry came back.

Or you could sing your own song about peace, said Cushla.

What's this? said Harry.

What do you want to sing? said Gerry, as if Cushla had not spoken.

I'm not singing, said Harry, not a hope. He said it three times, hands up in refusal, protesting all the way to the settee, where space had been made for them.

He began to sing "The Town I Loved so Well," a song about how the Troubles had changed Derry. Everyone joined in; everyone but Cushla. As she listened, it struck her hard what an outsider she had become. In school and in college she had been surrounded by Catholic girls like her with whom she had swapped illicit copies of Edna O'Brien books and secrets. Cushla was the only one who lived outside Belfast, albeit just a few miles away. As things in the city worsened, she had begun to lose touch with them, and on the rare occasions they met now, they treated her like a tourist. She felt like one here, watching how easy the others were in themselves and with each other.

Harry lowered his voice for emphasis as he sang the last line, a cry of hope for better times. Fuck this, he said when the cheering subsided. I'm depressing myself.

The couple were back at the stereo. A Disney record came on and they began to do a marionette dance to a song from *Pinocchio*. She followed Gerry and his friends to the kitchen, where he made a big show of pulling out a chair for her. On the back of his shirt there were five small interlocking rings in a pattern like the Olympics logo, where the soldier had poked him with his greasy gun. She had a vision of him under the broken pipe. He would have a better night without her, but she couldn't ask him to take her home. The pregnant hostess was behind them, tipping crusts from a paper plate into the bin. Cushla had forgotten to ask her name and it was too late now. She smiled at her. The woman blew her hair from her face and rolled her eyes.

The people of Ballymurphy don't want power-sharing, Joe was saying, they want a fucking revolution.

Sorry, Gerry said. I'm neglecting you.

You're not, she said, checking her watch under the table. It was a quarter past eleven.

Gerry says your ones have a pub? said Harry.

Yeah, said Cushla.

There's hardly a bar left up our way, said Joe. Most of them have been blown up.

The ones that haven't don't inspire a lot of confidence, said Harry.

Aye, said Joe. They just haven't been blown up yet.

They both laughed.

Cushla did not care for the accusation that was implicit in their patter, that her family's lives were easy because the town they lived in was "mixed" and had seen little trouble. In the pub, Cushla had heard people say it was "very mixed," pursing their mouths in distaste because they had to share the place with Catholics who barely made up 10 percent of the population. Eamonn didn't even buy a Belfast newspaper for the pub anymore because of what the selection might say about him.

It's not that great over our way either. My brother stands behind the bar every night afraid to open his mouth in case he offends somebody and ends up on a loyalist hit list.

Do me a favor, said Joe. It's not exactly a war zone. Try getting stopped and searched by British soldiers every time you go out the door.

If it was a competition, Joe had won.

She went upstairs to use the bathroom. One of the doors off the landing was open, the bedroom bunged with fake Louis XIV–style furniture, white with gold beading. On the bed there was a mound of coats, sheepskin and leather and fake fur. She heard a moan and went

36

into the room. The furry man was facing the corner, in a gap to the left of a wardrobe. Cushla was about to ask if he was all right when she noticed a leg, frilled at the shin with partially removed hosiery, clinging to the back of his thigh. She fled, the wardrobe creaking rhythmically in her wake. She felt a lick of desire.

# 4

They pushed through the foyer, the smell of face powder and cigar smoke cut sometimes by the damp night air that swept in every time the doors opened. They found a spot at the edge of the room, by a ledge that ran the length of a vast window, and Gerry went to the bar. A couple sidled in beside Cushla, murmuring appeasements. They appeared both well-to-do and scruffy, the woman in an astrakhan coat that glistered under the strong lights, the man with fine bones and floppy, thinning hair. They were looking toward the entrance as though they were waiting for someone. The man raised a hand and they shuffled a little away from Cushla to make room for a tall man with a broad back. As he moved, his elbow jabbed Cushla's arm. He turned to apologize and said, There you are. Her heart lurched up into her throat. It was Michael Agnew.

He introduced her to Penny and Jim, remembering her name and telling her they were great friends of his.

Jim clapped his hands. Would you like a drink, Cushla?

My friend's getting me one.

He left Penny looking from Michael to Cushla. How do you know each other? she said. She was smiling, but there was something else in the look that made Cushla feel uncomfortable. And where was Michael's posh Dublin wife?

I know everybody, said Michael. Have you seen *Philadelphia, Here I Come!* before, Cushla?

I know nothing about it, she said.

Jim came back, his fingers threaded around three whiskies. Their glasses made a genial ring as they clinked. Cushla looked at the floor, wishing she had something to do with her hands.

Gerry returned with lager dripping from his wrist, sideburns constricted into tight curls. He handed Cushla a rum and Coke and took a slug from his pint, wiping his mouth on the back of his hand. Michael was looking at her expectantly.

Gerry, this is Michael Agnew, she said.

Hello, said Gerry, his mustache a fringe of beer froth.

Michael said hello, then introduced Jim and Penny.

After a few interminable seconds, Jim punched Michael lightly on the shoulder. We thought you'd gone underground, Agnew, he said. Almost imperceptibly, they turned away.

Gerry raised his eyebrows at their backs. You know who they are, don't you? he said.

Michael was in the bar one night. I've only just met the other two, said Cushla, her voice scarcely above a whisper in the hope that Gerry would lower his.

He asked her if she went to the theater much, a variation on "Do you come here often?" A pathetic question to ask on a second date. She wanted to tell him she had hardly been out in two and a half years, that since her father died she had cleaved herself to her mother and the house, in a sort of heartsick stasis, but who'd want to hear that? No, she said.

Thanks for coming, he said. I thought you were avoiding me.

Why would I do that? she said. She had been avoiding him. When he dropped her home from the party he had launched himself across the gearstick at her, his tongue out before he'd reached her lips, lunging twice to find her mouth. An excruciating effort he must have thought was expected of him.

OK, well that's good. I was afraid it would be awkward.

As she opened her mouth to answer, an announcement came over the tannoy, *The performance will start in five minutes*, and she was spared the trouble of replying.

Gerry said he was sorry they were so far from the stage, but Cushla liked their seats at the very back, watching the audience come through the side doors, edging along the rows. Another announcement, *The performance will begin in one minute*. Far below, Penny took her seat, then Jim. Michael was behind them, bending sometimes to talk to someone as he inched across. When he reached his seat he paused, his back to the stage, eyes moving slowly over each row until they seemed to rest on Cushla. She looked to her left, expecting to see someone holding a hand up at him in greeting, but the woman next to her was reading the program.

What were you going to tell me about those three in the bar? she asked Gerry.

The man's a historian, lectures in the university. She's an artist.

What about your man Michael?

He's a barrister. He made that documentary about the 1798 rebellion that caused ructions. He's been outspoken against internment, defended a few of the civil rights crowd when nobody else would touch them. He's all right, he said.

"All right" meant he was not a bigot.

The house lights fell and the stage lights rose. Two actors played the main character, showing his public and private selves as he prepared to leave for America. Gar Private was played by a big man with a north

Antrim accent. There was terrible anguish in his lines, in his delivery. Sometimes her eyes wandered to where Michael Agnew was sitting in the third row from the front. His face was tilted slightly to the left. There were people all around him, but he looked quite alone.

At the interval, they went downstairs. There was a long table of drinks in the foyer with receipts tucked beneath them. Gerry hadn't ordered in advance and left her again for the bar. She went to the ledge where they had stood earlier, both their coats clutched against herself, Gerry's jacket with its rusty sheen facing outward, making her arms sweat. She had put on a dress cut in a low V at the front; black jersey printed with beige-stalked lilies, their blossoms lime-white. It had begun to cling, and as she lifted the fabric from her chest she was aware of someone standing in front of her. It was Michael, holding two whiskies. All the times she had tried to construct his face, she had given him dark brown eyes but could see now that they were lighter than that. Hazel, flecked with pieces of gold.

He offered her one of the glasses. I ended up with two by way of a happy misunderstanding, he said. Cushla hated whiskey. She took it from him so he'd stay. He asked her if she was enjoying the play.

I didn't think the two-actor thing would work, but I love Gar Private. It's sad, but, she said. There was merriment in his eyes as he watched her speak. She wondered if he found her silly, but then he nodded slowly, as if she had given the correct answer.

He had seen the original production in the Abbey in the sixties, he said, and asked her what else she liked about it.

I like how he calls the place Ballybeg. Small town.

Do you speak Irish? he said. She liked that he didn't call it Gaelic.

I did it for my A levels. And in teacher-training college. There's not much use for it here.

You have an Irish name, he said.

It's not a proper Irish name. It's one of those made-up ones, like Colleen.

What does it mean?

It's from an endearment. *A chuisle mo chroí*: the pulse of my heart. My da wouldn't have known that. He got it from the John McCormack song.

The pulse of my heart. If anyone heard her.

I knew your father, he said. He was a beautiful man.

He was, she started to say, but his words had slayed her. She took a sip of the whiskey.

I'm sorry, he said. I've upset you.

Don't be. It was lovely, what you said.

When he began to speak again she could feel his breath below her ear, and her shoulder began to curl up involuntarily, as if it was trying to meet his mouth. Some friends and I are trying to learn Irish, he said. We meet every couple of weeks and murder it at Penny's kitchen table. Maybe you'd teach us.

Gerry was between them, then, thrusting another drink at her, only slightly less flustered than on his earlier return. Michael took the empty tumbler from her hand and gave an ironic half bow as he backed away. After the whiskey, the rum and Coke tasted sugary and artificial. She drank it down to be rid of it. An announcement told them the performance was about to resume, and they joined the throng moving toward the stairs. Michael was ahead of them, between Penny and Jim. When they took their seats, he didn't look for her.

There was a lightness in Gerry's step as they walked to his car, as if he had gotten something he was dreading out of the way, an exam or an interview. He put on the Horslips tape that had been playing when the soldiers stopped them and told her about his summer in Israel. The hippie girl from Brooklyn who manned the lookout tower in a sun top, a rifle slung across her chest. The heat haze on the hills. The sense of community. In other ways it's worse than here, he said, if you can imagine that. He wouldn't go back. What were you and Your Honor talking about? he said.

Is that not how you address a judge? He's a barrister, said Cushla.

Oh, excuse me.

He said he's learning Irish.

Exoticizing the natives. Fuck's sake.

Cushla turned away from him and looked out the window. Beyond it the dark acres of the park seemed to stretch for miles. It wasn't like that, she said. He just sounded interested.

Aye, right, said Gerry.

Cushla didn't reply.

When he pulled up outside her house, the hall light was on, a pinkish glow at her mother's window. She pictured Gina sloped against the pillows in the gloom and didn't want to go in alone, to feel the absence of her father. She asked Gerry in for a cup of tea. By the time she had put the key in the lock she was already regretting it.

# 5

Cushla got off the train from Belfast just after four. The sun had come out and the wet platform seemed to be steaming. She exited the station and walked along the esplanade, turning right at the end to go through the tunnel to the pub. Its walls were dabbed with words sacred and profane. FUCK THE POPE AND THE VIRGIN MARY. FOR GOD AND ULSTER. MARTY LOVES DIRTY TITS. Cushla wondered if Dirty Tits was a girl, or if Marty liked tits that were dirty.

The car park was full. Under the round window that was supposed to look like a porthole, the anchor that was attached to the wall had rusted where the black paint had peeled away.

Inside, dust was suspended in tobacco smoke, glittering. The stained glass in the long window on the west-facing wall was throwing gaudy shapes around the room. In the sunlight, the wood was dull with layered polish and the upholstery was shiny from spills and the rub of backsides. The old mirrors advertising bygone distilleries were bleary. The cleaning was supposed to be Gina's department. The room had the creeping decrepitude that lingered about her, with her too-long nails and bleeding lipstick. She used to come in on a Monday with rubber gloves and a housecoat. Cushla couldn't remember the last time she had. Eamonn could have reminded Gina, but Cushla suspected he didn't want her around.

There was horse racing on the television, men gaping at the screen, tension in the set of their shoulders. As the winner passed the post, a tiny man with a purple nose leaped from his bar stool and shouted, "Yeow." Leslie crumpled a beaten docket and tossed it into the ashtray. On Saturday afternoons, Cushla's father would sit her at the counter with an orangeade and get her to put the invoices in alphabetical order. Now her mother was behind the bar; she was meant to be working, but when a customer tried to order from her she smiled beatifically and took a sip of her gin.

Has she been on the gargle all day? Cushla asked Eamonn, who was at the end of the counter, as far away from Gina as possible.

That's her second one.

She must have had something before she left the house.

Fuck's sake, he said. I don't know what she had but she's neither use nor ornament in here.

Cushla looked at her mother. She was still ornament. Still pretty, with her wrinkles blurred by cigarette smoke, her skin softened by the low light. Don't be horrible, she said. She went to Gina and kissed her cheek, laying the things she had bought in town on the shelf, the bag from the bookshop on top.

How was town? said Gina.

Wet. It took ages to get through the security. They made everyone open their umbrellas.

Dear God. What sort of being would put a bomb in an umbrella?

Cushla began taking down the dust-furred Toby jugs, the ceramic Black & White dogs. She filled the sink with soapy water and lowered the knickknacks in. She took down the liqueurs no one ever ordered. Advocaat with its crusty yellow neck. Galliano that smelled like ice cream. Green chartreuse in a square-sided bottle that doubled as an ashtray; there was a black smudge where someone had ground a cigarette. Probably Gina.

That anchor needs a lick of paint, Cushla told Eamonn.

Least of my worries, he said.

She washed and dried and buffed, wiped the shelves, put back the now sparkling tat. She was reaching up to replace a cardboard Babycham fawn when her mother slid off the stool and stepped toward the counter.

Michael Agnew was standing at the bar, Gina reaching her hands to him. Cushla lifted away the overflow tray from beneath the taps, sloshing flat beer down the sink. She hadn't seen Michael since the night at the theater. The evenings she helped Eamonn—several times a week now, which both baffled and pleased him—were a cycle of apprehension and dejection. Choosing her clothes, applying makeup so painstakingly it didn't look like makeup. Watching the door. She thought about him all the time, allowing herself fleets of fancy where she was alone with him in the bar or sitting beside him in the Lyric when the lights went down. Other scenarios that verged on sordid that she tried to put out of her head. Now he was here, she didn't trust herself to speak to him.

Gina was talking in her telephone voice. Cushla had rarely heard her use it away from the hall table, but there was something about Michael Agnew that made you want to be better than you were. Her mother went to the optics and, holding a tumbler under the Jameson, asked Cushla to bring the remainder of the sandwiches to Michael. There were two left. The cheese and pickle one looked fresh but he chose the other, egg and onion sodden with the juice of a cut tomato. The selection seemed like penance. Cushla unwrapped it and put it on a plate with a tin of salted nuts on the side that he hadn't asked for, handing him a knife, a paper serviette. She stayed near him. He ate with big quick bites, like the children in school after PE.

Gina was moving up and down the length of the bar, lifting the odd empty glass, talking to the customers, a mince to her walk that Cushla found appalling. Eamonn's mouth was tight. Gina was getting in his way.

Michael pushed his plate away and thanked Cushla. He pointed vaguely at the bag from the bookshop.

Is that yours? he said.

Yeah. She passed it to him, regretting having drawn a rainbow of tester lipstick on the back of her hand in Boots earlier.

Ah, he said, when it was out of the bag. I've read this.

She had bought a copy of *The Black Prince* by Iris Murdoch because it looked like hard work and might stop her obsessing about him. Is it good? she said.

It's very literary. Shakespeare references, complicated relationships. A bit farcical at times. Mind you, that's almost every one of her novels. He replaced it, smoothing the paper bag. Have you thought any more about coming to our Irish nights? he said.

Cushla found herself blinking at the phrasing. Maybe there was something in Gerry's remark about Michael "exoticizing the natives." It sounded as though he and his friends played at being Irish once a fortnight, which was probably about right. Michael's color had risen. Irish conversation nights, I mean, he said, flustered. It seemed like he was asking her out.

OK, she said.

They would meet on Monday. He would pick her up outside the house at seven. He would drive her there so she would know where to go in future. His voice had dropped to a whisper. Maybe he was asking her out.

What did your young man think of *Philadelphia, Here I Come!*? he said.

Gerry's not my young man. He's a fella from work.

Michael lit a cigarette and didn't say anything.

. . .

When they got home, Gina put a tray of bacon rashers under the grill. She served them in floury baps blobbed with HP sauce. They ate in front of the television, the burned, lardy taste reminding Cushla of Saturday evenings when her father was alive. There was a western on. She and Eamonn had watched it as children. He had been wearing a cowboy suit, a wooden pistol in the holster, and laughed at Cushla for weeping as the Indians were being massacred.

A game show, the hostess twirling like a figurine on the lid of a jewelry box to show off her ball gown. A contestant, slathered in shaving foam, trying to remember the labor-saving devices and toys that had just juddered past him on a conveyor belt.

I can't see the point of those machines that wake you up with a cup of tea, said Gina.

That's because you have me.

It's nice you're in tonight, said Gina. You've been out a good bit lately. She was smiling, but her eyes were shining, as if she was trying not to cry. Cushla felt a stab of guilt and resolved to tell Eamonn she would not be available for the three shifts she had volunteered for: it was enough that she would see Michael on Monday. She stretched on the sofa, a cushion behind her head, and felt her body sink into sleep. When she woke there was a trail of slobber on her chin. Michael Parkinson's guest was Helen Mirren. She looked fabulous, Cushla thought, in a black dress with tiny straps, twirling a long feather in her fingers. Parkinson asked her about being sexy. She made a joke of it, tried to change the subject, but he kept at her, referring to her attributes. Specifically her bosoms.

Dirty article, said Gina.

Isn't he.

I meant her.

# 6

Clothes on her bed, over the back of the Lloyd Loom chair in the corner, drooping from hangers on the front of the open wardrobe door, where they had been considered briefly and rejected. She settled on a bottle-green georgette blouse over jeans; the gray parallels had looked wifey with the top's pussycat bow. She had twice applied eyeshadow and taken it off, but the intention was still on her face. He would be here in a few minutes. She would have to do.

That's nice on you, Gina said when Cushla went downstairs, her mouth pleated at the corners, as if she begrudged the compliment.

Cushla reached for the spark guard. A flame leaped in the grate, catching the notches in the crystal tumbler Gina had tried to hide on the floor beside her chair. Cushla slammed the guard in place, brass jangling against marble.

You're sending all the heat up the chimney, said Gina.

That coal keeps exploding, said Cushla. And will you try and finish each cigarette before you light the next one?

I'm never going to hear the end of it, said Gina. Earlier, Cushla had found the remains of a Silk Cut in the laundry basket, burned out in the molten gusset of an eighteen-hour girdle. Gina said she only wore one the odd time, as if the offense was in needing support underwear and not in almost burning the house down.

I'm away.

Where are you for? said Gina.

I'm going to the pictures with Gerry Devlin, said Cushla. When she invited him in after the theater, he had not attempted to stick his tongue in her mouth. She now thought of him as a friend. And he was a plausible alibi.

The teacher? she said. Will he not come in to say hello?

I told him to wait outside.

You should be looking a fella a bit more sophisticated.

If she knew.

Michael's car was outside the house next door and the extra yards felt like miles. Cushla sat in the passenger seat, clutching her basket to her chest. She had emptied it of schoolbooks and packed it with the Irish texts she hadn't opened since college: a dictionary, a vocabulary book, a phrase book, a grammar book. The seat was as far forward as it would go and her knees were uncomfortably high. She had a sudden picture of Michael's wife, an uncharitable thought: a slight, nervy woman, pressed to the glove compartment, slatternly in herself. She was so taken with the image it was a moment before she realized he was speaking to her.

I'll adjust it, he was saying. He reached down beside her and released a lever that made the seat roll back. The skin on her calf prickled at the nearness of his hand.

I hope you don't mind that I picked you up. I thought it would be the easiest thing for the first time, he said.

The first time.

I don't mind, she said. She took in a breath to settle herself but got a lungful of him instead, a clean, manful smell of soap and tobacco.

How are you getting on with Iris Murdoch? he said.

She cleared her throat. I'm not sure I know what's going on, she said. In the dark his profile was coarse. A forehead that protruded slightly, the line of his nose uneven, as if it had been broken. A full, belligerent set to his mouth. He smiled and his features seemed to soften.

Will you stick with it? he said.

Yeah. I hate not finishing a book.

That's a good policy. Although sometimes I think life's too short.

On the main street, someone had changed the quote from the Bible that was displayed in a glass box outside the apricot-painted Pentecostal church. *The wages of sin is death.*

You Catholics think you have a monopoly on sin, he said.

The gigantic tin 99 that normally stood on the curb outside Fidel's mother's shop was bulging from its doorway. There was a light on upstairs, a couple of figures at the window.

There's a "No Surrender" meeting going on up there, she said, pointing at the first floor. Pity it's clashing with your Irish night.

He had stopped at a pelican crossing. She could sense his head turn very slowly and began to panic that she had gone too far. Their eyes met. He burst out laughing.

Past vast aircraft hangars, the hulking bent heads of the yellow cranes in the shipyard, the hoppy smell from the animal-feed factory beyond the docks seeping into the car as they crossed the Lagan. High Street was ahead of them. Another river runs beneath that street, he said. The city got its name from it. *Béal Feirste*, the mouth of the Farset. It flows through a tunnel under the road now. You can almost sense it, in the breadth and curve of the street, that it's following a river's course. I have a drawing from 1830. People in frock coats walking on the quays, a boat docked beside them. Amazing, really.

His voice was so beautiful she felt as if she was being read to. But the way he said *amazing*, the second *a* long and open. What was she doing in a car with this man, with his genteel accent and urbane manners? Something was rearing up in her, and when they passed the City Hall she heard herself say: My mother comes from behind there. She was trying to tell him she was not like him, but he glanced at her, his face full of encouragement. It disarmed her, and she found herself telling him one of Gina's stories from the war. A GI walked her home from a dance one night and she didn't want him to see how small her house was. There was a light on at one of the upstairs windows on the east side of the City Hall and she stopped, saying: You can leave me here. Daddy's still working in his study. Cushla had delivered the last part in Gina's telephone voice.

Your mother's a character, said Michael.

That's one way of putting it, said Cushla.

He drove up a narrow street. It was blocked at the end by concrete bollards shaped like treasure chests. There was no space to do a three-point turn, no driveways to reverse into. He rested his arm across the back of her seat, turning his head to look out the rear window. A lock of her hair was trapped under his elbow and she felt a tug as he reversed all the way back down. Before he set off, he lifted the curl and laid it on her shoulder, looking at her for a moment.

They were on the Malone Road, passing the big house Cushla's father had grown up in.

Did you visit your grandfather often? said Michael.

She had forgotten, or tried to forget, he had known her father. Perhaps he knew already where Gina was from. Knew Cushla was making a point by telling him. We went to see him a few times a year, she said. A maid in uniform served us lime cordial from a Waterford crystal jug while my mummy sat glaring at me and Eamonn in case we let her down.

I married above myself, Gina said sometimes, making a joke of it. But Cushla could not forget how she was on those visits, every word stammered like an apology for being a millie who had nabbed Oliver

Lavery's eldest son. It didn't help that she hadn't filled her house with children; nine pregnancies and all she had to show for it was Eamonn and Cushla.

Michael turned onto one of the avenues. It had a barracks on the corner, an elegant, understated fortification, the old mansion and fencing painted pigeon gray, a lookout tower on stilts at the edge of the garden, innocuous as a treehouse. Toward the end of the street, he drove between a pair of imposing posts onto a tarmac driveway fuzzy with moss, parking neatly, as if he'd done it many times.

A chipped pot of primroses sat on each side of the front door, which was heavy and coated thickly in navy blue gloss. Michael pressed the bell. Cushla had relaxed in the car but now her chest was tight.

Jim answered in his stockinged feet, bifocals on his head the way women wear sunglasses. *Fáilte*, he said.

Impressive, said Michael. He placed his hand on the small of her back, his touch faint but deliberate. She glanced at him. After you, Miss Lavery, he said, pressing her in ahead of him.

The hallway was high and wide and cluttered. Burgundy paint above a dado rail, tobaccoish Anaglypta below it. A curved wooden chair from the thirties, its seat cushion covered in a William Morris patterned fabric. A large watercolor, a hill beneath a cold blue sky, the dead sedge and heather coral colored. She paused in front of it.

Isn't the light wonderful? said Michael.

It's like somewhere in America you'd see in a film. Arizona or Nevada, she said.

It was January in Donegal. Penny loves the light in winter, said Jim.

The air in the kitchen was warm and garlicky. Penny was wearing a washed-out pink-and-green-checked apron that flared at the waist, over a black sweater dress. Cushla was admiring your painting, Michael said, kissing her on each cheek.

Thanks. It's the only thing I've ever made that I like, said Penny. I'm mucking around with sculpture now.

Jim poured them wine from a bottle covered with woven straw, and they did that wordless salute again, clinking against her glass as an afterthought.

Victorian jelly molds in various patterns and patinas on a long shelf that ran above the kitchen window. A stripped-pine dresser behind the table crammed with silver teapots and ceramic tureens, jars and tins with French labels. *Pâté de campagne, beurre de homard, confit de canard.* Penny laid a heavy blue-and-white platter on the table with both hands. There were anemic-looking biscuits on it smeared with something baby pink and shiny, like Angel Delight. Jim passed Cushla the packet. It had an image of a man in a wig like a sheep's fleece. This is Doctor Oliver of Bath, after whom the biscuits were named, he said. Does he remind you of anyone?

Bugger off, said Michael.

Jim left the table to answer a rap at the door. Voices in the hall, loud then soft, as though they did not want to be overheard. Cushla realized with a pang that they were talking about her.

She recognized Victor from current affairs programs on television. He was short and wiry, wearing a sleeveless khaki jacket with pens protruding from the breast pocket. He was a little out of breath, which gave the impression he had been running around Saigon. Jane had hair the color of toffee and huge brown eyes rimmed by spidery lashes. She said hello in a small voice.

The insides of Cushla's jaws were dry from the wine, as if she had been drinking black tea. She lifted a biscuit and bit it.

What do you think? said Penny.

It's nice, she said, but I didn't expect it to be fishy. They laughed, although whether with her or at her she could not tell. All except Victor,

who was peering at her through the smoke from the cigar he was tok-
ing on in urgent puffs.

Michael tells us you're a native speaker, he said, a slight stress on
"native."

Cushla remembered again what Gerry had said. I did it for my A
levels, she said. "My" had come out as "me." She felt her color rise.

Penny took the platter away and dumped a clatter of bone-handled
knives and forks and a bundle of linen napkins in its place. She lifted
an oval earthenware dish from the AGA and rested it on a rusty trivet
in the center of the table. Its contents were burnished and bubbling,
dark juices dripping down the sides.

Cushla got up. Can I do anything? she said. Penny was buffing the
inside of a wooden bowl with a scrap of garlic. She handed Cushla a tea
towel and asked her to take plates from the warming oven. Behind
them, Michael was saying: Diplock courts . . . no juries . . . not what I
signed up for. The space between the oven shelves was narrow and
Cushla felt a singe on her wrist as it touched hot metal. For a second she
thought she might cry, not in pain, but with frustration. She reposi-
tioned the tea towel and went around the table laying a plate at each
place. Michael watched her reach across him.

You burned yourself, he said. The mark was livid, already rising. He
led her to the sink and held her hand under the cold tap, his thumb on
her pulse. Her heart was clobbering in her chest and she wanted to run
from the house.

Poor Cushla, said Penny, I should have done it myself. Her tone was
kind, but it was the sort of thing Eamonn or Gina might have said.

Cushla slipped into her seat. The others were passing Penny their
plates. Cushla need not have handed them out, but nobody told her.

Moussaka, said Jane, as Penny dug a collop of food from the dish.
Where did you find aubergines?

Lila brought them in her suitcase when she came home for reading week, along with the taramosalata.

You have a daughter? said Cushla.

Penny laid a bowl of crisp lettuce dressed with lemon juice and oil on the table and a basket of crusty bread, torn rather than cut. We have two. Lila's at Cambridge and Alice is at Heriot-Watt, she said, as though Cushla should know where that was.

Jane told them about a contract from Brazil she was working on for an engineering company.

Jane's a Portuguese translator, said Michael.

Do you get a lot of work? said Cushla.

It's as lucrative as one might imagine, said Victor. Jane laid down her knife and fork. For the rest of the meal she spoke when she was spoken to, which wasn't often.

Afterward there were Irish coffees and roughly cut, crumbly fudge. *Sláinte*, said Jim. That accent again.

Michael took his jacket off. She hadn't seen him in his shirtsleeves before and couldn't help staring at his shoulders, the part of a man's body she always noticed first.

Right, said Jim. Let's do this. They were all looking at Cushla.

She took the books from her basket and laid them on the table. Talk among yourselves, she said, and we'll see where you are.

Victor lit another cigar. Tell us about the Irish word for *no*, Cushla.

She knew where this was going. There is no word in Irish for *no*.

*Ní hea*, she said.

That doesn't mean no, though, does it?

It can mean no.

It means "it isn't." It's a tad slippery, don't you think?

They were watching her, waiting for her to answer. What do you mean by slippery? she said.

Evasive. Noncommittal. If someone offers you a drink, how do you say *no*?

*Níor mhaith.* I don't want.

That sounds like a proclamation.

The word had a particular resonance for nationalists, but she could not tell if he was goading her. All evening there had been something arch in the way he spoke to her, but he hadn't been much better with the others. Perhaps some word association of her own was making her see a slur where there wasn't one. Or maybe he was wondering what Michael was at, bringing her along.

She asked them simple questions in Irish; only Michael seemed to have more than a few phrases. He leaned over her book sometimes to see how a word was spelled, his face an inch from hers. So close it was torture.

It was almost eleven when they left. Jim saw them out. When Michael and Cushla were in the car, he called something over his shoulder and slipped back inside, shutting the door abruptly. Cushla pictured him bursting into the kitchen to the others, and was distraught at what was being said in her absence. Beside her, Michael was oblivious.

At the end of the road, something glinted in the fence around the barracks. Gunmetal, or maybe she was imagining it. Instead of driving back the way they had come, he turned right then left into a cul-de-sac lined either side by a long terrace of tall Edwardian houses, parking in front of the last but one.

Back in a tick, he said, leaving the engine running. His feet on the gravel, the rattle of a key in a lock. Light blooming in a window on the middle floor, Michael bent over a table, reaching for something. The room dimmed, the door slammed, and he came back down the steps swinging a holdall that he put on the back seat.

This was my grandparents' house, he said. It was divided into flats when they died. The other two are rented out.

Did he really think they were not so different? Cushla's grandfather had been a teenage runaway from the Falls who won a complex bet and used the proceeds to set himself up as a wine and spirit merchant. Gina said he made most of his money during Prohibition, "smuggling brandy to Al Capone." Cushla's father always laughed it off, but Gina insisted it was true. Oliver Lavery had left the streets for a tree-lined avenue on which his Protestant neighbors considered his gains ill-gotten and kept their distance. Cushla thought of him as lonely. A widower dressed like Fred Astaire, ambling down the road to the Eglantine Inn at four every afternoon in his spats, leaning on a cane. Michael's grandparents were likely to have been among the disapproving neighbors.

Back down the road, past the university, spotlights trained on its ornate tower and buttresses, its immaculate lawn. The road split, then widened. He drove on, waiting at a red light beside the Europa Hotel. Its windows were boarded up again.

The state of it, Cushla said. One of the children told me in The News that they call it the Hardboard Hotel now because it's the most bombed one in Europe. The other kids laughed.

It looks awful, regardless. Ugly bloody thing to throw up beside these beautiful Victorian buildings. The Grand Central bothers me more. The army taking it over was an outrage, he said.

The Crown Bar on their right, the Grand Opera House—also boarded up—on the left. She had never thought of the city as beautiful before. The lights changed and he moved off. A car came fast out of a slip road and his arm flew up, an automatic movement, as if he was trying to stop her from going through the windscreen.

Across town, skirting the cordon around the city center, its empty streets. A prostitute in the shadow of the Albert Clock. The wind lifted a curtain of her bleached hair and she felt above her head for it, the air about her sparkling with damp. Back over the river. Men on the deck of a ship, hunched against the cold, beyond them the black lough. For a mile or so Michael's was the only car on the road. It felt as though they shouldn't be out.

I brought you a book, he said, for when you get fed up with Iris. It's on top of my bag.

When, not if. As though he knew her. She reached behind. The cold leather of the seat. The holdall, bunged with clothes, soft material, flannelette or brushed cotton. He was bringing his dirty laundry home to his wife. She snatched her hand away.

I can't find it, she said.

He pulled into the hard shoulder and retrieved it, handing it to her before setting off again. The dust jacket was missing, its green leather cover split and furred at the corners. *Betsy Gray*, she read aloud. The edition had been published in the sixties, but it looked old.

It's well read, she said.

It's about the ninety-eight rebellion. I read it often. To remind myself that I come from a great liberal tradition, he said.

The shipyard cranes were on their left, colossal yellow angles in the sky. Gina's brother worked two shifts there before his workmates realized he was a Catholic and mangled his hand. Afterward he held his cigarette between his thumb and the stub of his middle finger, all they had left of his digits. Quite the liberal tradition, thought Cushla, putting the book in her basket. She couldn't think of anything more inspired to say than thanks.

The trouble started with industrialization. They used sectarianism to divide the workers, he said. Cushla wondered who he meant by "they."

Are you a socialist or something? she said.

59

Is that very surprising?

Well, yeah. It is.

Why?

Because you're not a wee man in an anorak. Or a hairy student.

A strong labor movement would sort this all out, he said.

Like last year, during the strike? she said.

Of course not. It would have to include Catholics.

They could start by giving us jobs. I can't see that happening, can you?

One has to be hopeful.

They were outside her house. He asked her if she would come with him next time. She said she would.

How do you say that in Irish? he said.

*Tiocfaidh mé.* I will come.

He took her hand and put his thumb on her wrist. The blister had swollen into a plump cushion of water. You were embarrassed when I ran the tap over your burn, he said.

I felt stupid. Your friends must think I'm pathetic.

She knew the kiss was coming but was surprised by its clumsiness, the chink of his teeth against hers, the scrape of his chin. It made her feel tender toward him and she found herself kissing him back gently to soothe him. He withdrew his hand and rubbed it across his face. My circumstances are complicated, he said. I realize how hackneyed that must sound. I won't always be able to get away.

But sometimes you will?

Yes.

OK, she said, because it was all he was offering.

# *Dúil*

## 7

Two men have been arrested in south Down in connection with an arms cache that was found near the border.

A lion escaped from the zoo. Jumped over back gardens all the way to the Shore Road, where it was apprehended by security forces.

The body of a man was found on waste ground in East Belfast in the early hours of the morning. He has not yet been identified.

We'll miss Davy today, said Cushla, taking in the empty chair beside Jonathan.

I won't miss the stink, said Lucia. Zoe giggled.

Ten lines, said Cushla.

But, miss.

Twenty.

Cushla went to the blackboard and wrote:

IF YOU CAN'T SAY SOMETHING NICE, DON'T SAY NOTHING AT ALL.

That's from *Bambi*, said Zoe.

You could learn a lot from *Bambi*, Zoe. And you can do twenty lines for laughing. The girls bent scowling to their pages.

You forgot to say a prayer, miss, said Jonathan.

That's because I'm going to teach you the Hail Mary in Irish, she said. She had forgotten, but it would kill the first part of the morning. She rubbed out the *Bambi* quote and wrote the prayer on the black-

63

board. They lined up to sharpen their pencils in the parer that was clamped to her desk, turning the crank and examining the lead before returning to their seats.

Lucia and Zoe came to Cushla's desk to show her their work. Zoe had drawn cascading stars in the margin. Lucia had corrected the grammar and written *Don't say anything at all.*

Good work. Go back to your seats, said Cushla. Rewarded for the good, punished for the bad. She pictured Michael Agnew in his robes, hair tamped down beneath the wig. The boys and men paraded in front of him, refusing to recognize a British court, answering in Irish they had taught themselves in Long Kesh. No juries, not what I signed up for, he had said.

She had not seen or heard from him since the "Irish night" the previous week. Countless times she had replayed the evening in her head, searching for the word or gesture or pronunciation that had repelled him, that had shown she was too young, too unsophisticated, too Catholic. It seemed piteous now that she had opened her college Irish books at Penny's messy, elegant table, desperate to impress him. Perhaps she had been too obviously besotted with him. Every time he lifted his glass or shifted in his seat she found herself gazing at him, as if she had never seen a man in her life. Several times she had raised her eyes to find one of the others looking away, as if they had been watching her, and once she saw Victor mouth something at Jim, who replied with a swift shake of the head, as if warning him to stop. She was tormented by what might have been said after they left, that she was the butt of Victor's jokes, had made Michael a figure of ridicule. She had embarrassed them both.

The children had finished copying the prayer. She read it slowly from the blackboard, pointing to each word with the yardstick as she said it, relishing each syllable, the sonorous, guttural blur of it. She turned, expecting to find them bored. They cheered. She laughed and took a bow. Even if he rang her and asked her to join them again, Michael Agnew and his arsey friends could teach themselves Irish, or whatever they thought they were at. She would put him out of her mind.

She began lessons with a spelling test and moved on to the next block of words, telling the children to think about how two letters could make a single sound. If you put *a* with *i*, she said, it makes an *ay* sound. She wrote words on the board. Rain. Pain. Stain. She said them aloud, but her mouth didn't make an *ay*: a mean sound came out, more like *ie*. She thought of Michael in the car, when he had said "amazing," and her stomach turned with longing. He had found her wrong.

When the bell rang for break, she was out the door before the children. In the staffroom, Gerry Devlin had made her a mug of tea. His shirt was printed with peacocks. There had been no mention of another date, and she had begun to look forward to seeing him by the kettle.

How's your morning? he said.

Dire. I made two girls write an ungrammatical line from a Disney film twenty times. They were slagging the wee McGeown fella. He's not even in.

Someone was talking about that child earlier. His father is in hospital.

Is he sick?

He got a hiding or something.

He was attacked?

Gerry shrugged. That's what it sounded like.

Back in the classroom, she handed out the songbooks and turned on the radio. The song began, "The Streets of Laredo." There was heat and dust in it, a dying cowboy begging water to wet his parched lips. Davy would have been reeling about the room, taking the bullet slowly then slumping over his desk. What had happened to his father?

After lunch, the children who had gone home to eat brought news.

Davy's da is in hospital.

He got beat up.

They near killed him.

*The body of a man was found on waste ground in East Belfast in the early hours of the morning. He has not yet been identified.* Davy's father had initially been reported as a fatality. They must have left him for dead.

There was a knock at the door. Two girls from P7 had brought a note from Bradley with the pompous instruction: *Bring your charges to the hall immediately.*

The classrooms were emptying lines of children into the corridor. They moved in silence along the terrazzo floor. Word of the attack had gone around the school.

Bradley was on the stage with Father Slattery. He took a step forward and tugged the lapels of his brown suit once, as if he was about to launch into a stand-up comedy routine. You will have heard that the father of one of our pupils is in hospital, he said. It is not a time for idle gossip. The best thing we can do is say a prayer.

Slattery moved in front of the headmaster and the children put their hands together, in readiness for Our Fathers, Hail Marys, Glory Bes. Hands up who has heard of *Romper Room?* he said.

A girl from P4 raised hers. It's a TV program, she said. Miss Helen gets kids to sing wee songs.

Do you know what else a romper room is? Giggles, now. Cushla waited for Bradley to do something, but he just stood there.

Loyalist murder gangs have romper rooms, said Slattery. In the backs of their bars, their social clubs.

Some of the other teachers had begun to shift on their feet. Gerry Devlin stepped away and began walking along the edge of the room, slinging the strap of his guitar around his neck, a *crios* belt woven in shades of red and yellow and green. He went up the steps and onto the stage. Bradley leaned forward and said something to him, but Gerry kept walking and stood by the priest. He swiped his thumb downward across the strings of his guitar and began to sing. His song for peace was even worse than Cushla remembered. Bad rhymes that didn't fit the tune, slabbered in clichés about love and forgiveness. At first there was just Gerry's voice and the trill of his pupils. It was excruciating, but anything was better than listening to Slattery. Take away the hate and violence, Cushla found herself singing, bring love into our hearts. By the end, everyone had joined in. Everyone except the two men on the stage behind Gerry Devlin. Bradley looked like he was waiting for permission to leave. Slattery was motionless, his eyes on Gerry's back.

Afterward, Cushla made her way through the lines of children to where Gerry was standing by the wall.

Thanks for the moral support, he said.

I couldn't let you make a dick of yourself all on your lonesome. Fair play to you, Gerry Devlin. You're the only one had the balls to shut that lunatic up.

A scent of poached chicken and root vegetables had replaced the stale smoke that normally greeted her when she got home from school. The soup appeared when Gina was trying not to drink. She was at the hob, scraping chopped parsley from a board into the stockpot. She had been to the hairdresser, gone a shade lighter. Her skin had a peachy luster.

You look lovely, said Cushla.

It's called Viking, said her mother, lifting her hand to her temple. There was the faintest tremor.

It suits you.

They were talking about that McGeown man in the hairdresser's, said Gina. The dumpy one from the estate said she'd often seen him staggering home, full. Bad bitch. As if that's an excuse for beating him to a pulp.

One of his kids is in my class. I had him here with me a couple of weeks ago. Do you remember him?

Of course I remember, said Gina, the answer coming so fast it was clear she didn't.

*She could hardly walk*, Cushla wanted to say, that's what the child said about you. I should go up to see them, she said.

There's enough soup to feed an army, said Gina, crossing to the overstocked pantry. They had run out of food toward the end of the Ulster Workers' Council strike the previous year and over her dead body would bastard loyalists leave them hungry again. She filled two shopping bags and they left for the estate.

Wouldn't you think they could have given them a house at the front? said Gina as they passed through the gray quadrants. She had been born above a pub in 1920, during the first Troubles, days after her parents had been burned out by their Protestant neighbors. Wherever she went, she looked for an escape route.

Two women in geometric-patterned housecoats were standing in a garden three doors up from the McGeowns'. Cushla said hello. They didn't reply.

Tommy answered the door, hands on the hips of washed-out gray cords, a thin acrylic jumper with an argyle pattern barely reaching the belt. My mummy's not here, he said.

Take them bags off our Cushla, and let us in, for God's sake, before I drop this pot, said Gina.

They followed him into the house. Davy was on a rust-colored velour settee, snuggled into Mandy, his sister. He got up and stood uncertainly in front of Cushla. My daddy was the victim of an attack, he said, as if they were in class and he was giving her The News.

Cushla dropped to her knees and took his hands. I know, Davy, she said. He looked disappointed, as if he had expected more from her.

The kitchen was spotless but claustrophobically cluttered. Bleach-faded worktops stacked with Tupperware. A Formica table pushed into a corner, five small stools under it, one sticking out. A clotheshorse hung with socks and jumpers and towels partly blocking the back door, the wall above it clouded where it met the ceiling, as though an attempt had been made to wipe away mildew.

It's good drying weather, said Gina. You could hang those outside.

The neighbors keep cutting down our washing line, said Mandy.

They throw dog's dirt over the fence, said Davy.

Charming, said Gina. She was at the hob, stirring. Mandy was setting the table.

Davy unpacked the bags. When he saw something he liked, he held it up to show the others. Are you better in yourself, Mrs. Lavery? he said, waving a packet of pink wafer biscuits. Gina pursed her lips and began buttering a stack of bread. Cushla had to suck in her cheeks to keep from laughing. Tommy, Mandy, and Davy sat down to eat. Gina stood over them, ordering them to have second helpings, teasing them for not eating their crusts. Cushla sometimes thought Gina overbearing in company, but this evening she was grateful to her.

Cushla gave Tommy her phone number. He wrote it in a small black notebook that he took from his back pocket. He stood in the hall to see them out, looking beyond them at the teenagers she had seen surround him, who were now sitting on their wall. One of the boys was striking matches and flicking them onto the path.

Fuck this, Tommy said, and took a step toward the door.

Gina caught his arm. You'll go back inside, she said.

They've come to taunt us, Tommy said, tears springing into his eyes.

I know, love. But there's not a bloody thing you can do about it. Now get in and mind your brother and sister.

Tommy dragged his knuckles across his cheeks and nodded. Cushla and her mother walked down the path to the click of locks and bolts. As they reached the car, a match landed on the ground an inch from Gina's foot and one of the teenagers said something they couldn't hear that sent the others into titters. Gina shoved the empty pot into Cushla's arms and strode toward them. Take yourselves off, she said.

It's a free country, one of the girls said.

Now, said Gina. Their faces were close, each waiting for the other to back down, and their hair was the same shade. After an interminable minute, the girl slid off the wall and the rest sauntered after her.

Cheeky wee bitch, said Gina when she was in the passenger seat. A free country, indeed. It's a bigoted hole.

You shouldn't have gone near them.

Intimidation, that's what it is.

Cushla looked back at the house. Davy was at the window, the net curtain behind him. Tommy's arm appeared briefly, pulling him away.

Cushla's three-point turn became five, and they left the close to the sound of mirthless laughter. Gina reached for the handle to open the window.

Christ, Mummy. The McGeowns have to live here.

They have nobody.

What do you mean?

The girl in the hairdresser's said the mother's a Prod.

I know that. Slattery and Bradley don't like her for not coming to Mass.

Well, as far as the ones round here are concerned she's worse than a Catholic for marrying one. And her family don't speak to her.

In the house, Cushla didn't object when Gina poured herself a gin and turned up the volume on the radio news. Davy's father's attack had been downgraded to an assault and was the second item, after a fatal shooting. Getting hacked to bits doesn't get you the top slot, said Gina. What sort of hellhole are we living in?

The phone began to ring. Cushla went to the hall to answer it. The sound of coins dropping. Hello? she said.

It's Michael. I'm in a phone box, he said, as though this was the most surprising thing that had ever happened to him. Would you like to know what else is in the phone box?

A feeling of ease was washing through her body. I'm afraid you're going to tell me anyway, she said.

Several chips in an alarming shade of yellow. A beer can printed with the image of a young lady called Cheryl who has an implausibly large bosom. A pale slimy thing which I won't examine closely, as I fear it is a used prophylactic. He paused and said, I'll be passing your door in two minutes. I could pick you up.

She looked toward the kitchen. Gina was trotting across the tiles in the direction of the gin bottle. OK, said Cushla.

She combed her hair with her fingers in front of the hall mirror and took her trench coat from the banister. I'm going for a walk, she called. So much for never seeing Michael Agnew again; one phone call and she was streeling from the house.

His car was between the Laverys' and Mr. Reid's. He glanced at her as she sat in the passenger seat. She felt ugly, in her plaid skirt and jumper, and pulled her coattails across herself.

He was driving away from the town. I called to the pub, he said. I thought you'd be working.

Not tonight.

Good day? he said. There was a shadow where the collar on the white shirt should have been, a light trim of grime. Another smell, mixed with the laundry detergent and leather, ripe and elemental. Grayish chaff on his chin and jowls. He looked vaguely wrecked. Beautiful.

The father of one of my pupils was attacked last night, she said.

The man who was found this morning?

Yeah.

Christ, he said. I heard about that.

The estate was on their left, drab against the bright fields. The family live in there, at the very back, she said. It's a mixed marriage. She watched his profile for a reaction, but if there was one she couldn't see it.

Apparently he went for a drink after work and left at ten to get a bus. He must have been dragged into a car, because he was found a mile and a half away, said Michael.

How do you know that? said Cushla.

We hear everything in chambers, he said.

Jesus, said Cushla. All he did was walk down a street?

It's not about what you do here, he said. It's about what you are.

She told Michael about the letters on the wall, the shit-flinging neighbors. The other children tormenting Davy because of the smell of frying on his clothes. That he considered it newsworthy that his father got a job.

Past the cemetery where they had buried her father, its sloping lawn and slim lanes of headstones. The army barracks, rolls of barbed wire on top of high fences glinting weakly in the evening light. Up and away from the town, and into the hills. The hedgerows had been cut back hard, except where the gorse was bustling and straining from the straight blocky lines. Michael's house was farther out this road. Why was he bringing her here?

He pulled in by an iron gate that was visible only for a moment to a passing driver.

She told him about Slattery's terrible address to the children, Gerry's singing, how she joined in to take the bad look off him. I haven't a note, she said, and it's the worst song in human history.

He laughed, a sound she felt in her lungs, and she thought she would do anything to make him happy.

What about you? she said.

Busy.

There was so little he could tell her.

They got out of the car. He took her hand and helped her up onto a hump that edged a narrow gully. The fields were dotted with ewes and lambs. The sky was cloudless, the hills across the lough petrol blue, ribbed with white dashes, bungalows, rows of houses; the water dark where it narrowed toward the shipyards, the city sprawled around it.

He stood at her right shoulder. The valley is a natural amphitheater, he said. Depending on the wind direction the sound can carry all the way over here. Sometimes you can hear bombs.

I went to college on the Falls. If you go up the mountains on the other side you can see the army helicopters hanging over the streets and flats, said Cushla, like an alien invasion. He didn't answer and she wondered if she had crossed a line. In the pub, she would not have mentioned that part of Belfast, let alone commented on the military presence.

It must be intrusive, he said. Living with that level of security.

He pointed out the Cave Hill. Samson and Goliath, the cranes in the shipyard; he said that only in this place would mechanical devices be given biblical names.

He asked her what she planned to do for Easter. She had no plans, a fact that had not bothered her until now.

Nothing, really.

But you'll have a family lunch on Sunday, I'm sure, he said.

We're not really that sort of family, she said. Does that sound awful?

No. There are all kinds of families, he said, and was quiet.

She didn't ask if he had plans; she didn't want to hear the answer. Lest he found her aimless, she told him she had bought eggs that she would hard-boil so the children could paint them in school. He stepped over the gully, one long stride, and began to pluck flowers from a gorse bush. When he stepped back he offered them to her, dropping them into her cupped hands. The stems were tough and needly. He told her to put them in the water with the eggs. That she would see why when she did it. That one should never give gorse as a gift because it was unlucky for both the giver and the receiver. That he was happy to take his chances with bad luck if she was.

The sun had dropped. I should go home, she said.

In his car, he put the key in the ignition but didn't turn it, shifting on his hip to face her. He touched her where her neck met her collarbone. You like that, he said, as her shoulder rose to meet his fingers.

Apparently so, she said.

He dragged the side of his hand across her clavicle and down her breastbone, so slowly it was almost painful. She heard herself take in a breath. He was on her then, his hand flat on her chest, his tongue in her mouth. He tasted strong, almost fetid. She opened her hand to touch him and there was a flurry of yellow as the gorse blossoms settled on them. He drew away and laughed, turning up her hand; she had been holding the gorse so tightly her palm was dented with red dashes. He kissed it and began to fill it again with the bruised flowers.

They went back down the road in silence. Outside her house she reached for the door handle but hesitated, not knowing how to part from him. The light had not quite fallen and she could not kiss him or touch him without risk of being seen. What happens now? she wanted to ask but could not bear to hear herself sound desperate. He was holding the steering wheel, the backs of his hands speckled with age spots. He looked at her and flexed his fingers. I'll phone soon, he said.

Her mother was at the kitchen table, bra unfastened under her jumper, the cups sitting high and pointy on her sternum, her real breasts drooping below them. Cushla could sense the start of a bender. A paschal slide into self-pity. Where did you disappear to? said Gina.

I went out to get these, said Cushla, holding out the bruised flowers. Gina flinched. Nature repulsed her. She had never brought Eamonn and Cushla to the park or the beach. Once, when she was small, Cushla steeped rose petals in water overnight, an attempt at making perfume. The next morning she found the jam jar upside down on the draining board, the slimy remains of her tincture in the plughole.

Cushla took down their biggest pot, an aluminum fish kettle, from the top of the cupboard and put in water, the eggs, the flowers. Her hands were stinging and fragrant with coconut. She stayed at the hob, listening to the rumble of the water as it gathered heat, the faint clack the eggs made as they bobbed against each other. When they were done, she dredged them one by one from the water with a slotted spoon and laid them in a colander in the sink. The shells had turned yolk yellow.

She joined her mother in the sitting room. What are you watching? she said.

Some courtroom thing.

A barrister was in his chambers. He had a bulbous nose and piercing eyes that he kept narrowing below his wig.

The get-up of him, said Gina.

Cushla sat on the sofa. The barrister's name was Rumpole. He was defending a young Black man accused of stabbing someone outside Lord's Cricket Ground. He advised the man to plead guilty, but he insisted on pleading innocent.

That doesn't mean he's innocent, Gina said.

That's not the point. His job is to defend him. Everyone's entitled to a defense, said Cushla. As soon as the words were out she felt ridiculous. She had got a lumber off a barrister in a car and now she was an expert on the criminal justice system.

Speaking of which, Michael Agnew was in the paper today, said Gina. Criticizing the Diplock court system. He'll not win any popularity contests saying things like that out loud.

He's right. It's an unfair system. Three judges, all probably Protestants who went to the same school, and no jury. Where's the paper?

I lit the fire with it.

How did Daddy know him?

Your uncle Frank was in some early civil rights organization about ten years ago. Michael Agnew was involved as well. There weren't too many Prods lining up to do that.

Was Daddy involved?

Jesus, no. He had to keep his nose clean behind that bar. But we saw plenty of Michael in those days.

Was he ever in this house? she asked.

He came to a few parties. Me and your da had great parties, said Gina. She lit a cigarette, staring at the floor as she took the first drag; happy memories made her morose.

Is he still friends with Uncle Frank?

How the hell would I know! said Gina. The Laverys don't come near me. Anyway, what has you so interested?

You brought him up. I'm just trying to make conversation.

Gina regarded her for a moment then looked back at the television. Cushla would have to be careful.

Rumpole had a son who was about to leave for America. He was so preoccupied with the case they only got to say good-bye briefly, at lunch. They were awkward with each other, the son churlish, defensive. Rumpole had not been a good father.

Rumpole's wife was alone in the house, drinking. He went home to find her pacing the floor, as if she wanted a row, but she poured herself another drink and put a meal in front of him. They ate without speaking. At the end he said to her, Who am I, exactly?

Who am I? thought Cushla.

# 8

She was passing the longest hoarding in the UK, according to the papers. Messages flashed by. USE THE CONFIDENTIAL TELE-PHONE NUMBER . . . IF YOU'RE SUSPICIOUS DIAL 999 . . . DON'T LET THE BOMBER GET <u>YOUR</u> CAR . . . DON'T LET CHILDREN PLAY WITH TOY GUNS . . . , the final ellipsis leaving endless possibilities. DON'T FALL FOR A MARRIED PROD TWICE YOUR AGE . . . DON'T AGREE TO SEE HIM EVERY SINGLE TIME IT SUITS HIM . . .

Michael had phoned just before seven, as Cushla was finishing Gina's traditional Good Friday collation of a fish-finger sandwich soggy with melted butter and malt vinegar. He was at dinner and would be at the flat by ten. Come and see me, he said. As "yes" came out of her mouth, she had felt a first twinge of resentment. He would never give her more than this. For her there would just be liaisons arranged an hour or two in advance, couplings in lay-bys, evenings at his friends' house under unconvincing pretexts. When her thoughts flitted—briefly—to his wife, the guilt at what she was doing to her did not take. The image Cushla had of her rival was protean. Visualizing her was like playing with one of the cardboard dress-up kits the girls brought to school sometimes. There was a flourishing selection of imperfections from which she could draw when her conscience pricked. A complexion like grapefruit or a scouring of broken veins. A wheedling voice or earlobes made freakishly long by heavy jewelry. It took little to summon these visions; the simple fact that this woman was keeping Michael from her was enough.

When she reached Michael's flat, the curtains on the first-floor window were open, the room filled with warm light. She parked beside his car and checked her face before getting out. He was leaning against the doorframe. She liked how the gravel slowed her as she walked toward him, the flounce of her dress at her knees. That he was watching her. She mounted the wide steps two at a time and inhaled deeply to settle herself. He pulled her inside and shut the door with his foot. His eyes were glassy. It's yourself, he said, kissing her full on the mouth. You look good. It's the dress you wore in the Lyric.

He was wearing a black polo neck under a houndstooth sports jacket. So do you, she said. Like a Malone Road James Bond. Or your man from the Milk Tray ad.

I'm not familiar with the work. Do you want a nightcap? he said, kissing her again. It was like drinking whiskey.

No. It's a day of fasting and abstinence.

Oh dear. I've been doing neither. Cup of tea? His mouth was still on hers.

No.

She felt his lips open into a smile.

There was a lamp on in his bedroom, a dowdy beige one with a tasseled shade. Large, dreary pieces of Victorian furniture. Books, newspapers, an ashtray on a nightstand. The air was faintly savory. She took her coat off and laid it on an overstuffed chair upholstered in salmon-colored velvet. When she turned back he was crouching at her feet. A paisley sleeve was protruding from under a pillow on the bed. If she hadn't come he'd be changing into his pajamas. But she had, and he was unzipping her boots.

She woke with her nose in the hot, scalliony hair of his armpit, his hand splayed on her hip. She lifted it off gently and slipped out of his bed, lifting her dress from the floor and pulling it over her head.

The bathroom had black and white tiles set like bricks. She put paper in the toilet to deaden the splash of her piss and sat on the seat. A Mabel Lucie Attwell rhyme was nailed to the back of the door. His toiletries were spartan. Shaving cream in a pot beside a stubby brush, anti-dandruff shampoo, a bar of lemon soap. A single toothbrush in a beaker. The mirror over the basin gave up horrors: cheekbones peppered with granules of mascara, a scuffed chin, hair so charged with static it looked like she had rubbed it with a balloon. She washed her hands and held them to her nose. They smelled of him.

As she entered the bedroom he raised himself on his elbow and wiped his hand over his face. She sat on the edge of the bed and bent to kiss him. There was a needling of stubble as their chins met and he pulled away. Are you consumed by self-loathing and regret? he said.

Why would I be?

Because you woke up with an ould lad.

Maybe I like ould lads.

There had been something perfunctory about the previous night. The brief inquiry about birth control—the previous year Dr. O'Hehir had prescribed medication to regulate her periods, although it wasn't until she read an article in *Cosmopolitan* that she realized he had put her on the pill. The efficient way Michael removed her clothes, the thorough foreplay. The sex was almost performative, a series of set pieces. She wondered now if he had been anxious to impress her. He shifted on his elbow and winced. The right shoulder was so high it looked like it was lifted in laughter. She put her finger on the bump of bone where his clavicle met his arm. How did that happen? she said.

A rugby injury, he said. His color was rising. She had made him aware of himself.

Does it hurt?

Not as much as it did in 1940.

She put her hands flat on his chest. The hairs there were gnarly, one or two of them white. She drew back the covers and lay beside him. He traced the outline of a flower on her dress, just above her breast. "The Meadow of Asphodel where abide the souls and phantoms of those whose work is done," he said.

I thought they were lilies.

You're funny.

Yeah. Even when I don't mean to be.

He kissed her for a long time, caressing her arse through the fabric of her dress in maddening, swirling loops. You're not a virgin, he said.

Afraid not. Are you disappointed?

Last night I rather hoped I was going to get to deflower you, he said, sliding his hand between her legs. It felt as though all the heat in her body was rushing to his fingers. She reached for him, so wet she took him in easily. He made a small noise that sounded like relief and rolled her onto her back.

Go slow, she said.

At college she'd had a boyfriend called Columba, an engineering student from Fermanagh with a face like a martyr who read Graham Greene in the pub. The day he graduated he told her he was immigrating to Canada and asked her—without enthusiasm—to go with him. Her father was dying, she said, an excuse that suited them both. They got drunk and at closing time he led her by the hand to his bedsit in the Holylands. The sex was short and uncomfortable but not disastrous, and they spent his final month in the city on his moldering mattress, drinking Vat 19 from mugs and learning to please each other, liberated by the knowledge that he was leaving. She was grateful, as she moved under Michael Agnew, to have had someone to practice on.

She loved the weight of him on her, the solemn and mildly distracted look that settled on his face as he got into his stroke. The grunt that seemed to issue from the depths of him as he finished. That he stayed inside her until he was soft.

The letter box flapped. He got out of bed and walked naked along the hallway. His head was jutting forward, legs slightly bowed, giving him the appearance of a prowling animal. He returned with the Saturday papers, a pair of black glasses on the end of his nose. As he reached the bed, he caught her looking at him.

So it's true, he said, getting in beside her.

What's true?

Catholic girls are nymphomaniacs.

She laughed. He tidied her arms and legs so that she was lying with her head on his chest, and opened the paper.

There was a photograph of a woman pushing a pram, one of the Divis towers rising in front of her.

What bloody idiot thought it acceptable to house families on those concrete corridors? he said.

I did teaching practice round there. The kids came to school knackered because the army shine beams from the helicopters into the flats during the night.

Appalling, he said, and she found herself looking up at him.

You sound so reasonable, she said.

I don't know what you mean.

Everyone else takes a position. Like "those towers are full of Provos and they deserve all they get." Or "they're lucky to be getting a place to live for nothing." You don't do that.

It's depressing that you find that remarkable, he said.

They rose at eight. The kitchen was a narrow galley off the sitting room. While Michael made tea, Cushla sat on a chair at the dining table. It was covered in grim-looking legal texts, box files with handwritten stickers. There were a couple of books, Liam O'Flaherty's *Dúil* and de Bhaldraithe's Irish dictionary. She picked one up. A name was inscribed on the inside page in *cló gaelach*, the old Celtic script: *Siobhán de Buitléar*; "Joanna Butler" was printed underneath it.

He came carrying a tray of art deco china.

Who is Siobhán de Buitléar? she said.

He glanced at her hands as he laid down the tray. I've been swotting up, he said, as though he hadn't heard her, handing her a foolscap notebook. I have to stop every few words to look things up.

She put the book facedown on her lap. On the jotter he'd written the word *dúil* and below it "desire, liking, fondness, craving. Yearning? Want? Like *saudade*, maybe?"

What's *saudade*?

Soh-dadge, he said. It's a Portuguese word, like *dúil*, I think.

You'd make a good teacher, she said. I don't feel like I've just been corrected.

He poured, added milk, stirred. The cup handle was flat and triangular and she had to hold it daintily to get the tea to her mouth. He left the room. She could hear water running, the toilet flushing, the open and shut of a drawer. She picked up the book again and looked at the signature in English. The *r*'s were fussy, like miniature capitals; it was how the nuns at school from down south had made the letter. She wondered about the girl with the careful hand who had once owned it.

She got up and walked around. The drawing of High Street he had told her about was on the wall above the record player. She had visualized little boats, but they were sailing ships. On top of a glass-fronted cabinet bunged with crystal and old Belleek china there was a photograph of a group of boys in shorts and rugby jerseys. She found Michael at once, among the tallest, his arms folded.

He returned with tidy hair, wearing an Aran cardigan. You're like one of the Clancy Brothers in that thing, said Cushla.

I thought you'd appreciate that, he said. He was behind her, his arms around her waist.

And you are absolutely delighted with yourself here, she said, putting her finger under his chin in the photo.

I rather threw myself at sport that season, he said. Otherwise it was a dreadful year.

What was so bad about it?

A boy in my dorm hanged himself. At the start of the term.

Jesus Christ.

We stood at the end of our beds as they carried his body away. We were not allowed to go home. The school overlooked our back garden, and for weeks I watched my sister play with our dog and counted the sleeps until half-term. There were forty-three, by the way. Sleeps.

He mumbled something about music and crossed the room to the stereo, where he began sorting through a stack of tapes. Without the camouflage of robes and manners and whiskey he seemed vulnerable. She went to the window. It was the first time she had seen his street in the daytime. There was a magnolia tree in his front garden, gnarled branches pimpled with green buds, a single white, starry blossom on the bare bark. The houses seemed to be washed in pink light. There was bossa nova playing from the speakers, and when he came to sit at the table, he pulled her onto his knee. She looked up at the curlicues and finials and smiled.

They left the flat together, getting into their own cars. He trailed her through the city. At a red light she checked her mirror, curious to see what other people saw. He was surprisingly unremarkable, just a middle-aged man in a decent car, and it was oddly thrilling to think of what they had been doing an hour earlier. As they approached her house, she checked the mirror one last time. He touched two fingers to his forehead in farewell and drove away, out the hill road. Something twisted in her. While she was looking at the pictures on his walls he was washing her off him. Making himself presentable for his wife.

She went into the house on her toes, laying her keys gently on the hall table. As she mounted the first step, the kitchen door opened and Gina bustled into the hall.

What are you doing up? Cushla asked.

What are you doing coming home at nine in the morning?

She scrambled in her head for an excuse, eventually muttering she'd had car trouble and stayed over at Gerry's. She placed a foot on the second step, but Gina had moved forward and was looming into her face.

Hoho! Car trouble indeed. You must think I'm some fool, she said, nostrils flaring.

Dear God. Are you actually sniffing me? said Cushla.

You'll get yourself a reputation, carrying on like that, said Gina, her expression almost triumphant.

I am twenty-four, said Cushla, belting up the stairs, suddenly conscious that Michael's smell was on her. Twenty. Bloody. Four.

Below, the vacuum cleaner roared to life. Gina was permanently sozzled, but she wasn't stupid. As for Eamonn . . . if he got even an inkling that Cushla was sleeping with a customer, let alone a married one, there would be hell to pay. She stripped to her underwear and got into bed. As Gina bashed the Hoover against the skirting boards, Cushla thought of all the mornings that had led to this one: waking alone, making her mother's breakfast, going to school in her dowdy clothes. The way Michael had looked at her earlier when she took him in; as if he might devour her. She drew back the covers and examined her body, to see what he had seen. The slight dip of her belly, the breasts that were neither big nor small. She put her hand inside her knickers and pushed her pelvis into the mattress, using her thumb like he had. She came quickly and lay looking at the ceiling, feeling as if she had woken somewhere very far away.

# 9

The body of a man was found off the Shore Road by a woman out walking her dog.

I wouldn't thank you for a dog, said Gina. You'd be odds-on to find a corpse.

Sporting fixtures around the island have been postponed due to inclement weather, including tomorrow's Irish Grand National.

Cushla switched off the radio. Her earliest memory was of looking through the railings at Fairyhouse Races on Easter Monday. They were so close to the post that clods of earth flew up as the horses passed, flaying her cheeks and new blue coat. Her father carried her into the bar on his shoulders, proclaiming her the winner. She glanced at Gina, who was blinking as though trying not to cry.

Are you ready? said Cushla.

Aye. But I'm not a hundred percent today, said Gina. She was a hundred percent hungover, eyeballs juicy, the skin around them puckered. They had been avoiding each other since the fight the previous morning, Cushla discomfited by the knowing way with which her mother now regarded her, Gina furious not to have received an explanation.

There was a line of blue on the horizon weighed down by dirty cloud. A biting wind had come up. Gina teetered down the driveway and arranged herself haughtily in the passenger seat. Cushla's father had driven cars with slippy leather seats and walnut dashboards. They suited Gina better than Cushla's did.

Cushla put the Easter eggs they had bought for the McGeowns on the back ledge. As she straightened herself Fidel came loping up the driveway, a plastic carrier bag under his arm.

Happy Easter, he said, dipping his knees to wave in the window at Gina. There were flecks of white matter in his beard, dandruff or food. He offered Cushla the bag.

What's this? she said.

Creme Eggs. My ma got in too many and they'll not shift now. Give them to those McGeown kids.

Cushla thanked him and offered to drive him down the road. He blew on his hands and got into the back seat.

To what do we owe the pleasure? said Gina.

Fidel brought chocolate for the McGeown kids, said Cushla.

Good, said her mother, as though he was only doing what he ought to be doing. The previous day they had gone into his shop to buy Easter eggs. Gina told him who they were for and—as if it was his responsibility, as a prominent local loyalist, to make amends in the form of confectionery—insisted he knock 10 percent off the price.

Are youse going to church? said Fidel.

Mass, said Gina. We're going to Mass.

Well, say one for me, he said.

They left him at the bottom of the road. He slapped the roof of the car before Cushla drove off.

Acting the big fella, said Gina.

You can't see the good in anybody. As for that mouth of yours. *We're going to Mass*, she said, imitating her mother's voice. You'll get our Eamonn killed.

Rubbish.

The church was packed with families in new Easter clothes and women her mother's age in thin coats and thick hats, the daily communicants. Gina did the bare minimum: Mass on Sunday but never on holy days of obligation. She blamed Vatican II for her lack of enthusiasm, said it wasn't the same since they abolished the Latin Mass; to Cushla's knowledge her mother did not have a single word of Latin.

They sidled into a space near the confession boxes. The heavy paintings that marked the Stations of the Cross seemed to be tilting from the walls, as if they might fall on top of them. Jesus is condemned to death. Jesus carries his Cross. Jesus falls for the first time. Jesus falls for the second time. Jesus was a ringer for James Taylor, his facial expression unchanged from one station to the next, regardless of what degradation was being visited on him.

The McGeown children were two rows ahead. Tommy was dressed in a dark gray jacket with wide lapels, a white shirt. He looked like his father, eyes a murky blue, face squarish. He was going to be handsome. Davy and Mandy had the fair coloring and pale blue eyes of their mother. The day Cushla brought the dyed eggs to school he had refused to leave the classroom at break time, saying he needed to finish painting his. He had brought it to her desk—it was like a piece of spongeware, spotted with tiny brown rabbits on tufts of scutch grass—and cried when she admired it.

Slattery came out of the sacristy and seemed to glide toward the altar, silver embroidery glistening like filigree at the edges of his white vestments. Gina made a clucking sound with her tongue. Done up like a Christmas fairy, she said. He's good to himself.

His sermon was not a celebration of the Resurrection but a dirge about Christ's Passion. Torn with scourges. Mockeries and insults. Obedient to the point of death. Hold on to your faith, he said. They want you to walk away from it. They'll pick you off on building sites, on your driveways. They'll leave you lying in an entry, with a dog sniffing at what they've left of you. Cushla could see Tommy's profile. His chin was raised, his eyes on the altar.

Outside, sleet was slanting across the stone steps, the sky leaden. They were addressed quaintly. Mrs. Lavery, Miss Lavery; publican, teacher; known to everyone. Cushla sent Gina to the car and waited for the McGeowns. She offered them a lift. Tommy began to say no, but the sleet was coming down hard and he accepted reluctantly. Davy sat in the middle of the back seat, so far forward he was almost on the hand brake.

There's a couple of bags on the ledge behind you, said Cushla. Open them.

This is going to be wheeker, Davy said. You should see their house.

Gina let out a snort. That child's a geg, she said.

Cushla left her mother home, as Eamonn and his family were coming for lunch. Tommy got into the passenger seat, beside Cushla. At the turn for the estate she caught him looking at her. She expected him to be embarrassed, but he didn't look away.

Davy was counting out Fidel's eggs. Four each, he said, dancing with his hands.

Nice one, said Tommy, when they reached the house. He handed Mandy a bunch of keys and told her he would be in shortly.

Thanks, Miss Lavery. For looking after our kid, he said. She could hear something in his voice. A smirk. Or derision.

It's Cushla, she said. And don't be silly, I've done nothing. How's your daddy?

Do you really want to know? he said.

Yes, she said, I do.

He listed his father's injuries, with the strange composure that had been on him the day he quizzed Davy about Slattery.

A sob had gathered in her throat and she didn't trust herself to speak. Tommy inclined his head slightly, eyes glittering. Sorry you asked? he said, and got out of the car.

Back home, Gina was putting a leg of lamb in the oven. What's wrong with your bake? she said, glancing at Cushla.

Tommy told me what they did to his father, said Cushla. She recounted his afflictions slowly, as Tommy had. Fractured skull. Both legs broken. Smashed jaw. Cracked ribs. Collapsed lung. Ruptured spleen. They slashed his hands and wrists with a nail hammered into a plank.

Gina stood shaking her head, as if she was trying to drive the words out. Keep an eye on those kids, she said eventually, especially that older fella. He's at a bad age.

Cushla peeled potatoes and parsnips and carrots. She carried the skins outside in a basin. Their neighbor, Mr. Reid, was in his garden. There was an apple tree strung with fat balls, the lawn blooming with drifts of snowdrops and crocuses; beds that would be bright with color were turned over and ready for planting. The Laverys had a wan clutch of daffodils that came out sulking in spring and a single diseased rose bush. He wished her a happy Easter and took the trimmings for his compost heap, returning with a bunch of forced rhubarb wrapped in the *Belfast News Letter*.

Mrs. Reid had died before the Laverys moved in. There were no children, just a nephew who had taken over the running of Mr. Reid's lemonade factory a few years earlier, a small man with a big car who seldom visited. Cushla almost asked Mr. Reid to join them for lunch but couldn't picture him at Gina's table. It would be strained enough without the hardship of keeping the conversation neutral, avoiding religion, politics, the Troubles. Gina pretending to be sober. Eamonn trying not to curse.

Eamonn arrived half an hour late, a bottle of wine in each hand,

Bull's Blood and a sweet German white. His daughters, Emma and Nicola, ignored Gina's outstretched arms and put their faces in their mother's skirt. Gina watched, a smile on her mouth that hadn't reached her eyes. They ripped open the eggs she gave them and began eating. Marian told them three times to say thanks before giving up and plopping into a chair.

Cushla plated the vegetables while Gina hacked at the meat.

We should do this more often, whispered Cushla.

Marian's put on a quare lot of weight, said Gina.

You can't help yourself, can you? said Cushla.

As they ate, the girls got on and off their seats, asking to be brought to the toilet, pulling faces at the food. Gina watched them, her neck and chest splotched red, the wine showing on her in a way the gin didn't.

Anything strange or startling, Cushla? said Marian.

No.

Ha! said Gina. Apart from staying out all night.

Marian giggled. Who with?

A wee teacher, said Gina, willing to enter an alliance with her sworn enemy to humiliate her own daughter.

What's going on? said Eamonn, looking up sharply.

Nothing, said Cushla.

There'd better not be, he said. What about your job?

Eamonn! said Marian. Leave her alone. She's a single girl.

She'll stay bloody single as well, giving it away for nothing, he said.

Cushla stood to clear the table. I have no privacy, she said.

Eamonn slapped his thigh and laughed. Do youse hear her? he said.

Cushla scraped and rinsed the plates. Eamonn was right. A teacher Cushla trained with had been sacked without a reference after someone wrote anonymously to the bishop that she was living in sin with her boyfriend. The last Cushla heard of her she was working in a shoe shop in Wolverhampton.

She opened the oven to check the crumble she had made with Mr. Reid's rhubarb. It was not quite ready and she returned to the table.

How's business, Eamonn? said Gina. Cushla's stomach heaved.

It's all right if I can keep the wages down, he said.

It's a nightmare running the place with so few staff, said Marian.

I'm well aware of what the place needs to run, said Gina.

Marian gave Eamonn a meaningful look. He lowered his head and put a forkful of meat in his mouth.

We were hoping you'd be able to help a bit more, Marian said. We never see Eamonn. As if to reinforce it, the girls clambered onto his lap.

I can work more in the summer, said Cushla, but Marian was looking at Gina.

I've been doing the cleaning, she said, but it's hard when the girls haven't started school. And it's not going to get any easier.

What does that mean? said Gina.

Marian's hand hovered at her middle then came to rest on her belly. I should let you tell them, Eamonn.

He had tipped the untouched food from his daughters' plates onto his and was mashing gravy into a cut potato. Number three's on the way, he said, his mouth full.

When? said Gina.

End of July.

Gina's lips twitched with numbers, calculating the dates. Marian was five months gone. They hadn't told her. She moved her chair back with uncharacteristic dignity and left the kitchen.

From the sitting room, the scratch of the poker in the grate, the clink of bottle against tumbler. Cushla took the crumble from the oven and put it in the center of the table. Congratulations, she said. You two make nice babies. And they did. The girls were like children from a Victorian Christmas card, all honey-colored curls and rosy cheeks.

How is she, anyway? said Marian.

Some days she's OK, said Cushla. It must have been loyalty that was making her lie. Gina was never entirely sober. She had always been a binger, beating gin into herself for three or four days straight, emerging from the bedroom new and unsteady, as if she'd been purged of whatever tormented her. Marian had been coming to the house since she was fourteen, had seen their father hand Eamonn money for the chippy on evenings Gina was holed up in the bedroom, too drunk to cook a dinner.

Marian folded her arms across her chest. Well, she's half-cut today, she said.

The girls were swinging from Eamonn's neck. We should tip on, he said, and they leaped off him in relief.

In the hallway, Marian put her head into the sitting room and said, Thanks for having us, Gina.

Cushla lifted her head in time to see her mother make a reptilian movement with her neck, recoiling from the sound of her own name in Marian's mouth. Right you be, she said. She didn't get up.

They prepared to leave, Eamonn settling the girls in the back, fussing at toggles and buttons, squeezing a snatter from a small nose with a tissue. Marian saying something when he sat in the driver's seat that made him lean suddenly to kiss her. Instead of driving down toward town, he pulled out and onto the hill road, the car horn sounding a cheerful toot.

Cushla closed the door quickly, thankful her mother had not seen the direction in which they had gone. But when she turned, Gina was behind her. They went to the golf club, she said. I bloody knew it.

Eamonn was no golfer, but pubs in the north were not allowed to sell alcohol on Sundays—which gave him his only day off—whereas clubs were. Every week he and Marian had Sunday lunch in the clubhouse with her family, and they clearly regretted breaking the habit. Any wonder they left, said Cushla. You could have cut the atmosphere with a knife.

She's so far gone she's showing, said Gina. Her ma was probably told as soon as our Eamonn pulled out of her.

That's disgusting. And Marian knows you hate her, said Cushla. Why did you tell them about me?

Respect, said Gina. I want to be treated with respect.

Well, try sobering up then! said Cushla, stalking to the kitchen and banging the door behind her.

She took the crumble from the table, the only pudding she had made since O-level Domestic Science, and stabbed at it with a spoon. It was shrunken and jammy, the topping an unappetizing dun color. She had fancied, when she asked her mother to host lunch, that there would be hours of good food and conversation, like at Penny's table. Michael said there were all kinds of families. Cushla's was an unhappy one. What was his like?

When she had finished clearing up, she went to the sitting room and shook coal on the fire from the brass scuttle. Her mother was silent, but her body was taut, as if she was ready for combat.

The phone began to ring. It's hardly for me, Gina said.

Cushla went to the hall to answer it. The sound of coins dropping again. Michael? she whispered.

It's me, Cushla. Tommy.

Is everything all right?

Great. Our Davy ate all his chocolate by four and broke out in hives.

Oh God, she said, lifting the phone and sitting on the third stair. He'll be sick.

Too late. I told him he should have cut out the middleman and flushed it down the toilet.

Cushla laughed. How are you doing?

Grand. I just wanted to say sorry. About earlier. I get angry. Like I could kill them. She heard the strike of a match and he breathed in deeply.

It's OK.

Aye. Well. Thanks for the eggs and all.

You're welcome, Tommy. And stop smoking.

Yes, miss, he said, taking another drag and exhaling theatrically. For a moment neither of them spoke. Then he said, Is it OK, like? Me ringing you up.

Of course it is. Any time at all. The line began to beep and he was gone.

She replaced the receiver. Maybe her mother was right and Cushla could help them, not just Davy, but Tommy too. It made her feel good. Grown up, useful. She wished she could talk to Michael, right now, and tell him. The telephone directory was on her left. She pulled it toward her and hesitated before opening it. She found his entry: Agnew, M. & J., his address beneath it. She put her finger by the 9 and turned it. Then she turned 2-3-9-0. She held her finger over 6, her heart pounding. She withdrew it and replaced the receiver.

# 10

Davy's backside was protruding from beneath the net curtain. Goal! he said.

Come away from there, said Tommy. You don't even like football.

I might if they'd let me play.

They won't, so get down.

Davy emerged from the cloud of white nylon and launched himself onto the settee, where Tommy was sitting with his hand closed around the notebook in which he had written Cushla's number. His knuckles were nicked and swollen. Trevor's a good laugh, Davy said. Him and me would get on great if he was allowed to talk to me.

Aye. They're all a barrel of laughs round here, said Tommy.

Listen, said Davy, cocking his ear stagily. Trevor's singing a song.

Is it the one about being up to his knees in Fenian blood? said Tommy.

It's the one about Mr. Bradley.

Davy, don't, said Mandy, with a look at Cushla.

What's this? said Cushla.

Wait till you hear, said Davy, leaping to his feet.

Mandy's hands flew up to her eyes. Oh God, she said.

Davy began a lolloping march up and down the length of the sitting room. The song was to a jaunty, music-hall tune:

*"Our wee school's a great wee school, it's made of bricks and plaster.*
*The only thing that's wrong with it is our wee baldy master.*
*He goes to the pub on Saturday night, he goes to church on Sunday.*
*He prays to God to give him strength to slaughter us on Monday."*

Cushla looked from Mandy to Tommy. The three of them dissolved into giggles. Davy said he had an even better one. Simmer down, wee man, said Tommy.

I thought you liked poems, said Davy, hurling himself onto the settee again.

I don't think that was strictly a poem, said Cushla.

Our Tommy writes poetry in that notebook he keeps in his back pocket, said Davy.

Cushla could almost feel the heat from Tommy's ears. Shut you up, he warned.

He won't show them to us, said Davy.

He's doing English for his A levels so they might be really good, said Mandy.

I did English too, Cushla said. What texts are you reading?

*A Passage to India. The Woodlanders. Persuasion.* Hopkins's and Browning's poetry, he told her.

What Shakespeare?

*Hamlet* and *The Winter's Tale.*

What's your favorite?

*Hamlet.* Although he fannies about a good bit instead of getting the job done.

I liked *The Woodlanders,* she said, to avoid hearing Tommy's views on vengeance. But not as much as I loved *Far from the Madding Crowd*. And *Tess*. And *Jude the Obscure*. Oh my God.

Tommy lifted his chin. Is it that good? he said.

It was months before I opened another book. I was afraid of what I might find between the pages.

I can't get to the library. My mummy's at the hospital every day and I don't want to leave the kids alone.

Kids, said Mandy, putting on a deep voice. What are you?

Tommy got off the settee and went upstairs. They could hear him thudding about overhead and then loud music came on.

You've put him in bad form, said Davy.

He's always in bad form, said Mandy. He was punching the wall out the back last night.

When she was leaving, Cushla stood at the bottom of the staircase and called his name. There was a sound of feet hitting the floor of the room he shared with Davy, the creak of a door. "Make Me Smile (Come Up and See Me)" was playing from a radio, an absurd contrast between the lyrics and the sour twist of his mouth.

Great song, she said. I'll bring *Jude* next time.

He went back to his room without a word.

She drove down the road, past her house. It was hard not to pull in and check on Gina, but she didn't want to give in. Her mother had been peevish since Sunday, ranting about Marian, that she was dragging the girls up, that she had the bounce on Eamonn, that she dressed like a barmaid. The previous night, Cushla had finally lost her temper. The girls were afraid of Gina because she didn't know how to talk to children, she countered. Eamonn could have told them about the baby, but he chose not to. And at least Marian didn't sit on a stool behind the bar, getting pissed when she was meant to be working.

It was not yet five. Eamonn's white Capri was the only car outside the pub. Inside, the room smelled of Handy Andy and lavender furniture polish; Marian had been doing Gina's cleaning. She was sitting at the bar, between the girls, who were drinking lemonade from Babycham glasses, bags of crisps ripped open in front of them.

I used to do that, said Cushla.

About five years ago, said Eamonn.

Very funny, said Cushla.

Minty and Jimmy were farther along the counter. Eamonn leaned across the bar, his nose wrinkling. You smell like beef and damp fanny, he said.

Cushla sniffed at her top. It's the smell of the McGeowns' kitchen, she said.

Eamonn's eyes flicked from Minty to Cushla, his mouth forming an O, shushing her. Keep your oar out, he said.

Why?

Cos it's none of your business.

Is the house bogging? whispered Marian.

No, said Cushla. It's immaculate. She can't hang her washing out, so the kitchen's moldy.

Any chance youse could change the subject? said Eamonn.

Marian made a face at him and began rooting in her bag. She produced a bottle of perfume and sprayed it at Cushla. It was heavy and floral, sickeningly so, but the gesture was sisterly and Cushla found herself smiling. The girls held their wrists out and Marian misted them too.

Smells like the inside of a huir's handbag round here today, said Eamonn, looking over Cushla's shoulder. She turned to see who he was speaking to. It was Michael. She felt a rush of elation so strong she didn't trust herself to speak. He was wearing ordinary clothes, tweed and brown corduroy. There was a newspaper under his arm.

How's Cushla? he said quietly, as Eamonn passed him a whiskey.

Good. How are you?

All right, he said.

There was a shriek. Emma had slid off her stool and landed on the floor. Marian tried to haul her up, but there was too much bulk at her middle. Eamonn came from behind the counter, scooping the child off the carpet. Her cry had risen to a wail, and Nicola had begun to howl too.

I tried to phone you, said Michael.

Gina had said the phone had rung twice when Cushla was out, but the caller had hung up when she answered, and she had credited the prank calls to "wee bastards." Cushla had almost hoped it hadn't been Michael. She didn't like to think of him sneaking out to a phone box like an adolescent.

Never a dull moment, said Marian. She gathered the girls' coats and she and Eamonn brought them through the door to the car.

It's been difficult, said Michael. Easter holidays and so on. You'll come to Penny's next week?

*Tiocfaidh mé*, she said. It was overwhelming, standing so close to him.

He smiled. Can you get away for an hour?

Now?

Right now.

I'm going to the pictures.

Oh? Who with?

Gerry.

He finished his drink and handed her the tumbler. I'll have another, he said, swinging his backside onto a stool.

Eamonn came back. Get the finger out, princess, he said, and Cushla went behind the counter. When she put the glass in front of Michael he did not acknowledge it. She wiped broken crisps from the counter into an ashtray with the side of her hand, trying not to look at him. The bar began to fill up and she was aware of him hunched over the counter, among the regulars and a few strays, including a dapper wine victim from the Salvation Army home, a tarnished medal attached to his jacket by a greasy loop of ribbon. Conor, a schoolfriend of Eamonn's who had recently resigned from the RUC, had come in too. He had thought the force needed more Catholics, but six months in a station in south Armagh, waiting to be blown up, had tested his commitment to integration. He had developed a series of facial tics, and when Eamonn put a pint in front of him, his mouth gurned enthusiastically.

Gerry arrived, wearing his leather coat, looking around anxiously.

A man walks into a bar, said Eamonn.

He's here to see me, said Cushla.

Eamonn let out a low whistle. Is he the boy had you out all night?

Please don't, she said.

Gerry pulled out the stool beside Michael and sat on it. It was the stuff of nightmares. She had phoned Gerry on Easter Monday, complaining that she was bored, in the hope that he would ask her out. Disgusted as Gina and Eamonn were at the idea of her sleeping with Gerry, at least he was single and the right religion. She moved along the counter and introduced him to Eamonn, praying her brother would not say anything more. She could feel Michael's eyes burning on her skin. Gerry mentioned Leeds United and Eamonn visibly relaxed; they were both fans and, for the next few minutes, chatted as if she didn't exist. There was a good chance the club would make it to the European Cup Final. They might even win, which would make them only the second English club to do so. Bremner, Lorimer, Giles, great side.

Nice guy, like, said Eamonn, coming to where she was skulking beneath the television. Go round and sit with him.

The nearest empty stool was at the far end of the bar. Gerry carried it over and she tried not to look at Michael while they made space—horrifyingly—between them.

Recognizing Michael, Gerry said, How's about you?

Hello again.

We're going to see *Chinatown*, said Gerry. It'll be my fourth time. Lavery here hasn't seen it.

I see, said Michael, taking a pen from his pocket. He unfurled his newspaper, snapping it open, and began filling in words on the crossword.

Farther along the bar, Fidel lifted the English tabloid he bought daily that was full of sport and busty women, waving it at Michael. Wee Jimmy here did the crossword as well, he said. He began reading the nonsensical words the old man had written. Blibs. Sttor. Amicth. Beside him, Jimmy's eyes were bright, a gormless smile revealing dentures too big for his gums. Michael glanced up sharply, then slapped his paper onto the counter.

Leave Jimmy alone, said Cushla.

Fidel spread his hands. I'm only having him on, he said.

Minty began telling a dirty joke, looking at Cushla slyly from time to time. She missed the set-up and was only half listening, distracted by Michael's proximity. She glanced at him and their eyes locked. He was furious. For a mad moment her hand rose from her lap. She put it under her thigh, afraid it would betray her by touching him. The beer tap sputtered and Minty delivered the punchline: "I always forget to take my tights off."

Gerry turned to Michael and made a face. The old ones are the best, he said.

Quite, said Michael.

Gerry went to the gents'. Michael lit a cigarette, glaring at her briefly as he took the first drag.

You smoke like a teenager, said Cushla. As if you're afraid you'll be caught.

He's rather taken with you, said Michael.

Are you joking?

He drained his drink. The glass made a small, irritated bang as it hit the mahogany. When are you coming to the flat again? he said.

When are you there?

His gaze was steady. That's a reasonable question. I'm there most of the time.

But not all the time.

Not all the time, no.

Will you be there tonight?

He shook his head, almost imperceptibly, and crushed the cigarette into the ashtray. He wrote something on a corner of the newspaper and tore it off, tucking it under his glass.

Do you want another one, big man? called Eamonn from the taps.

No. Must dash, he said, getting to his feet. He looked at Cushla as though he was going to say something but turned on his heels and left. On his way out, he stepped aside to let Gerry pass. There was a Belfast phone number written on the sliver of paper. She tucked it into her bra.

Eamonn lit a cigarette and blew a jet of smoke across the counter. You know, he said, I think that man is all right. Then he says something like "must dash" and I think he's a flute.

The film was in the final week of its run and there was no one else in the cinema. They sat in the very center. It was cold and Cushla draped her coat over them like a blanket. I hope you're not planning to feel me up or something, Gerry said.

You should be so lucky.

. . .

The film was beautiful, in a seedy way, although she shrieked when Jack Nicholson's nostril was slit, which Gerry found hilarious. And she loved how Faye Dunaway carried herself, elegantly damaged, draped in those exquisite clothes.

They watched all the credits. I enjoyed that, she said, as the lights went on.

Enjoyed. Is that it?

OK, it was great. And nice to see it on a big screen. The last film I saw in a picture house was *Klute*.

I'll have to drag you out more often. He kicked at the curbstone with the toe of his boot. I don't fancy you, you know, he said.

That's hurtful. Like, how am I supposed to feel? said Cushla.

He burst out laughing. You're good craic.

So are you.

They hugged and got into their cars. Cushla locked her doors. They weren't far from where Seamie McGeown had been found slashed and battered.

When she got home, Gina was already in bed. Cushla emptied ashtrays, flicked off the lights in the sitting room. As she put her foot on the bottom stair, the phone rang.

The pause. You're home, he said.

Yeah, Michael. I'm home.

Alone?

Gerry's here. And half a dozen soldiers. I've promised them a good time. Where are you, out of interest? she said, although his voice was so low she knew he was trying not to be overheard.

I appear to be jealous, he said. An unhelpful development.

I never know where you are or what you're doing. So I won't be getting myself to a nunnery anytime soon.

I'm sorry.

Good, she said, and hung up.

Upstairs, she pushed her mother's door. The radio wasn't tuned in properly and was emitting a fuzzy hiss. She crossed the room and switched it off.

You're back early, said Gina, making her jump.

Jesus. You scared the shite out of me. Why were you lying in the dark listening to that horrible noise?

I didn't notice. Eamonn rang. He likes Gerry.

Everybody likes Gerry. He's likable.

He said Michael Agnew was there, in shocking bad form. Herself mustn't be well again. Joanna Butler, she said, putting on a brogue.

Cushla felt as though she'd been punched. *Siobhán de Buitléar* was his wife. Do you know her? she said.

I used to. She wouldn't be in circulation, if you know what I mean.

I don't know what you mean.

The nerves, I told you before. Any wonder, married to him.

What's wrong with him?

Fond of the women, by all accounts. Sure he'd charm the knickers off you.

Cushla spotted cigarettes on the bedside locker, hidden behind a lamp. She snatched them away. I'm going to bed, she said.

The phone rang a few other times as well, said Gina. When I got to it no one was there.

Kids messing, said Cushla, kissing her mother's cheek. Night, Mummy.

In her bedroom, she lifted the window sash. Splinters of paint tinkled onto the sill. She sat on it to smoke a cigarette. A car passed the house in a fizz of rain, disappearing around the bend toward the hills. Somewhere out that road, a woman who had once signed her name in girlish *cló gaelach* was with a man who used her old schoolbooks to make other women want to sleep with him.

# 11

The secretary of state says the recent spate of killings in the west of the city is part of an internal Republican feud and insists the IRA truce is still in place.

The Protestant Action Force has claimed responsibility for the shooting dead of two men in a bar in the New Lodge area.

"Bye Bye Baby" is still number one.

My daddy's getting better, said Davy. The others were taking out their books and did not appear to have heard.

She gave them a spelling test, confusing them by calling out the same list of words twice. Jonathan pointed out her mistake and she rounded on him, telling him to do as he was told and not to be such a busybody, the words flying from her mouth. The boy's face flushed with shame and she turned to the board to avoid looking at him. She wrote the first verse of "The Owl and the Pussycat," the staccato tap of chalk against board going through her, and told the children to copy it. She left the room, aware of the glances they were exchanging in her wake, and ran along the corridor to the back door. Outside, she leaned against the nubbly pebble-dashed wall. Her chest was tight and she was trembling all over. What was wrong with her? The thought of Joanna Agnew had troubled her for the length of time it took to smoke a cigarette. Was it that her body had become her conscience, sending shudders through her to remind her of her badness? She stayed outside until her breath returned to normal, and went back indoors. Along the corridor, she expected to hear giggles and whispers, but there was not a sound. She was not usually a cross teacher; her outburst had frightened them.

When the bell rang at three, Davy moved slowly. He was shy of her and she felt like a harridan. Come on, she said, forcing cheer into her voice, helping him put his pencils in their case, a camouflage-patterned canvas one with red ink in the corner like a bloodstain. She left the car park and passed the main entrance of the school, parking outside the parochial house. Davy stayed in the car and Cushla walked around the corner to the newsagent's. She hovered in front of the magazines. The cover of *Cosmopolitan* showed a woman swathed in green satin, full red lips around a rosy apple, as if she was about to perform an intimate act on it. Cushla brought a copy to the counter with a *Beano* for Davy. His father had left Intensive Care and the children had been allowed to visit him. Davy had been quiet in school and, when she asked how his father was, said he was sleeping and covered in bandages.

The local paper was set aside every week under Cushla's name. The woman who served her asked her twice to spell it, calling her "Cursula." For the umpteenth time Cushla wished her parents had called her Anne or Margaret or Rose—not Mary, with its connotations of Marian shrines and rosaries—any name that didn't mark her out so obviously as a Catholic. She felt guilty for the thought, which, she realized, also marked her as a Catholic.

As she approached her car, she saw a gaunt backside protruding from the passenger window. It was Slattery. She began to walk faster, and he looked up at the sound of her heels.

Father? she said.

Miss Lavery. I was just talking to our young friend here.

Right, well, I need to get him home, she said. She got into the driver's seat and slammed the door. Davy, close your window, quick.

He wants me to go to him for private catechism. Do I have to? he said, as she pulled out.

No. You certainly do not, she said, handing him the comic. She checked the rearview mirror. Slattery was standing on the pavement, watching her drive away.

I don't even know what catechism is, he said.

Neither do I, and it hasn't done me any harm, she said. Is there anything good in that comic?

Dennis's da brought him to a museum. Gnasher is pulling apart a suit of armor because he wants to chew the slipper. Only it's not a slipper, he said.

He flipped through the pages absently all the way up the road. At his house, he rolled it up and carried it under his arm, as if it was the evening paper.

Tommy answered the front door, in jeans and a red T-shirt. He held a hand up at her briefly in greeting. He should have been at school.

Mr. Reid's camellia had begun to shed soggy petals onto the Laverys' driveway, emphasizing the grimness of their garden. We should do something out the front, she told Gina in the kitchen, laying her purchases on the kitchen table. Grow flowers. Do some weeding.

Nobody's stopping you, said Gina, pulling *Cosmopolitan* toward her. She read the headlines aloud: ARE YOU A LOVE ADDICT? (QUIZ). HOW TO STOP STIFLING YOUR FEELINGS AND BECOME A TRULY SEXUAL WOMAN. MAKE YOUR BOSS YOUR GREATEST ALLY AND GET HIM TO PROMOTE YOU. Mother of God, she said.

Davy had looked so small and fearful in the car, worrying at the strap of his bag. What did Slattery mean by private catechism? There was no point in telling Bradley; she would have to make sure the priest didn't take the child from class. She opened the local paper. A woman in Ballyholme had lost four and a half stone by giving up potato bread. The Catholic church in Sydenham had been damaged in another arson attack. The maypole was due a facelift. Opposite her, Gina tutted sometimes. She lit a cigarette and shoved the magazine in front of Cushla. Awful smut to be buying, she said.

Cushla flipped through the glossy pages but was too skittish to read even the captions on fashion spreads. It was five days since she had been to the pictures with Gerry and there had been no word from Michael. She had hardly eaten. It was as though a sickness had settled in her, an actual physical ache deep in her bowels. Sometimes she thought she was hungry, but when she went to the fridge, she was nauseated by its contents. She had looked at the phone number he gave her so often she knew it by heart but could not bring herself to dial it; not out of pride—she had abandoned that when she presented herself at his door—but because she could not bear to hear it ring out. She looked up at Gina and her head felt light. She should try to eat. I might cook, she said.

Her mother made a noise like a snort but, seeing an opportunity, poured herself a gin, saying she was celebrating a night off from the drudgery. The only cookbook in the house was the *Hamlyn All Colour* one. Some of the dishes looked horrific. Turkey suspended in aspic with segments of mandarin orange, unnatural-looking swirly puddings. She found a recipe for spaghetti Milanese and went hunting for ingredients. She had to use ham from a slipper-shaped tin you opened with a key, and mushrooms from a jar. The pasta was about a yard long, a purchase she had made in a deli in Belfast when she was buying canned shrimps for Gina, so she took down the fish kettle and filled it with water. There was a yellow tidemark around its sides from when she had boiled the eggs with the gorse blossoms. The sauce was more a matter of chucking things in a pot than cooking, but she liked the musty, minty smell of dried oregano. As she was about to bend the spaghetti into the pot, the phone rang. Gina was reading the magazine again, smoke snaking over her head, and made no move to get up.

Cushla half ran to the hall and when she lifted the receiver her hello came out high and breathy. She knew by the pause it was Michael. There were voices in the background, a television.

You've been exerting yourself, he said.

I'm cooking. She heard the ping of a till. Are you in the pub?

Yes. I came in looking for you. I can be there in five minutes.

The joy at hearing him dissolved. Michael, I haven't heard from you for days and you want me to drop everything.

I couldn't get away. Please meet me.

Jesus. OK. But don't park outside the house. I'll walk around the bend.

Who was that? said Gina when she went back to the kitchen.

Gerry Devlin. I forgot there was a meeting in the school about the Communion. I'll boil that stuff when I get back.

She waited on the curb in her trench coat. When he pulled up she got into the passenger seat. I'm not exactly playing hard to get, am I? she said.

He looked at her, just for a moment, and swung out onto the road.

Forty minutes later she was back in the house. Gina had managed to get drunk in her absence and was drumming on the table with her nails. That was quick, she said.

Really quick, said Cushla. She ran the hot tap and washed her hands, going at them with Fairy liquid and a nail brush until the gray-brown water ran clear from her fingers.

What has you so dirty? said Gina.

For God's sake, said Cushla, turning the gas on under the water again. Michael had driven her to a derelict farmhouse. He'd pulled her from the passenger seat and slapped her palms onto the roof of his car. She didn't know if she'd enjoyed it, but she loved the way he looked at her right before he hauled the gusset of her knickers aside and fucked her.

She folded the pasta into the pot and sat at the table, flicking through the magazine. The women in the photographs were heavily made up, showing flashes of glistening skin. She smoothed her plaid skirt and went to the cooker to drain the pasta. Some of the spaghetti had clumped into a gluey, corrugated sheet. She salvaged what she could and tossed it in the sauce.

Gina looked at it without enthusiasm when Cushla put a plate in front of her. Is that wee Gerry fella your boyfriend now?

What if he is?

I bloody hope he is. Staying out all night. All the phone calls. You'll be the talk of the town.

Cushla twirled spaghetti and raised her head. Stop making such a big deal about it.

Gina lifted a single strand and stared at it. Watch yourself, she said. You'll end up in the family way. She set down her fork and didn't touch the food again.

Cushla scarcely chewed hers, letting it slither down her throat. The ache in her belly had vanished. She was ravenous.

They went into the sitting room to watch television. Cushla lay on the couch and felt herself sink into the place between sleeping and waking. She sensed a hand on her, unsure if it was real or dreamed, and struggled upright.

That wee lad's in the hall, said Gina.

Gerry? Bring him in, said Cushla, rubbing her eyes.

Not him. The other wee lad.

Cushla stumbled from the room. Tommy McGeown was at the foot of the stairs. Oh, said Cushla.

Were you expecting someone else?

Yeah. I mean, no.

Michael, maybe? he said, tilting his head slightly in that way he had.

She could feel panic moving over her face. Tommy was watching her, his expression inscrutable. Did he know something? Had he seen them?

Relax, he said. That time I phoned you said "Michael?"

Right, she said, recovering her composure. Do you want a cup of tea or something?

Aye. Thanks.

He followed her into the kitchen. So this is the mansion our kid keeps talking about, he said, as she flicked on the kettle and took down mugs.

She almost said it was hardly a mansion, but was aware of how big the house was in comparison with the one in which he lived. You weren't at school today, she said instead.

Yeah. Not planning to go back, either. The sun was low. In the light his eyes were almost violet in color, so gorgeous it was an effort to look away from him.

You're so close to the end, Tommy. Would you not suffer it for the next few weeks? Sit the exams at least.

They're saying my daddy's injuries are life changing. He'll not be able to work.

Jesus, she said softly. But if you get a couple of A levels you'll be able to earn more money. Maybe go to university. Have prospects.

He laughed. What prospects would they be?

She could not argue with him. Her father had often reminded her that they were lucky to have a business, to be sheltered from the sectarian bigotry of the job market. It's good to have an education, Tommy, she said.

You in the Alliance Party or something? he said.

She laughed. No. I vote for them, though.

You're joking.

Tactical voting. To keep Paisley's lot out.

Nothing's going to change that way, he said. Anyway, my uncle says he can give me a job. He was peering at her cheekbone.

She felt her hand go up. She wiped the place he was looking at with her fingertips. Did I get it? she said.

No. He began to reach toward her face, but withdrew his hand.

She went to the hall mirror. There was a gray-brown smear where her cheekbone met her ear, the stuff she had scrubbed from her hands earlier. She buffed at it with her cuff and looked into the kitchen. Tommy was standing with his backside against the sink, watching her.

# 12

The tails of his white shirt were flopping over his trousers, damp patches clinging to his underarms. Cushla followed him to the bedroom, carrying her basket. His bed, sheets snapped tightly into hospital corners. Two white shirts hanging from the door of the wardrobe, pressed crisp like paper. The holdall open on the velvet armchair, pajamas on top, fully buttoned, sleeves folded behind as if they were on display in a shop. It was not the work of a slattern.

Good day? he said, pulling the shirt over his head and dropping it on the floor in the corner.

Grand, she said.

He kissed her and went to the bathroom. She took a bundle from her basket—knickers, tights, a toothbrush, cold cream—and left it on the far side of the bed, nearest the window. At home she slept in the middle of her bed; she liked the idea of having a side. A tap running, a cough. She paused in the corridor on her way to the sitting room. Michael was at the basin, soaping his underarms with a flannel like a laborer.

Papers spilling from a leather briefcase onto the dining table, otherwise the room was tidy. Tumblers gleaming on the tray that held the decanter. The hearth swept and dusted, brasses bright. The sort of cleaning Gina did, or used to do. Cushla sat on the sofa, a Chesterfield upholstered in maroon-colored leather, the paraphernalia of his evenings beside her on a folded card table. Pipe, tobacco, matches. Newspaper, glasses, pen. Siobhán de Buitléar's copy of *Dúil*. Cushla put it at the bottom of the pile so she wouldn't have to look at it.

They left his flat and started toward Penny's house, Michael carrying a bottle of brandy that he hadn't put in a bag, something delinquent in how he was swinging it by the neck. Sometimes his elbow grazed her arm, her breast. They were in step, her soles slapping the pavement in time to his. He watched their feet, laughed.

I'm not doing it on purpose, she said.

It's those long legs of yours.

At the door, Michael pressed the bell and leaned suddenly to kiss her hard on the mouth. They were drawing apart when the door opened. Penny was in the checked apron, smiling, then her face closed, as if she had seen something she shouldn't. She turned quickly and walked in ahead of them. When they reached the kitchen, the others were watching the door, and Cushla wondered what Penny's face might have given away.

Victor and Jane were already there. The six of them murmured greetings and exchanged kisses that didn't connect, except Victor's, which were more liquid than air. There was a charge of something in him. Drink or anger. Maybe both. Jane had painted a circle of pink blusher on each of her cheeks, the effect Pierrot-like with the layered mascara. They took their seats. Wine sloshing in glasses, the scrape of chairs. Melba toast heaped in a raffia basket. A squat cylinder of pâté in a silver dish, a butter knife jabbed in its center. Pearl onions and rings of sliced gherkin in a sugar bowl.

Penny would have a solo exhibition in the summer. Jim had been invited to speak at a conference in Scotland and their daughters would join them for a few days. Victor had been commissioned to write a book about the Ulster Workers' Council strike. Cushla thought he was looking at her as he told them. Michael asked Jane how she was. She said she had translated a short letter from Brazil for an engineering firm and the Portuguese was so bad it had taken two days. She became animated as she talked, and Cushla realized Michael had been aware of Victor's surly mood and was trying to put Jane at ease.

Penny placed a cast-iron casserole and a tureen of buttery potatoes on the table. Jim opened more wine. Make it last, he said as he poured. She bucked a full bottle into the stew.

Beef bourguignon is hardly a stew, said Jane, opening her eyes so wide she reminded Cushla of a ventriloquist's dummy, as if what was coming out of her mouth was being said by someone else. Cushla wondered if her commentary on the food was her way of claiming the right to be there. They paid her so little attention.

Michael said a boorish acquaintance of theirs had appeared on a drunk-driving charge and refused to recognize the court. When asked to explain himself he said, It's been painted since the last time I was here. They all laughed.

Does that happen a lot? said Jim.

Refusing to recognize the court? said Michael. All the Republican prisoners do it. His arm was across the back of Cushla's chair. She caught Penny looking at it, then looking at Jim.

Ha, said Victor. Gunmen and bombers thinking they're being treated unfairly.

They are being treated unfairly. The system would not be tolerated anywhere else in the United Kingdom. Or in any civilized country for that matter, said Michael.

I suppose you're buying this claim that they're political prisoners? Bloody yahoos, more like, said Victor.

She could sense Michael bristle beside her. He opened his mouth to speak, but instead grabbed his wineglass and lowered its contents. Jim and Jane were staring at the table. Penny got up and dumped a fistful of utensils in the sink. If it wasn't for the political situation, most of these kids would not be in trouble, said Michael.

And you're their champion. Good old Michael. Defending the indefensible.

There is no work for them. They are subjected to constant harassment. Every once in a while the police or army screws up so badly it results in a recruitment drive for the IRA, said Michael. His voice had changed, his diction crisp, the tone orotund, like a pastor.

Penny slammed the door of the cupboard under the sink, rounding on them. Please stop, she said.

Michael murmured an apology and Jim poured brandy into glasses engraved with a ring of fleurs-de-lis. Chocolates were passed around, dark bitter ones with powdery centers from a box Cushla didn't recognize.

Cushla bent to take the books from her basket, suddenly conscious that the others now knew she was more to Michael than an Irish teacher. She drew herself up slowly, hoping hostilities would be suspended by the time she was upright, but Victor and Michael were still eyeballing each other across the table. Start talking, she said.

Michael lit a cigarette and smoked it in silence. The others spoke haltingly, in sentences with atrocious syntax, accents so off she hardly recognized some words, but they went on. Aside from the obvious one, this was the real difference between her and them. They had the confidence to be foolish, to be wrong. She asked Michael a question in Irish and he looked surprised, as if he had forgotten where he was. He picked up her dictionary and she confiscated it. If you're stuck I'll translate, she said.

There are lots of words I'd like to know in Irish, said Victor.

Fire away, said Cushla.

Propaganda, said Victor, his eyes on Michael.

*Bolscaireacht*, answered Cushla.

Internment.

*Imtheorannú.*

Terrorist.

*Sceimhlitheoir.*

As she trawled the *foclóir* and her memory, she recalled a birthday party she'd attended when she was seven. Gina had dressed her in a fussy frock with a full skirt; the birthday girl and her friends were in pinafores and starched blouses. The gift she brought was ostentatious. She was introduced to Janets and Beverlys and Lindas who asked her to spell her name and was bewildered by the looks they exchanged on the fourth letter, unaware that Catholics said "haitch" and Protestants said "aitch." Later, she exclaimed "Oh God" when she won a round of pass the parcel, a mild response in the Lavery house that was met with hushes of "Don't swear, thingy." That had hurt most; even after they'd made her spell her name, they didn't remember it. She went home in tears, a flaccid balloon in one hand and a slice of cake wrapped in tinfoil in the other. Gina had railed at her, I hope you didn't let yourself down in front of that lot. She felt that way now. She shouldn't be here.

Are you all right tonight, Victor? Michael said. His voice was soft, but his body was hard, as if he was about to lunge.

Fine.

Are you sure?

Yes.

Excellent. Now pass the brandy, like a good fellow.


They were a few feet from the barracks on the corner. That was fun, she said. Her face was hot from the brandy but her body creased in a shudder at the cold the dark had brought. Michael put his arm around her and rubbed her hip to warm her.

Victor was goading me. It had nothing to do with you.

Interesting list of words, though. Words associated with my lot. Catholics. Nationalists. Republicans. Whatever you call us.

I made him stop.

Fuck's sake. It's awkward enough sitting there like the token Taig without you shaping up to biff your friend.

I dislike that word.

Biff? Remind me not to say it ever again.

Don't be flippant.

Taig? At least it's honest. What do you prefer? RC? Fenian? Mick?

They were in front of his house. She paused to root in her basket for her keys. Michael had walked a couple paces ahead and turned when he realized she'd hung back. You're not coming in? he said.

I'd better go home to my mummy. School in the morning.

He looked at the sky as though he was asking for strength. That makes me feel like a pervert, he said. His body had the faint stoop it had the first night, in the car park of the pub.

Sorry. She sounded petulant.

Come inside and don't be so bloody childish.

Childish? I've just had to take a load of flak from your friend.

I refuse to argue with you on the street.

You *refuse*, do you? she said, imitating his accent. That's a bit bloody pompous.

Please come in. He reached out his hand. She ignored it and stalked past him, toward his door.

They stood facing each other in the hallway. Have you any idea what it's like having to listen to that? All the time.

No. I don't.

I should have told him to fuck off, she said, instead of sitting like a good little native, letting him humiliate me.

It had nothing to do with you, I told you.

Bollocks, Michael. He asked me to translate those words because I'm a Catholic. To remind me of what my ones have been doing to his ones.

I'll have a word with him.

I don't want you to have a word with him. I just want to get through even one single day without being reminded I kick with the wrong foot.

Can we go to bed? he said. I've had quite a day.

She went to his room and took her boots off. He came back from the kitchen with two glasses, a cigarette dangling from his lips. There was a bottle of whiskey under his arm.

Do you mind if I finish this in here? he said, out of the side of his mouth.

Do you have to? You look like my ma, she said. He had kicked off his shoes and was lying on the bed, watching her undress. She slipped in beside him in her bra and knickers. He stubbed out the cigarette and arranged her so that she was lying across his chest, the covers tucked up under her chin. His left arm was around her, the hand cupping her breast. The bottle was in his other hand.

What's going on with you and Victor? she said.

He slugged from the whiskey. I've taken on a case of which he doesn't approve.

What case?

Three boys who were picked out of a lineup by a witness who could only be described as unreliable.

What did they do?

What are they accused of, I think you mean. Murdering a member of the RUC, he said. The slosh of whiskey again, a pop as he pulled the bottle from his mouth.

Why is Victor so angry?

He was one of the first reporters on the scene on Bloody Friday. Said it smelled like a butcher's shop.

Jesus.

Quite. It rather hardened his views on militant Republicanism. So he doesn't like that I take on certain cases.

He put the bottle on the nightstand and lit another cigarette. Sometimes I hate this place, he said.

# Chiaroscuro

## 13

Davy was waiting by her car, his satchel on the bonnet. He was running in slow motion, arms and legs cutting through the air like the blades of a windmill. He saw Cushla and began moving toward her. Steve Austin, astronaut, he said. A man barely alive.

You're like Three Legs of Mann.

I saw one of them on an Isle of Man 10p.

She unlocked her car and he hopped into the back seat.

Miss Lavery, a man's voice said behind her. It sounded so formal she thought it was Gerry Devlin pretending to be the headmaster, and she let out a guffaw and swung round. Bradley was a few feet away, the waistcoat of his suit doing an admirable job of containing the paunch above his belt. I hope you know what you're getting into, he said.

I'm just giving the child a lift.

It's too much. Sitting with him at break. The lifts. The lunches.

The dinner ladies must have told him she'd paid for Davy to eat school meals for the rest of the term. She had asked Bradley if the school would cover it, but he had turned it into a conversation about Betty McGeown's ineptitude as a mother.

I'm just doing my job, she said.

Bradley was looking at her car. Davy had wound the window down and was turning his head slowly, eyes coming to rest on them.

Look, I'd better go, she said, and got into the driver's seat. Dear God, Davy, what are you doing? she whispered.

Focusing very hard with my bionic eye.

Close the window.

Right, miss. One of his eyes was almost closed, the other staring at her. Gentlemen, we can rebuild him, he said. We have the technology.

She started to laugh, so he kept going. We have the capability to make the world's first bionic man, he said. Better, stronger, faster.

They were still giddy when they reached his house. It had been a few days since Cushla had spoken to Betty, so she went up the path with him. Tommy answered the door, in his own clothes. He put a closed fist to Davy's temple. There's a surprise for you inside, wee man, he said. Davy dropped his bag on the floor and went into the sitting room.

Tommy's hair had grown and he had to lift his chin to look at Cushla, which made him appear belligerent. Hiya, miss, he said.

You didn't go back to school.

Nope.

Ah, Tommy. At least sit the exams.

I'm done with it all, he said. Come in and meet my father.

Cushla's chest constricted. Michael said she had a face that showed exactly what she was thinking. What if Seamie saw revulsion in her? But Tommy had turned and she had no choice but to follow him.

The air was blue with cigarette smoke. Seamie McGeown was in the sort of armchair you saw in hospitals, his back to her. His head had been shaved for surgery and the downy regrowth reminded her of Davy's when he'd had an extreme haircut. Mandy was on the settee and Betty was in front of Seamie, perched on the edge of a stool from the kitchen, as if she might fly up. Come on over, she said.

Tommy stepped onto the hearth of the unlit fire to let Cushla pass. Above Seamie's right ear his skull was slightly concave, the edge of the dent marked by a crescent-shaped scar notched with horizontal dashes where the stitches had been.

This is Miss Lavery, Davy's teacher, said Betty. She's been awful good to us the last while. Her voice was loud and cheery, as if speaking to a deaf person. Her mouth was grim.

Without thinking, Cushla thrust out her hand. Seamie looked at it and slowly turned up his palms. The wounds were still wet. Other scars—crude red lines—traveled up from the heels of his hands, disappearing under the unbuttoned cuffs of his shirt. Cushla thought she might pass out. She took in a deep breath to steady herself and glanced at Betty, who shook her head almost imperceptibly, allowing her the moment. There was a box of cigarettes on the arm of Seamie's chair. He began footering at it, trying to take one without bending his fingers. Cushla was making things worse by watching, and she was relieved when Betty wagged a thumb in the direction of the kitchen.

A twin-tub washing machine was connected to the sink, a fresh-breeze scent of washing powder wafting from it. There was a nylon shopping bag on the draining board, a bar of Sunlight soap.

You must be glad to have him home, said Cushla.

Aye, said Betty. She lifted a garment from a bowl of sudsy water and began working at it with a nail brush, dipping, peering, scrubbing again. The vests and faded pajamas that were spilling from the bag were spotted with watery ocher stains.

Did you see the cut of our Tommy? said Betty, lifting her ham-colored hands from the water and dragging them across her tabard.

Maybe he'll go back next year. Have you spoken to the school?

He's eighteen. They say he can do what he likes. He's hardly here anymore. He's been knocking about with his cousins, she said, reaching to stir the soap-slicked water with the shaft of a sweeping brush. Bad news, them boys.

Oh! Cushla said. That reminds me. Davy can get school dinners for the rest of the term.

Who's paying for it? said Betty.

Cushla hadn't prepared an answer. The school, she said, a beat late.

Betty had stopped working and was frowning as she listened. That'd be handy, she said eventually.

As Cushla passed through the sitting room, Mandy was in front of her father, lighting the cigarette that was between his lips, Davy watching. Cushla called good-bye to them and went to the hall. Tommy came down the stairs as she opened the front door. He caught the edge of it with one hand; in the other he held the copy of *Jude the Obscure* she had lent him.

Best book I've ever read, he said.

I'm delighted you like it.

A smile was trying to escape him, manifesting itself in a deep dimple on either side of his mouth. It's great, he said. Dark, like, but great. Keep them coming.

It was an oddly cocky thing to say, and she felt color rise in her face. Your mummy's demented about you, Tommy.

The dimples vanished. She had reminded him that he was a schoolboy. Did you see what they did to him? he asked.

It's horrific.

He has seizures from getting his head kicked in. He can't concentrate long enough to read a headline in the paper. He's sitting in there with a bag of his own piss strapped round his fucking leg, like.

I hope the police find whoever did it soon.

I hope they find them before I do.

She laid her fingers on his cuff. His arm jerked, as if she had given him an electric shock. He stared at her hand for a moment and went back upstairs, slower now.

When she got to the end of the estate, she could hardly see for crying. A gully sucker was coming from the left. There was time to swing out ahead of it, but she let it pass, wiping her eyes with her sleeve and following its foul sludgy load down the road toward town.

Gina was in the hall, hands clasped. She had taken to hovering by the doors and windows to better monitor Cushla's movements.

You're standing there like one of the von Trapp children, said Cushla, putting her basket beside the phone. As if you're about to burst into song.

Gina placed her hands on her hips and tilted forward, louring. Were you crying? she said.

Seamie McGeown got out of hospital today. Mummy, you should see the state of him. His hands haven't healed. I nearly touched them, said Cushla.

I hope you didn't gurn in front of him.

No! But it was upsetting.

Dear Jesus, but I wouldn't send you for the midwife.

The phone began to ring, startling them both. Cushla reached for it, but Gina had grabbed it first and was calling out their number in her telephone voice. She made a face and handed Cushla the receiver. It's that wee Gerry fella, she said.

Cushla stared her mother down until she went into the kitchen. Fuck's sake, she said as she put the phone to her ear.

Delightful language. And does Gerry know your mother refers to him as "that wee fella"?

It's you.

Come tonight.

She opened her mouth to say yes but stopped. She would have to change, dress up in a way that looked like she hadn't dressed up—which was harder than actually getting dressed up—think of an excuse to make to Gina. I'm knackered, she said. Today was weird and I need a quiet night.

Bad weird?

Not great, she said, tears streaming again. She sniffed, making a wet snattery sound.

Oh, Cushla. What is it?

There was such tenderness in his voice she let out a whimper. I can't talk now, she said.

Let me look after you.

Upstairs, she threw a change of underwear into a bag and sat on the stool in front of her dressing table, looking at her reflection in the mirror. She was overcome with a feeling of utter defeat. She wanted to lie on her bed and sleep, but had been unable to say no to him. It wasn't because he had been kind to her. It was because each time she saw him she was afraid it would be the last time.

Crying made her completely unpresentable, and now her eyes were bloodshot, her nose pink and swollen. She dabbed on some foundation to conceal the worst of the blotches and reapplied mascara, but it just made her look as though she was having an allergic reaction. She ran downstairs to the kitchen, where Gina was standing by the open fridge.

I forgot I'd promised to go to something with Gerry, said Cushla.

But I got in a couple of wee steaks. I was going to make chips.

Maybe we can have them tomorrow night?

All right, said Gina.

Cushla put her arms around her mother and held her. Gina normally accepted such advances stiffly but, to Cushla's horror, her body yielded. Cushla pulled her closer, feeling wretched. I'm sorry, Mummy. I'll be in all weekend, she said, knowing as the words came out of her mouth that if Michael wanted to see her she would leave Gina alone without hesitation.

Go on out, love, said Gina, patting Cushla's back. There's no point the pair of us being miserable.

A boy carrying a violin case came out of the house next to Michael's, followed by a woman with short blond hair. She looked at Cushla's car—it was notable among the saloons and estates in the other driveways—then looked at Cushla, her expression one of amusement. How many women had visited him here? She took off across the gravel, kicking it up in her haste.

He was in a thin jumper with suede patches on the elbows, a brushed-cotton shirt with a soft collar. Mr. Reid clothes. He watched her blink the image away. What does that look mean? he said.

She pushed up on her toes to find his lips. Nothing, she said.

He took her hand and brought her inside. A window was open, a magnolia branch fingering the glass. The olive-green curtains had faded to khaki where the sun had touched them. An attempt had been made at tidying the papers on the table, and the whiskey decanter was full.

He told her to put on some music and went to the kitchen. She bent over the stereo and flipped through records she didn't recognize, jazz and classical and blues. She lowered the needle to the LP that was already on the turntable and stood in the archway.

Do you want to talk about it? he said.

Seamie McGeown got out of hospital today. Tommy brought me in to meet him.

Oh dear, he said. The suck of the fridge door, the soft dunt of it closing. That must have been awful.

She told him about the wounds on Seamie's hands, weeping like stigmata.

One hears about these attacks on the news, the shootings and bombings. But I think one has to hear or see the details to appreciate the suffering.

Do you come across a lot of that stuff in court? she said.

Yes. The evidence can be horrific.

Is that what's in those folders?

In some of them, yes.

He asked how the children were, and she told him Davy was the entertainer, Mandy matronly. That Tommy was angry.

Poor kid, he said. There are Tommy McGeowns appearing in front of me every day of the week. He was daubing toast with butter and mustard.

Betty was washing stains from Seamie's clothes. It wasn't blood, more like a fleshy color. I thought I was going to faint. I couldn't get away quick enough.

But you passed yourself. And looked after the children when their mother was at the hospital. Cut yourself some slack, he said, kissing her on the forehead.

He had been moving around the kitchen as they spoke. There was a grace about him, for such a big man, in the fling of his arm to open a cupboard, the brisk precision with which he took down the grill tray. A trumpet was playing, a woman's voice, clear and mournful, coming from the speakers. Excellent choice of music, by the way, he said.

It's the last record you played. I couldn't take the pressure of choosing. Who's singing?

He fetched the sleeve from the sitting room. There was a photo on the cover of a tiny woman with fair hair and a full frock. That, he said, is Ottilie Patterson. A County Down woman. He said she was married to a band leader and had sung with everyone from Lonnie Donegan to Muddy Waters. That a mostly Black crowd at a jazz festival in America kept Duke Ellington and His Orchestra waiting because they loved her so much they wouldn't let her leave the stage.

He had grated Wensleydale and was heaping it on the toast. He shook a bottle of Worcestershire sauce at her and said it would make all the difference, something boyish about him as he explained the modification.

You're cute, she said. Like the children at school when they put crisps in their sandwiches.

He handed her a bottle of wine and a corkscrew and told her to find glasses in the cabinet in the other room. They ate at the table. He pulled his chair so close to hers their thighs were touching. A newspaper was folded open on the crossword page. He filled in the answers before she had time to read the clues, stopping to top up their drinks or eat the crusts she had left on the side of her plate, until a corner of the puzzle was covered in inky-blue script. He paused as if he was stuck, read a clue aloud to her. She got it right and he said, Well done!

Piss off. I feel like you're teaching me chess or something and letting me win.

Sorry, he said, laughing. Did you ever finish that Iris Murdoch book?

I abandoned it.

Are you disappointed?

No. I bought it to take my mind off you. And then you asked to see what I was reading and based on my choice of book decided I wasn't a complete moron. So Iris has been lucky for me, she said. She had addressed most of the admission to her plate and lifted her head to look at him.

He left the table and went to the stereo to flip the record. Cushla sat on, wondering if she had misread him. They spent so much time alone it felt as though she could say anything, but maybe she couldn't. Had she sounded needy or clingy? If she wasn't here she would be at home with her mother, but there were lots of places Michael could be. He had friends, money. A family.

He came back with his pipe and began packing it. I liked you before Iris Murdoch, he said.

I need details, Michael.

He lit the tobacco and told her between puffs that he had liked how she stalked into the pub with a dirty big cross on her forehead. That he liked that she hadn't looked away when she caught him watching her in the mirror. That he liked her in the Lyric, when she was standing by the ledge, trying to look nonchalant. That he especially liked that she cried when he mentioned her father. That he loved her.

If you're saying that you'd better mean it, she said.

I do. You're supposed to say it back.

Another time. I've been doing all the running.

They fucked for a while on the chair and then on the sofa, the sound of a petrol lawnmower and the herby smell of cut grass coming through the open window. A door slammed somewhere, a woman's voice called out. His breath changed and he pushed into her harder, like he did when they were in his car and headlights from another vehicle lit up their bodies for a moment, as if it excited him that they might be caught. Another noise from outside, wheels crunching over gravel, and he eased her off him and rolled to his feet. Cushla got up and backed toward the kitchen, smoothing her hair and skirt.

Michael was by the window, holding his trousers up with one hand.

Who is it? she said.

I don't know. A car reversed in and took off again.

Did you recognize it?

No. It was one of those drab makes you aren't supposed to remember, he said, fastening his clothes. He poured himself a whiskey and drank it by the window, looking down on his quiet road.

# 14

The UDA have claimed responsibility for the murder on Monday of a Protestant man who was working on a railway line near Donegall Road. His Catholic workmate was the intended target.

Today is the first anniversary of the start of the Ulster Workers' Council strike.

Mud are number one, said Zoe. She was wearing a turquoise jumper threaded with sparkles, a "Love Is . . ." motif printed on it. Some of the other girls were in party dresses. Cushla began the usual routine of sums and spellings, but the children were skittery. The police were coming to the school to put on a disco for them.

After break, she led them to the assembly hall. The drapes on the tall windows to the right were drawn, the room lit only by a strip of traffic lights propped on the edge of the stage. A table from the canteen held a turntable, an officer of the Royal Ulster Constabulary, in crested peaked cap and pistachio-colored shirtsleeves, standing either side of it. The removal of their flak jackets, which were slung over a large beanbag, appeared to be their only concession to the gaiety of the occasion. A glitterball sat on the floor, winking dejectedly. Cushla weaved between the children toward the front of the stage, where Gerry was talking to a third policeman, a man in his thirties with the ruddy, athletic look of one who got a lot of fresh air.

This is Cushla, the other P3 teacher, said Gerry.

Miss Lavery, said the policeman, hooking his thumbs into his belt loops. She must have looked surprised because he said, I drink in your family's bar the odd time.

Oh yeah, said Cushla, although she didn't remember him. Will you be dancing?

You never know, he said, and smiled as he walked away.

Chatting up peelers, said Gerry. You could be tarred and feathered.

You're just jealous.

You're not my type, I keep telling you.

Cheeky get. Come on and see what these kids are at.

As they walked across the boards he caught her hand, pulling her toward him and then releasing her, sending her spinning across the floor. He caught her again and twirled her under his hand.

I can't dance, she said.

I can see that, but I'm brilliant at it.

Their pupils had surrounded them. Gerry had taken charge of her so completely, she had to do little but let him dance her around the floor. When the song ended, the children cheered.

Jesus Christ, she said, laughing.

Disco Peeler can't take his eyes off you, he said.

She turned and saw the third policeman climb the steps at the side of the stage. You talk shite, Gerry.

I mean it. He was watching you.

Eamonn was in a good mood. He said he was thinking of booking a band to play in the upstairs lounge they never used anymore, like the good old days. The bar had thrived for a couple of years after the Troubles started, drinkers driving out from the city to get away from the chaos. It hadn't lasted; most people were afraid to go out at all now. The boys were bickering among themselves about the acts they'd like to hear live: Lynyrd Skynyrd for Fidel—he felt an affinity with the Confederate Army—and Doctor Hook and the Medicine Show for Leslie. Minty was torn but eventually settled on Clodagh Rodgers; presumably having the "best legs in British show business" compensated for the fact that she was a Catholic from Ballymena.

The opening montage of the news gave way to footage of the strike, the red, white, and blue poster that read DUBLIN IS JUST A SUNNINGDALE AWAY an eerie prelude to a photo of a Dublin pavement scattered with twisted metal and tarry with blood. It was a year to the day since a group of electricity supply workers began industrial action to force the dissolution of the power-sharing government that had been functioning for a few months. Businesses and shops began to close. The pubs stayed open at first—an essential service, Fidel had joked as he swaggered about the place—but were soon ordered to shut. Cushla felt rage rise up in her as she watched. Paramilitaries openly parading on the streets; Brian Faulkner, the chief executive, announcing the collapse of the government. She rinsed a cloth in soapy water and began slowly wiping her way along the counter, observing the profiles of the regulars as they watched the television. It was so much easier to say nothing than to forget. This is what Cushla remembered.

Leslie coming up the path of their house with milk in a Lucozade bottle that still had the crinkly orange wrapper on it. Gina hugging him, her face a picture of gratitude and welcome. Later, she and Cushla had sat at the kitchen table, darkness sinking around them, drinking tea they had boiled on a Primus, which tasted of glucose. That was decent of him, Cushla said.

He did it to show us that he could, said Gina.

Minty in front of the locked gates of the high school, surrounded by a couple dozen of its students. Slattery had ignored advice from the police to close, and at three the children left to a chorus of "Who's in Derry? Who's in Derry? Fuck the Pope and the Virgin Mary." A missile came hurtling through the air and landed at the feet of one of the P1s; a crisp bag oozing what looked like a human turd. Cushla strode to the edge of the footpath and opened her arms at Minty, as if to ask him what was going on. He looked away.

And Fidel. One day, Cushla set out with Gina to visit her father's grave. Just before the entrance to the cemetery, someone had blocked the road with a tractor. The car ahead of Cushla's was waved through but hers was stopped by two men with tartan scarves tied around their faces, one of whom was holding a shotgun. A third man, in a balaclava, stepped forward and made a rolling motion with his hand. Cushla opened the window and he bent to speak to her.

Gina leaned across Cushla. Fidel, she said. Are you taking the hand out of me?

How did you know it was me? he said, glancing over his shoulder at the other pair, who were now reclining against the front of the tractor, smoking.

Your beard's sticking out the bottom of your mask.

He chuckled softly. No flies on you, missus, he said. Go on through, ladies.

Cushla thanked him and drove off. Over the following days, the bare larder and her car's empty fuel tank took up all her time. It wasn't until the strike ended that she realized how outrageous the encounter had been. That someone she had known most of her life had stopped her at a paramilitarized checkpoint that had been erected in the cause of preventing her kind from participating in government. And pretended not to know her.

She had cleaned to the end of the counter. The news had moved on

to a human-interest story, about the threat to traditional home baker-
ies from factory-made bread. A tall man in fogged-up glasses was ma-
niacally cutting soda farls without taking his eyes from the camera,
and blaming the Common Market for the drop in sales.

Eamonn flipped down the stout tap, a pint glass tilted under it. He
inclined his head at the door. Here comes Rumpole, he said. Look after
him, will you?

Michael hung his jacket on the back of a stool, lighting a cigarette in
the juvenile way he had, one eye almost closed. Cushla put a whiskey in
front of him. Sandwich? she said.

No, he said, holding out a pound note.

He was going home to his wife, she thought, and felt her lips push
into a pout. She turned away from him and went to serve someone else.

When you're ready, said Michael, his voice thick with irony. She
plucked the note from his fingers and went to the till, stabbing at the
keys. She returned with his change, leaving it stacked on the counter,
ignoring his open hand.

Newspapers were folded and tucked under arms, glasses were
drained. Eamonn left and there was just Michael and Jimmy at the bar
and a couple of men from the Super Ser Club, as Eamonn called them;
men who had drunk themselves out of marriages and into unheated
bedsits near the esplanade. Cushla checked they each had a drink and
cleared all the empties and ashtrays to the sink. Michael had pulled his
stool beside Jimmy's and was smiling as the old man made chop-chop
karate motions, as if he was singlehandedly taking on a battalion of
Japanese soldiers. Older people loved to talk about the war, especially
the Blitz. Belfast endured the worst single night of bombing outside of
London, but it was more than that; the doodlebugs had been nonsectar-
ian. They could talk about that war because this war was unspeakable.

She went toward them with a stack of clean ashtrays. I was sixteen,

Michael was saying. My mother saw something on the road and sent me out to investigate. The road was in pitch darkness, of course, and I crawled across the tarmac on my belly.

Was it a bomb? said Jimmy.

It was a pile of dung left by the rag-and-bone man's horse.

Do you remember World War One? said Cushla.

Jimmy chuckled, clamping his hand on Michael's shoulder. His fingernails were long, the tips pewter with dirt. He got to his feet. Good night, Your Honor, he said, and ambled out the door. Sometimes Fidel and the others patted their pockets when he was leaving, checking imaginary eggs. Behind his back, they pretended to shoot themselves, as if he was boring them to suicide. Michael had listened to him.

Why does everyone think I'm a judge? he said.

Because you're ancient and you talk lovely.

You're merciless.

Sorry. I was going to tell you a reason why I like you but I don't want to seem too keen.

Heaven forbid. What are you doing at the weekend?

# 15

A blast of cold air and diesel fumes propelled a boy Davy's age along the aisle of the train. Davy stood proprietorially beside Cushla, holding up three fingers of his left hand and the thumb of his right. A woman dumped a nylon shopping bag on the table and sat opposite, beside the boy. Cushla shifted to the window seat to make room for a girl of five or so.

The mother took a coloring book and a bundle of crayons wrapped in an elastic band from the bag. The girl began to fill in the black outline of an Indian chief in a wide feathery headdress, making the plumes fearsome with orange, red, and yellow markings. Cushla had brought things for the journey. June's *Cosmo*, a Dairy Milk, a can of Coke. The boy picked up the drink and, in unison, his mother and sister hissed, *Put it down.*

He's welcome to it, Cushla said. The mother smiled but pulled the boy's hand away when he reached for it again. He went at the picture. He couldn't stay within the lines and with every stroke his sister complained. Cushla watched him look slyly at her and lift a red crayon, curving his arm around the page to conceal what he was doing. When he revealed the finished picture, the chief's face was scarlet.

You wrecked it! the girl said.

He's a red Indian, said her brother. R. E. D. He's meant to have a red bake. Big Chief Dirty Bum, his name is.

The mother shot him a deadly look. I'm warning you, she said.

The boy put his lip out. When's Daddy getting out of jail? he said, as if his father would show clemency.

The mother glanced at Cushla and turned the page of the coloring book.

The boy had taken a packet of biscuits from the bag and was slotting them into his mouth like coins in a vending machine. His mother gave him a good-natured smack on the back of the hand and snatched them off him. They got off at Dundalk. Cushla had read in the paper that border towns down south were filling with families fleeing the north.

It was just after six when the train arrived at Connolly Station. People were surging along the platform toward her. Students swinging sausage bags bunged with dirty clothes, men in overcoats carrying briefcases. Girls in crimplene suits clutching vanity cases. Outside, the pavements were clotted with phlegm. Even after six years of carnage Belfast was cleaner. She crossed the road, hurrying to avoid the green double-decker that was reeling unsteadily toward a bus stop, her suitcase banging off her thigh. Halfway to the hotel her arm was numb, and she paused outside the Abbey Theatre to change the case to the other hand. There was a gypsy woman cross-legged on the ground. She'd say three Hail Marys for a couple of bob, she said. Cushla told her she had no punts and walked on, a curse spat in her wake.

The hotel's name was spelled out on a stained-glass canopy above the entrance. Cushla pushed the old mahogany door and went to the desk.

There's a room booked for Mr. and Mrs. Lavery, she said.

The receptionist looked behind her. And Mr. Lavery?

He's on his way.

I see, she said.

The room was large with a high ceiling, shrouded from the street by floor-length net curtains. A cast-iron fireplace, blocked up, a fern in a copper pot on the hearth. A bureau inlaid with green leather, a wardrobe on elegant, precarious legs, a dressing table with a three-way mirror. Heavy green drapes under a fringed pelmet. It reminded her of Michael's flat.

She hung her clothes in the wardrobe, put her underwear in a drawer. Her skin felt tacky, the city's grime clinging to her sweat. A corner of the room had been boxed in by boast walls to make an en suite bathroom. She ran a bath and lowered herself into the water. She lifted fistfuls of suds and soaped the places his mouth and hands would go. Under her arms, around her breasts, between her legs. Her watch was out of reach, and without natural light she had no sense of time passing. She got out and dabbed her skin with a towel, smeared it with baby oil. Cleaned off that morning's makeup, applied a new layer that *Cosmopolitan* said would appear dewy after the steam of the bath.

Downstairs, she ordered a Coke at the bar and sat in a leather bucket chair by the window. Beside her were two American couples in their forties with pints of Guinness they turned from time to time in admiration but didn't drink, and four whiskies they did drink. At another table, three nuns gulping tea and breaking pieces from plain biscuits, priests in twos and threes. At the counter, a lone priest parping on a cigar between mouthfuls of brandy. She looked out the window. A man left the religious bookshop across the road. There was a May altar in its window, a tall blue-and-white plaster Mary surrounded by vases of yellow flowers and white candles. He locked the door behind him, taking his glasses off and tucking them in the pocket of his jacket before walking slowly up the street in the direction of the train station.

The scratch of his chin against her cheek. How's Mrs. Lavery? He was in a gray suit, a knitted tie loose over a blue shirt.

Brilliant. It's like Vatican II. Did you just get here?

I arrived a few minutes ago. I watched you from the doorway. Your head was in the air.

You said you like me when I'm nonchalant.

He laughed. Come on, he said. We have time for a quick one before the play.

Rush hour was giving way to weekend. A newsboy on the corner, packing up. A mauve dusk falling on the rooftops. Boys in wide trousers waiting for girls under a Victorian clock, Michael's hand on her elbow as they crossed the street. A pub, long and narrow, with yellowy brasses and dark wood. She swung a bum cheek onto a stool at the counter.

What'll you have? he said. She was sitting sideways, her knee between his thighs.

Whiskey.

Seriously? His smell. Clean linen and lemon soap.

I am serious. I'm trying to fit in.

He needed a haircut. Or maybe he was trying to look younger. She pressed her mouth against his. His lips twitched, a hurried movement, and he drew back. What was that for? he said.

I felt like it.

He smiled, but then his eyes roved from the door to the drinkers behind her and back. He was concerned about being seen, she realized. Dublin was almost foreign to her. For Michael, it was a city he'd once lived in, the place his wife came from.

The gypsy woman was gone, the theater lit up from within. Another crowded foyer, people here and there he knew by name. Some he introduced her to, some he didn't: she tried not to think about why. She hadn't seen *A Doll's House*, she told him, but she'd watched *Hedda Gabler* on TV. Before she would have been ashamed to say so, afraid he would find her ignorant.

Wasn't it wonderful? he said, as they left.

Yeah, she said. And kind of disturbing. Nora is all the women I know.

Not you.

No?

You're far too argumentative.

She laughed, but felt uneasy. She dressed for him, tolerated the disdain of his friends, suffered his absences and lapses of contact; like Nora she had been "performing tricks" for him.

Across the big boulevard, the widest street in Europe, he told her. Cars parked along the curbs, bicycles swerving unsteadily under half-pissed backsides. It felt strange to be in the center of a city at night.

He brought her to a Chinese restaurant, a dim room with lacquered screens and red lamps. He ordered for them, ribs in a sticky glaze, chicken in a gelatinous sauce with chunks of pineapple. When the wine arrived he tasted it. Christ, he said, screwing his face up. It was the stuff Eamonn had brought to lunch on Easter Sunday.

Was it hard for you to get away? he said.

No, she said, and felt a stab of guilt. She had left school after lunch, claiming to have an urgent dental appointment. For Gina, who was having her roots done, she left a note on the kitchen table: *Mummy! I'm away to Dublin for the weekend. Back Sunday. C xxx.* What about you?

No.

Did you have to lie?

He took a long drink from his wineglass. I don't lie, Cushla, he said. I omit to mention things.

They walked back to the hotel without speaking. He bought a whiskey at the bar to bring upstairs. The priest from earlier was still at the counter, a stunned, rhapsodic expression on his face.

He's sitting there since I checked in, Cushla said.

It must be a lonely life, he said. His kindness made her ache.

Upstairs, they stepped out of their shoes. She took her nightdress from the drawer and went into the bathroom, leaving him propped against the pillows in his clothes, drinking. She removed her makeup, brushed her teeth. The nightdress was long and made of white cotton, with a fine lace trim. She liked how it looked with her hair down.

Michael had put his glasses on and opened *Cosmopolitan*. She sat on the side of the bed and applied hand cream the way Gina had showed her. One finger at a time, like putting on a glove.

Melvyn Bragg: The Man Who Makes 600,000 People Stay Home and Tune into Culture on Saturday Nights, he read aloud.

I'd stay in for Melvyn Bragg, she said.

He rolled so that he was propped on his elbow, looking at her. Do you think we're ridiculous?

Where did that come out of?

Do you?

Not when we're alone, but yeah, sometimes I do. Your friends think I'm some dolly bird you picked up in a pub. Which I kind of am, to be fair. And you're married, which makes me your bit on the side. We're actually worse than ridiculous.

Is that why you're angry? he said.

I try not to be, but I can't help it.

God did this, you know, he said. Put you in front of me when I've nothing to offer you.

An ugly sound woke her; a gull scrawking on the windowsill. It flew away, leaving a drip of gray fluid drooling down the glass. Michael was curved around her back, a hand on her belly. She lifted his arm and went to the bathroom. Her hair was matted, the nightdress creased like a wrung cloth. When she went back into the room he was sitting up, a sheet across his thighs. Take that bloody thing off, he said.

She felt her arms fly up and wrap across her breasts. What's wrong with it?

You look like Bertha Rochester.

She went to get into bed and he moved across to her side. Take it off where you are. Please.

She crossed her arms and lifted the sides of the nightdress, pulling it over her head as slowly as she could bear it. He took her hand and helped her onto the bed, lowering her onto his cock. She waited for him to kiss her, touch her, but all he did was put his hands on her buttocks. She began to move, watching his eyes, the slow blinks. Listening to the small clicks that came from the back of his throat.

As they finished, the clattering of delft outside the room, a rap on the door.

Jesus, she said, falling on his chest.

I ordered breakfast.

She climbed off him and pulled on the nightdress. On the corridor, she bent to lift the tray, cotton clinging to the mess he'd left between her legs. A door closed and she looked up. Two nuns were sweeping along the carpet toward her, eyes downcast. She murmured a greeting and reversed into the room.

You just said, "Good morning, sisters." With no drawers on.

Yeah.

She kissed his shoulder. Buttered his toast. Poured his tea.

A draft from the river that swept dust and litter from the pavement. Cushla narrowed her eyes at the light. He'd brought sunglasses. Wide, grand streets, a café with a smell of coffee that slowed her step. A curved Georgian building with blocked-up windows; he said there was once a tax on glass. Through the arch at Trinity College, across the cobbles. He pointed at where he'd sat in lectures, where he ate cheap lunches. Where he played cricket and won a yard-of-ale contest.

Back through the arch and a run through the traffic to cross the street. A girl in an Indian smock and man's leather jacket, squatting on the footpath, drawing a dragon in pastel chalk. He dropped coins in her hat and led Cushla into a shop that sold pipes. They were displayed in glass-topped cabinets lined with green baize. She told him it was like a jewelry shop for ould fellas and bought him a blackthorn pipe and a tin of Mick McQuaid.

They walked up Grafton Street. Buskers were playing guitars, huddles of youths standing about watching them. Something was wrong. She looked up and down the street and didn't know what it was until she was in the doorway of Switzers, sliding her handbag off her shoulder and holding it open. Michael laughed. You're not in Kansas anymore, he said.

There were bombs down here last year. Why's there no security?

There just isn't. Come on.

Inside, he passed her pairs of sunglasses he thought would suit her. She chose big Jackie O–ish ones with brown-tinted lenses. She put them on and felt unlike herself, as though she was a character in a film.

He brought her to a pub down a side street. Two women at a table under a bleary window, shopping bags at their feet. A ray of sunlight striking worn wooden floorboards. Michael ordered a pint of Guinness. Cushla asked for a Coke to slake her hangover. He protested softly when she insisted on paying, watching her smooth the corners of the unfamiliar money before handing it to the barman.

I love punts, she said. The way they put a beautiful woman on the pound note. The Brits have the Queen's head all over everything.

He lit a cigarette, watched the smoke curl up toward the ceiling. I know what we'll do next, he said.

It's weird how well you know Dublin. You being a good Ulster Prod and all.

A pause as he swallowed a mouthful of stout. I'm an all-Ireland sort of chap, he said.

As opposed to united Ireland.

Not necessarily. I love Ireland. I just don't think it's worth killing anyone over it.

He led her along streets she'd never walked before. They passed the parliament building and turned onto Nassau Street, which ran the side of Trinity College. Bouquets had been placed by a section of the railings, blooms sweating under cellophane wrapping. She told him she had seen this spot on the news a few days earlier, on the anniversary of the strike.

There were bombs in three locations, he said. Eleven people were blown to bits on the street parallel to our hotel.

He paused beside an old bookshop. There were slim volumes of poetry and fat history books behind a curved window. Cushla caught a glimpse of their reflection. The bulk of him, his face close to the glass, pointing. Her at his elbow, her face turned slightly toward him.

At the end of the strip of shops he turned right, onto a square. She followed him through the National Gallery, its high quiet rooms and echoey corridors. He stopped in front of a vast painting. Look, he said.

The woman from the Irish pound note was sitting in a chair, draped in sumptuous clothes in deep shades of blue and burgundy and purple, her arm around the shoulder of a little girl. To the left, a woman dressed like an exotic servant was carrying a platter of fruit. To the right, an older girl was leaning on a tallboy, watching them. At the back of the room a mirror was propped against the wall, reflecting the artist as he painted.

It isn't like looking at a family, said Cushla. The girl on the right seems lonely, standing there by herself.

Clever you. She's his daughter from an earlier marriage. Hazel was his second wife, an American he married in his fifties. She appeared in over four hundred of his paintings, and when he was asked to create an image for the banknotes he used her face as a symbol of Ireland.

What's the painter's name?

Sir John Lavery. He was a Belfast Catholic.

No way, said Cushla, smiling.

Michael told her that Lavery had become a portraitist, painting royalty, Winston Churchill, all the important figures of those days. That he had to tread a very fine line between his position in British high society and his support for the cause of Irish nationalism.

So he was good at keeping his gob shut. It must be genetic, said Cushla.

As they walked back to the hotel he told her about another of Lavery's paintings, of the trial of Sir Roger Casement. It is so quietly subversive, he said. Even amidst the pomp of a British court, it is the doomed figure in the dock to which the eye is drawn.

You're the only person I've ever met in my life who gets away with saying things like "to which the eye is drawn."

I must sound like an arse.

No. But I don't know what you're doing with me.

In the hotel room, he opened a window. They undressed each other slowly, to the sound of buses sighing and cars idling. Are you happy? he said, as they lay down.

For a moment she was afraid she might cry. Tomorrow she would be at home with her mother, lurking by the phone, waiting. Yeah, she said.

She was too happy. And not about to say so.

They got up at seven and dressed for dinner. He hailed a taxi from the hotel steps and told the driver to take the scenic route, naming streets and squares. They crossed the river, passed Trinity again. An old woman drinking from a bag by a canal, swans drifting on its oily surface. The hump of a bridge, a lock, the stench of stagnant water. Elegant iron streetlamps, the flat face of a Georgian terrace. Crackled doors under dirty fanlights, rows and rows of doorbells.

Such a beautiful street, said Cushla.

It's a kip, said the driver. Sure the houses are falling down.

They went down metal steps to a basement. The room was cavernous and warm, the tables laid with silver and starched linen, lit by candles. Michael knew the waiters by name, although that's not what he called them; they were Joe the sommelier and Paddy the maître d'. She let them choose for her, signature dishes she would remember, they said.

A slow meal, lulls between courses when he asked to see the wine list and noisily sloshed their recommendations around in his mouth. She thought of the lunch at Easter that degenerated into a row, how little they cared about what they ate, the crumble untouched amidst the main-course plates. Her gut burned with want. That she might get away from her family, her mother, and be with this man.

Sounds she could feel on her skin. His voice. Silver tinkling against porcelain. Corks popping. He said the last time he ate here Stanley Kubrick was at a table in the corner. He had been in Dublin filming *Barry*

*Lyndon*. The IRA sent him a death threat, ordering him to leave in twenty-four hours; he left in twelve. Maybe there were too many scenes of redcoat encampments, he said, British soldiers tramping around Ireland, Union Jacks billowing behind them. His actor friend, the man who was in *A Clockwork Orange*, said some of it had been filmed by candlelight and it looked like an Old Master. Michael couldn't wait to see it. The chiaroscuro. The slowness of it. We'll come back when the film is released, he said, go to see it in one of the big cinemas. We can eat here again, maybe in the winter, when they serve wild things.

*We'll.*

Another bar on a side street, a back room with a tubercular-looking jazz band, dressed in dark suits with drainpipe trousers. A woman wearing scarlet lipstick joined them to sing a song. Cushla recognized it.

*Saudade*, she said.

She closed her case and put it on the floor, beside Michael's. The room was as it was when they arrived a couple days earlier. Except the bed, which had a tumbled look about it. Michael came out of the bathroom, patting at his pockets for wallet and keys.

Are you right? he said.

Yeah.

He bent to pick up both their bags and followed her downstairs to reception. Two priests were ahead of him, paying their bill. Cushla told him she would see him outside the religious shop across the street in a few minutes. As she walked away, the receptionist asked Michael if he and his wife had enjoyed their stay. Sarky bitch, Cushla muttered.

Plastic bottles of holy water, Our Lady–shaped, that reminded her of Matey bubble bath. Books documenting the lives of the saints, holy pictures in gilt frames. She chose a missal for Davy—navy blue, embossed with silver writing—and plain silver rosary beads. There were prayers printed on cards near the till, the way supermarkets displayed sweets and chocolate. She chose a novena to St. Joseph her grandmother used to recite when someone was in trouble, that came in a plastic sleeve with a brassy, oval medal. Michael came into the shop as she was paying. Cushla watched the assistant put the items in a bag and saw them through Michael's eyes, the mass-produced piety of them. She had little faith, but enough to feel the badness of it. That she was bringing religious souvenirs home from a dirty weekend with someone's husband.

Who did you buy those for? he said, when they were outside the shop.

Davy McGeown.

He took the bag from her and tipped the prayer into his palm. He read the back of it aloud.

"Whoever shall read this prayer, or hear it or keep it about themselves, shall never die a sudden death, or be drowned, nor shall poison take effect on them; neither shall they fall into the hands of the enemy, or shall be burned in any fire, or shall be overpowered in battle. Say for nine mornings for anything you may desire; it has never been known to fail, so be sure you really want what you ask."

St. Joseph has it all covered. I should buy one myself, he said.

You're making fun of me.

He put it back in the bag and gave it to her. There might be something in it, he said. It's telling you to be careful what you wish for.

His car was parked a few feet away. He offered to drive her to the station, but she wanted to walk. He put his case in the back seat and took her face in his hands, kissing her forehead, her mouth, each cheek. Like a blessing. She stood by the curb, the debris of Saturday night strewn around her, brown paper bags blotted with grease and vinegar, dented beer cans. She watched his car until she could no longer make it out and started walking.

# 16

The First Holy Communion day was approaching. Endless talk of dresses. Long or short. Lace or satin. Veil or parasol. Cushla clapped her hands. Settle yourselves, she said.

The fire bell began to bleat. A few of the children fell silent, but there was a din on the corridor, voices and footsteps, and most were looking at the door. It opened suddenly. Bomb scare, said Bradley, turning on his heel to continue the evacuation.

The children left their seats and formed a line, standing still to allow Cushla to count them. She waited until the classroom next door had emptied before ushering her pupils out ahead of her. They left the building by the rear entrance. A squad car had arrived. As the children passed through the white-painted wrought iron gate that led to the church, she watched two RUC men amble across the car park, one with his hat in his hand. Real bomb warnings were given with code words. This one had probably been delivered in a recently broken voice by a pimply truant from the high school.

The church was humming with the chatter of three hundred children. Cushla's class crammed into the two empty pews behind Gerry's.

They're giddy, he said, joining her in the aisle.

They love a bomb scare.

We'd better get them singing, he said. He led them in the hymns that would be sung during the Communion ceremony. "Suffer Little Children," a crowd-pleaser, because some of the parents thought it was about children suffering through the Troubles. "Lord of the Dance," the children's favorite. "Faith of Our Fathers," Slattery's favorite, presumably because of its references to torture and death.

As if he had heard her thoughts, Slattery appeared out of nowhere, saying he wanted to have a word about their First Confession. Cushla had told the children they were too young to have sins, that they should make something up to tell Slattery: they had been fighting with their brothers and sisters, perhaps; given cheek to their mothers; forgotten to say their prayers. Slattery spoke of original sin, of Adam and Eve and the temptation in the garden of paradise. Of remorse, guilt, sorrow. You'll make your First Confession on Saturday, he said, and I promise you one thing: expect no leniency from me. He told them people would know the extent of their sinfulness from the length of time they knelt in the pew to say their penance. He handed each of the children a picture of Padre Pio—did he always walk around the place with dozens of those in his pockets?—and told them about the wounds on his hands that bled like the wounds of Christ. As he passed one to Davy, he bent and said something into his ear. Cushla bolted across the floor, but when she reached Davy, Slattery was walking away, smoothing his pockets.

A draft swept up the aisle. The two RUC men had entered the church, casting a long shadow on the waxed woodblock floor of the narthex. The school was safe.

The lunch bell rang as they passed through the gate to the school grounds. Cushla and Gerry went to the staffroom, sitting on the windowsill to eat. Gerry had brought a couple of sandwiches wrapped in tinfoil, and a green banana. Cushla ate cottage cheese from a tub. It contained scraps of pineapple and smelled like boiled sweets.

Your lunch is disgusting, he said.

Cushla kicked his ankle. Did I offer you any?

He laughed. I've to go to a wedding, he said. Fancy being my date?

Yeah, she said.

When Cushla dropped Davy home after school, Betty was waiting on the doorstep. She came striding down the path, stretching her pink cardigan tightly across herself. Cushla wound down her window and said hello, but Betty peered into the back of the car and told Davy to go indoors. He clambered out and hovered beside her. Go, she said.

Is everything OK? asked Cushla.

Did you report me?

Report you for what?

For not looking after the children.

No! Why, what happened?

I had a social worker here today. Standing in my scullery. Opening my fridge. Asking where the kids sleep.

I don't know anything about it.

They said the school contacted them. You're the only one from the school who's set foot in my house. Did you tell them I'm not coping?

No! said Cushla. Her voice was high and tight.

Betty straightened up and glanced back at the house, where Davy was at the window. I am managing, she said. I'm doing my best.

I know you are, Cushla began, but Betty had turned away and was walking up the path.

Cushla drove down the road to town, too fast, overtaking a van. Bradley's car was still in the car park. She went in the back door, heard the clang of tin bucket on terrazzo, smelled the burn of Jeyes Fluid and stale vomit from the caretaker's mop.

She knocked on Bradley's door and pushed it open. He raised his head and put down his pen, letting out a long sigh. To what do I owe the pleasure, he said.

I've just been at the McGeowns' house.

Sit down, Cushla. She almost told him to fuck off, but there was such contempt in his voice she found herself doing as he said.

Did you send a social worker up there? she said.

You came to me with concerns regarding the McGeown child, which I recorded. Bear with me while I find them, he said, and began leafing back through the pages of his diary. He located the entry in seconds; he'd been expecting her. He moved his hands across the page to smooth it, then picked up the pen again, pointing the nib at a paragraph in neat Quink. You told me, and I quote: "That woman is struggling." I am obliged, as principal of this school, to pass on any concerns regarding the welfare of pupils to the relevant authorities.

I was trying to make you feel sorry for her so Davy could get free school dinners.

So you exaggerated.

No. She is struggling, but she's a great mother. I just thought she could do with some help.

This isn't a game, you know. Pupils from this school have been taken into care. I had to report a British Army captain's wife for burning her child with a cigarette. I cannot be seen to overlook children who may be at risk. I suggest you modify your language in future, and act at all times with rationality and integrity. Can I help you with anything else?

No, she said. This time she closed the door after her.

She sat in the car until her hands were steady enough to start it. The army captain's wife had been reported by the nurse who checked the children for nits and rickets, not Bradley. Before Cushla's time a child had come in with blood on the seat of his short trousers and Bradley had sent Slattery round to the house to have a quiet word with the father—he made the man put his hand on the Bible and swear not to go near the boy again. Slattery himself should not have been allowed near children. Bradley wasn't concerned about the McGeowns. He was marking Cushla's card.

At the house, she put the key in the door, praying for the chicken smell, but there was nothing. The radio was on in the kitchen, an afternoon program playing light music. Gina wasn't at the table. Cushla called her and, when there was no reply, ran upstairs. The bathroom door was ajar, and before she pushed it open she got the smell, sour and chemical, like the caretaker's mop. Gina was in the bath. The cold tap was running gently, and she was shuddering. Ribbons of blood were swirling on the surface of the water, dripping from a cut on her eyelid.

What happened? said Cushla, twirling the tap closed and pulling out the plug.

Gina stretched her face, as if limbering up to speak, but the words that came out of her were scarcely intelligible. Cushla soaked a facecloth in the bathwater and squeezed it as tightly as she could, holding it to her mother's brow. Gina began listing forward, and Cushla shook her shoulder and placed her hands on the cloth. Keep it there, she said.

You left me . . . all by myself, Gina said.

Cushla got a couple of towels from the hot press and draped one around her mother's shoulders. The wash basin was flecked with sick. She put on gloves and began to pick the detritus from the plughole and drop it in the toilet bowl. A lurch of nausea shot from her own stomach and she dry-heaved, her elbow pumping awkwardly at the flusher.

When it was all cleaned up, she filled the basin with warm soapy water and dragged Gina upright and out of the bath. She was swooning, so Cushla put her sitting on the closed lid of the toilet bowl. The blood had not soaked through the cloth and Cushla told Gina to keep pressing. She daubed at her mother's body with the other towel; that Gina let her was testament to how pissed she was.

Cushla found a plaster big enough to cover the cut and dropped a nightdress over her mother's head, Gina holding her arms up like an infant. She led her into her room and flopped her onto the mattress, turning her on her side and pulling the blankets up around her. As she looked back from the doorway, something glinted under the bed. She knelt on the floor and pulled out a Gordon's gin bottle. She began opening drawers, rummaging among knickers and camisoles. There were two empty half bottles among her mother's tights. In the wardrobe, she picked up a large handbag. It clinked. She opened the smaller bags and found a quarter bottle in each: it gave a literal meaning to handbag-size. They were even hidden among her father's jumpers. She checked the spare room and found more. Cushla thought of her mother walking down the street to the off-license in town. How humiliating it must have been for her.

Gina slept, unaware of the evidence Cushla was gathering in her arms. Downstairs, Cushla lined the bottles on the hall table, behind the telephone. She went to the kitchen and ferreted through the cupboards. In the fish kettle in which she had cooked the spaghetti just a few weeks earlier there were five. Three behind the pipe under the sink. Cushla paused, remembering how she'd had to pump at the flusher of the toilet, and ran upstairs to lift the cover of the cistern. A green bottle was bobbing against the ball cock. She removed it and stood at the end of her mother's bed. A hurstle was coming from Gina's chest, an almost-snore, heavy with dolor.

There was a packet of cigarettes by the phone. Cushla lit one and sat on the bottom step. Sunlight was coming through the fanlight above the front door, catching the emerald green of twenty-nine empty Gordon's gin bottles. She finished the cigarette and went to the sitting room to get rid of the butt. There was a bottle on the hearth, a couple of inches left in it. She put it with the others and picked up the receiver, dialing the number of Michael's flat. It rang out.

She got an ashtray and sat on the step, smoking one cigarette after another. Just before six she tried the flat again, and again he didn't reply. She dialed the number of the pub. Voices risen in laughter, the ping of the till, a whoosh as the cycle on the glasswasher came to a halt.

Hello? Eamonn barked over the din.

Mummy's drinking is out of hand.

What?

Mummy's pissed all the time, she shouted. There are bottles all over the house.

I'm up to my ballix here, wee girl, he said. The line went dead.

She opened the telephone directory and found Michael's listing, memorizing the house number, road, townland.

Outside, a tabby cat slunk under the hedge. She got into her car and drove out the hill road, past the estate. She pictured Betty McGeown scraping plates, dumping them in a basin of sudsy water, turning away to reverse vests and pants on the clotheshorse. Past the barracks, the cemetery. Left onto the country road, past the lay-by where she and Michael had looked at the lough, where he'd picked the gorse and placed it in her hands. The road narrowed, the hedgerows became neater, shoulder high and angular like the walls of a maze. A sign for a Baptist church, the old Irish name of the townland anglicized. A village: his village. Tea room, antique shop, Pentecostal church. A strip of nineteenth-century cottages, the British Legion. A crossroads. She found herself turning left, as if her little red car knew where to go.

Number 18 was on the right. A Japanese car, olive green, not yet rusted, Michael's car blocking it in. A large house, built in the thirties or forties, painted white, crisscrossed with mock-Tudor slats of dark timber. A spartan garden, flanked each side by Castlewellan Golds, a cherry blossom in the center of the lawn. To the right of the door, crazy paving with floribunda roses sticking out of the cracks. A garden that didn't get much attention. Like his wife.

The curtains were open, venetian blinds slatted across the windows. She pictured him at a stripped-pine table, the wife fluttering around him, serving a meal; sitting on the edge of the chair opposite him, watching him eat. The thought was unbearable. Cushla reversed into his driveway, allowing a car to pass, before driving off.

She took the bends sloppily on her way back down the hill, spiky branches scraping the car. She pulled into the lay-by. She was quaking. She got out and stepped up onto the side of the gully. The sky was purple where it met the sinking sun. Lights had come on across the lough. She picked a piece of gorse the size of a buttonhole and rubbed it.

She stayed until it was almost dark, smoking the rest of Gina's cigarettes, and drove home. From the path she could see Gina, asleep in her armchair, in the nightdress Cushla had pulled over her head in the bathroom. Her legs were parted, her head tilted back hideously, as if she'd had her throat cut. Cushla left her keys beside the rows of bottles and went into the sitting room. She drew the curtains and put her hand on Gina's arm. Her mother gasped and her head jerked forward. You left me alone, she said.

Do you want a cup of tea?

Aye, go on.

Cushla filled the kettle and sat at the kitchen table, emptying her basket. She shuffled through the exercise books until she found Davy's. She had asked the children to write about their favorite place. *Anywhere we're all together*, he had written. *That's my favorite place.* Cushla felt sick. Because of her meddling, Betty had been visited by social services. What had she done?

# 17

Victor's car slipped into the parking space beside hers. He was on the asphalt before Cushla, a lit cigar in his mouth.

No Jane tonight? she said, feeling self-conscious as he watched her get out of the driver's seat.

She's a tad off-color.

We'll miss her, said Cushla, for the want of something better to say.

I like your—he moved a hand in the air around her, as if he was tracing the outline of her body—outfit. She had put on a white cotton smock threaded with ribbons in sugary colors, pinks and lilacs and pale blues, over jeans. She thanked him and began to walk to the entrance of the gallery, where Jim was waiting. He kissed Cushla's cheek as she passed and said there were glasses of paint stripper on a table to the side. The room was crowded, Penny in its center wearing a floral dress, her hair held off her face with a slide, giving the effect of a victory roll, having her photograph taken between a portly man with horn-rimmed glasses and an elegant red-haired woman. There were men and women in studiedly untrendy clothing nursing glasses of wine and speaking without moving their bodies. Victor disappeared for a moment and came back with two glasses of white wine, grimacing broadly through clenched teeth at its sharpness. Cushla was trying to think of something to say when someone began pinging the side of a glass. The man with the glasses introduced Penny and her exhibition.

Agnew's late tonight, said Victor, as the speeches finished.

He said he'll come as soon as he can get away.

Ah, he said, as though there was a hidden meaning in what Michael had told her that she had missed.

She stepped away from Victor to look at the paintings. She understood now what Penny had meant by salon style. The canvases were arranged haphazardly all over the walls, as if it was a cluttered drawing room. There was a field of bog cotton, troughs and holes like sunken baths of mercury. Ardglass Harbour was an arrangement of broken angles from white to slate gray that showed light and shadow on the water, the flimsy masts of boats. When she got to the end, she turned back to the room. It was almost empty. Michael hadn't come.

She went to Penny, who hugged her. I love your work, said Cushla.

It doesn't matter if you like it or not, darling, said Victor. It just *is*.

Shut up, Victor, Penny said pleasantly. I'm glad you like it, Cushla. I just wish they had hung the paintings lower, like I asked. One shouldn't have to tilt one's head back.

Cushla said good-bye, that she would see them soon, but the older woman squeezed her arm and told her supper was in the warming drawer of the AGA, that she was sure Michael would show up shortly, that Cushla had to come to theirs.

In her car, she pretended to fumble in the glove compartment and waited until the others had left before pulling out. Michael had said he would be late, but it was over an hour now. Was there an emergency at home? Had something happened to his son? Had something happened to him? She made a detour, bypassing the turn for Jim and Penny's house and driving to the end of Michael's road. His driveway was empty. She looked up at the flat, remembering the mood that had come on him after the strange car appeared. He had been preoccupied, practically distrait. And he had reacted so quickly, almost as though he had been expecting it. He had openly criticized the court system, but what of the folders full of murders? Maybe he had made enemies among the gunmen too. She reversed and went back the way she had come, praying his car would be there, but on the elbow of the road saw that only Victor's MG was on the pavement.

In Dublin, Michael had brought Cushla to a delicatessen off Grafton Street where she bought a box of Italian biscuits, intending to bring it to the next Irish night. She retrieved it from the boot and carried it to the house, anxious about going in alone yet relieved not to be empty-handed.

He brought you to Magill's! said Penny as she accepted them.

Jim handed her a glass of wine and asked what else they had done in Dublin. Victor let out a disparaging chortle, his eyes smirking at Jim over the lip of his glass. Cushla's face felt hot as she told them about the play and the walk around Trinity and the dinner. She didn't tell them the hotel was like a seminary and that she heard what *saudade* sounded like in the back room of a bar. She excused herself and went to the downstairs loo. The toilet bowl was ornate, the original mahogany seat corroded by decades of piss. Shelves that ran the length of the opposite wall were stacked with literary magazines and books on gardening and DIY. A box of lily bulbs had begun to sprout, green shoots protruding through the seams of the cardboard, giving off a funeral scent. She washed her hands and saw in the mirror what they saw. A dalliance, someone not to be taken seriously.

Cushla heard her name as she put her hand on the kitchen door. Victor was sitting with his arms folded, looking chastened. She couldn't bear to imagine what he had said. She lifted her wine, but an undulating dread was washing through her. Where the hell was Michael? She put the glass back down.

It was almost ten when he arrived, apologizing to Penny, asking how the evening had been. He sat heavily and found Cushla's hand under the table. Sorry, he mouthed at her.

Hard day at the office, darling? said Jim, as he filled Michael's glass. It sounded jovial, but he looked concerned.

You could say that, he said, lowering the wine as if it was water.

Penny took a shepherd's pie from the warming oven and placed a bottle of HP sauce beside it. Michael lit a cigarette, drawing hard on it while she loaded food onto plates and passed them around.

Jim said a poet friend of theirs had sent a draft of his new collection to his publisher. His editor said they were war poems.

Do you think this is a war? Victor said.

If it's not, I'd love someone to tell me what it is, said Michael. His hand was still on Cushla's. With his free one he refilled his glass.

The government is talking about it as a law-and-order issue, said Victor.

Westminster? Ha. The policing is atrocious. You would not believe what I saw today, Michael said. Even Cushla found herself turning to look at him. They've made a film called *Policeday*, he went on. It opens with a couple of officers chasing sheep across a country road. In another scene a man asks for directions to the Belgian Consulate in a language that sounds like Hungarian. My favorite part was the interrogation. A smart-aleck detainee and a couple of detectives with a line in witty banter. Like something you'd see on *The Sweeney*. A propaganda film intended to make the RUC appear impartial.

He looked around the table for a response and, when none was forthcoming, lit another cigarette.

The peelers put on a disco in my school, Cushla heard herself say.

Michael gave a short laugh. You never disappoint, do you? he said. Describe the scene.

Three uniformed RUC men with a glitterball and a strip of traffic lights. Flak jackets piled up on a beanbag. If they had weapons they must have been concealed on their persons.

Did they dance?

No. They stood stroking their mustaches, watching us.

Did you dance?

Reluctantly. Gerry Devlin dragged me up for "Billy Don't Be a Hero."

Was it fun?

The children found it highly entertaining.

They had been tilting toward each other and he was looking at her mouth as if he was about to kiss it.

Is that something the police do? said Jim.

School discos? Apparently. Community outreach or something, said Cushla.

Why did they go to your school? asked Victor.

Because there are lots of places they can't go, I suppose. Our school is probably considered safe because it is not in an area considered to be a hotbed of Republicanism, she said slowly, as if she was speaking to a child. Below the table, Michael patted her thigh in approval.

The police have a difficult job, said Victor.

Made more difficult by their own prejudice, said Michael.

Oh, come off it. Is this going to be your next hobbyhorse?

What precisely does that mean?

You've already pissed off the judiciary. You're going to find yourself very isolated, if you aren't already.

I feel like we should be speaking Irish, said Jim.

Good old Jim, said Victor. Changing the subject.

Michael asked Jim for whiskey. Penny rose to clear the table and Cushla got up to help her, offering to wash because she didn't know where anything lived. Michael was saying that if the police were so impartial, how come half the kids who appeared in court were black and blue?

Cushla frothed the water in the sink with her fingers and began dunking the plates. She felt Penny's eyes on her and looked up.

We are worried about him, said Penny.

Why?

Everything looks so clear to him and it'll do him no good here. And he's drinking too much.

What can I do?

That's not for me to say.

When they sat down, Penny opened the biscuits and put them in the center of the table. The next person to mention politics will leave by the window, she said.

Michael said he had a question about Irish that couldn't wait until the next official Irish night. Jim and Penny looked relieved that he had dropped the other subject. Victor was staring at the table sourly.

Can you explain the *tuiseal ginideach*? said Michael.

The genitive case, said Cushla. It's hard, but we can start with easy stuff. Like possession. The cat's tail, for example. *Eireaball an chait*. The tail of the cat.

The wife of the historian, said Jim.

*Bean chéile an staraí*, said Cushla.

Excuse me. The husband of the artist, said Penny.

*Fear céile an ealaíontóra*. Cushla exaggerated the pronunciation, gargling the consonants in the back of her throat, hoping to irritate Victor. She told them how to make a noun slender. About masculine and feminine.

Friend of the lawyer, said Victor. Is that feminine and slender?

*Cara an dlíodóra*, said Cushla. It's masculine, actually.

The table in his flat was littered with folders, ring binders, tea-stained cups and saucers. An empty whiskey bottle beside the empty decanter; another bottle, a couple of inches in it, by a stack of papers. He reached for it and shook the dregs into a dirty tumbler. Cushla went to the window. It would be midsummer in a few weeks. The sky was night blue, the street a weave of shadows. You have work to do, she said. I should go.

Stay with me. I'll be done in a while.

She drew the curtains and placed her hands on his shoulders. They were rigid with tension. He rummaged in his pocket and produced a key.

I had this cut for you. Come and go as you please, he said, twisting to give it to her. She waited for him to say more; the moment seemed significant. But he merely stroked her hand and reached for a pen.

She cleaned her face and brushed her teeth, heard a bottle clink against a glass in the sitting room. It had shocked her to hear Penny mention Michael's drinking. Of course he drank, but so did everyone else she knew, and it seldom showed on him. He spoke without slurring, his complexion was neither rosaceous nor jaundiced. He handled a car smoothly, his cock stiffened every time he put a hand on her. But maybe she was not in a position to judge; she was a part-time barmaid, had been practically reared in a pub, and lived with an alcoholic mother. He could be permanently flutered and she would think it normal.

The quilt was wrinkled, the sheets stretched taut beneath it, as if he had slept on top of the covers. She took a book from his nightstand. It had pen-and-ink illustrations of the wildflowers and trees of Ireland, each entry accompanied by folklore. The one for gorse contained the lines with which he'd mesmerized her in the lay-by. She read for a long time and fell asleep. She woke with the corner of the book jabbing her cheek. There was a strip of gray dawn between the curtains. She reached for Michael and, realizing he wasn't there, sat up. When her eyes adjusted to the light, she saw that he was sitting in the armchair in his clothes, a glass in his hand.

*Cara an dlíodóra*, he said. Are you my friend, Cushla?

# 18

Gina had put on a milky-gray crepe dress and matching coat. She looked vulnerable, ethereal, as she slid into the pew. Cushla had expected her to be angry about the legion of empties on the hall table, but Gina had beheld the arrangement with an expression of suffering. The bottles had colluded with her: look at the pain she's in, they seemed to be saying.

The children arrived in their frocks and suits, Cushla directing them to the reserved rows at the front of the church. Davy trotted in, wearing a sky-blue jacket and trousers. Instead of coming to Cushla he hovered by the holy water font. Seamie McGeown's thin frame appeared in the doorway, Betty linking one of his arms, Tommy the other. Beside him, you could see how like his father he was. Betty had not, to Cushla's knowledge, been in the church before. She felt a stab of guilt that the woman had come because she was afraid of losing her children.

You're very dapper today, Davy, said Cushla when they were level with her. The blue of his suit made his eyes leap from his face as he looked from her to his mother, who was busying herself with the cuff of Seamie's jacket. Mandy prodded Davy's elbow and he rooted in his pocket, producing the missal and rosary beads Cushla had given him; gifts she had bought out of love, that now seemed like a threat. Cushla could feel Tommy's stare but did not meet it.

The previous day, the children had made their First Confession, filing in one at a time to kneel in front of Slattery's grim profile. Davy had been first but was given an interminable penance, kneeling in the pew while the others came and went. Cushla thought about going to Bradley, who was standing by the entrance to the crying chapel, but remembering the revenge he had taken on the McGeowns for her insolence, said nothing. Eventually Tommy strode up the aisle and pulled Davy off his knees. He marched him toward the door, a hand between his shoulder blades. Slattery had left the confessional and joined Bradley. Tommy stopped dead in front of them. I don't know what point you're trying to make, he said, but it's not right. Cushla had followed them out. Tommy lit a cigarette at the bottom of the steps and began walking, Davy trotting beside him. Cushla broke into a run, and on hearing her footsteps, Davy turned and hurtled toward her.

I didn't do anything really bad, miss.

I know you didn't, she said, her hand on his head.

He said I'm a bad boy.

You're not a bad boy.

Come on, you, Tommy said, dragging Davy away from her. She pleaded with them to wait and went to her car. She found the bag from the religious shop in her glove compartment—she had planned to drive to the house with it later—and gave it to Davy. He opened it slowly, showing the contents to Tommy as if they needed to be vetted. As she looked at Davy now, shuffling uncomfortably in his Communion suit, she understood how very hard it would be to fix things.

The Apostolic ladies had decorated the church with white and yellow flowers, and Slattery's homily was notable for an absence of references to extreme sectarian violence. The children tripped up the aisle to receive the host without incident, efficient now at the flick of the tongue, the inclination of the head, the move of the fingertips to the brow. The

Father, Son, the Holy Ghost, amen. When the choir began to sing "Bridge over Troubled Water," sniffling started, women rooting in handbags for tissues. Cushla looked up at the gallery. Gerry Devlin's face appeared over the railing. He held up a thumb at her. A new crowd-pleaser.

Afterward there was a party in the school canteen. At the far end, tables had been pushed together and were laid with tall stainless steel pots of tea, stacks of cups inverted on saucers, plates of buns and sandwiches. The room smelled of salad cream and cake. Gina went around pressing a 50p coin into the hand of every child in a suit or white dress. She left Davy until last, crossing the room to hand him an envelope. He opened it and took out a fiver. For a moment he forgot himself and tugged at the edges of the note with both hands as if he was checking its authenticity. Betty pulled him to her and spoke into his ear. He stopped his capering and stood solemnly in front of Gina to thank her. Gina ruffled his hair, oblivious to the color on Betty's cheeks. The gift was extravagant. Embarrassing.

Cushla joined them, remembering not to offer Seamie her hand. She watched him reach slowly for a teacup on the table. Much as they repelled her she could not help looking at his scars. The wounds had closed, but the new skin was thin and bubblegum pink. His hand moved vaguely around the handle and there was almost audible relief from his family when his thumb and finger made contact with the delft.

Tommy went to the buffet table with Mandy and Davy.

Did Tommy ever go back to school? said Cushla.

He has a laboring job with his uncle.

That's great.

Great? said Betty, her voice sharp with anger. That wee lad has brains to burn.

Maybe he'll go back someday, said Cushla. Do a night course or something.

Betty was looking across the room at her children. She glanced at Cushla. Maybe he will, she said, her voice lowered to its usual pitch.

She's afraid of me, thought Cushla.

G ina had asked Gerry Devlin to the house for dinner. He arrived at five and presented Gina with a box of Terry's All Gold. She gave him a beer from the fridge and made a show of seating him in Cushla's father's chair. He sat, smiling, unaware of the compliment he was being paid.

Something smells good, he said.

Cushla had insisted on cooking. There was a roast chicken and potatoes; peas from a tin with a blob of mint sauce, the way Cushla's father had liked them; a gravy boat of Bisto. Mr. Reid had given her a head of pamphrey that she had boiled and tossed with butter. Gerry finished his beer and refused another, switching to water. He remarked on the length of time Davy had been left in the pew for his penance, said he was surprised Cushla hadn't gone buck mad with Bradley, since she was a bit of a targe at school. Gina said she was a pain in the arse at home as well and began to tell stories of Cushla's unreasonable behavior. For once, Cushla was grateful for the negative attention.

That was nice, Gina said when they had finished eating, making no effort to keep the surprise from her voice.

Cushla hadn't made pudding. Gina suggested they have Irish coffee. Cushla's heart sank. Gina appeared not to have been drinking since her fall, and Cushla had let herself entertain the idea that the last time had been the last time.

The rotary whisk jangled loudly against the side of the glass bowl as she whipped cream, and at first she didn't hear the phone. She rushed past the kitchen table and lifted it on the eighth or ninth ring. Gina had said something to make Gerry burst out laughing and Cushla said hello three times before she could make out a voice.

Who is with you? It was Michael, speaking so softly she could hardly hear him.

Gerry and my mummy. Who's with you?

He breathed out slowly, almost a sigh. How was the big day?

Lovely.

The sound of footsteps, a voice calling, Dad! A young man, not a boy. The line went dead.

She pictured Michael depressing the button to silence her. What scene was playing out in the Agnew house? A dinner with stilted conversation, the boy an unwilling mediator between parents who hated each other. A glass being topped up, over and over, looks exchanged over the flow. Or worse, the drinking was done in secret. Maybe the boy knew his mother's hiding places. Maybe he walked into the kitchen with a knot in his gut, like Cushla did, wondering which mother was going to greet him. But there had been no hint of strain in his voice. "Dad!" had been a happy sound.

Who was that on the phone? said Gina.

Wrong number. Cushla turned in time to see her mother part her lips to let smoke waft upward, veiling her face. There was something grotesquely sexy in the act.

Gerry brought their dirty plates to the sink and went back to the table with a damp cloth, brushing debris into his palm and wiping vigorously.

There's plenty of rearing in you, said Gina, her voice vibrating with feeling. I'll go in and light a wee fire.

While the kettle was boiling, Cushla washed up. Gerry dried, buffing briskly. She imagined him in a school uniform, cleaning up after a meal his father had cobbled together at the end of a day's work in the awful, bewildering months after his mother died. Cushla took down the Irish coffee glasses her father had bought in Killarney, with the gold rim and ring of shamrock around the base.

Your ma thinks we went to Dublin for a dirty weekend, said Gerry, watching her make the drinks, his back to the worktop.

Shit.

I don't mind covering for you, but you need to let me know, so I don't land you in it. Who were you with that you can't tell anyone?

I can't tell anyone.

Is it one of the fathers from school?

No!

Is it Bradley? Slattery?

There's something wrong with you.

Is he married?

No.

I think he's a Prod.

Why do you say that?

Because a nice Fenian boy like me wouldn't expect you to stay out all night. He'd be happy with a quick diddy ride in a car.

That's disgusting. Look, I'll tell you, but you have to swear to God not to tell a soul.

I swear.

It's Brian Faulkner.

Fuck away off.

It is. That's why I can't tell anybody.

He was sniggering. Does he talk dirty with marleys in his mouth?

Oh, aye. Very Malone Road, she said, in Michael's accent. It felt good to make fun of him, it made him seem real. And now someone knew she was in a relationship, if that was what it was; mostly it felt like a situation.

They drank the Irish coffees in front of the television, passing the box of chocolates between them. Gina said there was so little whiskey in hers she doubted Cushla had done much more than shake the bottle at the glass. Gerry looked at Cushla. He had seen her make them, must have noticed that she gave Gina a fraction of the booze she put in the other glasses.

*Songs of Praise* came on. The congregation were dressed in their Sunday best, faces raised to the pastel-colored light from a rose window behind the altar. The church was festooned in Union Jacks, and wall plaques remembered fallen parishioners. The camera switched to the front pew and a line of natty little men wearing berets and blazers, medals pinned to their chests.

I love this program, said Gerry.

You do not, said Cushla.

I'm a choirmaster. Listen to them, belting out the songs.

Agreed, said Gina. Not like our ones, mumbling.

On the rare occasions Gina watched, it was to ridicule the fussy hats and gormless faces of the congregation. She didn't even join in with the prayers at Mass. The only time Cushla had ever heard her sing was when Cushla's father was alive and she performed "I'm Just a Girl Who Cain't Say No" at a party, pretending to pull up the sides of her skirt, to guffaws from the men and knowing looks from the women.

Gerry stayed for another couple of hours and Cushla walked him to his car. He hugged her and put his key in the lock but hesitated before he turned it. Joking aside, he said, I don't know what you're up to but be careful. You could lose your job.

She felt a little flicker of disquiet, but the phone began to ring again and, kissing Gerry's cheek, she ran inside, praying it was Michael. It was Tommy.

Oh, said Cushla, unable to keep surprise from her voice. Why was he ringing her?

She heard a faint fizz as he drew saliva into his mouth. I told my mummy that you wouldn't be that good to us and then report her, he said. You wouldn't, like, would you?

Of course not.

That's what I thought, he said. The strike of a match, a deep intake of breath. I'm working now. General laboring stuff to start off with, but the money's good.

Your mummy is really hoping you'll go back to school.

He exhaled through his nose. She can hope away, he said.

Ah, Tommy, don't say that. There's no reason why you can't go back someday. I'll drop a book or two round, she said. If you keep reading all will not be lost. OK?

Yes, miss.

# In Calvary's Flow

# 19

A duck patrol, soldiers hunkered down, the last man—a boy, really—walking backward, scanning the pavement with his gun. A Saracen, then another. BRITS OUT dabbed on the wall outside the leisure center, the only venue available at short notice—the hotel Gerry's friends had booked for their wedding reception had been firebombed.

Inside, the floor was marked for basketball with colored tape, and trestle tables had been erected and covered with white cloths. They were seated with people she remembered from the party: Harry and Joe and the hairy chap she had last seen with a woman wrapped round his hips. Once the tables were full the room was almost pretty; Cushla's father used to say that people were the best decoration of all.

After a starter of orange juice they were served turkey and ham. It had a comforting school-dinner flavor, with its scoops of mash and gelatinous gravy. There was a stampede to the bar before the speeches began. Gerry bought Cushla a drink. So did Harry and Joe. When they were all seated again, the father of the bride rose slowly and cleared his throat. He said how proud he was of his daughter, that she had been a busy, happy wee thing since the day she was born. He said her new husband had better look after her, or he'd be getting a visit. Cushla felt a tear form at the corner of her eye. She had no father. The only man she would ever want was married already. Then she had a vision of Gina as mother of the bride—as full as the Boyne and telling anyone who'd listen that her own wedding dress was three sizes smaller than Cushla's—and the tear shrank back into the duct. The groom stood next. He said that when he was a child he asked God every night to make sure he married someone good, and that it was a bonus she was beautiful as well. The best man got to his feet and took a piece of paper from the inside pocket of his jacket. As he began to speak, there was a whirring sound overhead that got louder and louder. Everyone's head tilted back to look at the ceiling. Then the double doors burst open and boots stomped across the floor. It was the duck squad from earlier, a helicopter hovering over the building to guide their passage. The best man sat down and took a slug of his beer.

Another sound had started at the back that swelled as it traveled through the hall, a rushing hiss. The soldiers passed the top table, each of them stealing a look at the bride, who was resplendent with outrage at the intrusion. They moved between the guests, guns swinging left to right, sometimes knocking the backs of chairs. As he passed Cushla, the squaddie at the rear glanced at her. There was terror in his eyes. Cushla felt her mouth form the word *hello*, an impulse born of pulling pints for members of the security forces. She lowered her gaze, hoping to God no one had noticed.

A cheer went up as they left. They hadn't stopped to ID anyone, hadn't ordered anyone out.

Fucking harassment, so it is, said Joe.

Most of the guests had left their seats for the bar and it was fifteen minutes before the best man stood again and held aloft a crumpled piece of paper. I'll read the telegrams first, he said. This one is from Derry; it came through the window wrapped round a brick.

Looking well, Lavery, Gerry said.

Ha-ha.

He chuckled and offered her another drink, but she insisted on buying a round.

A man her own age was leaning on the counter. He had enormous, soulful gray eyes, the rest of his features squashed into a face broader than it was long. He asked her if she was here for the bride or the groom. Her name. Which school she had gone to. Where she lived.

Nice spot, he said. Quiet, like.

She didn't say her family had a bar. He asked who Gerry was, how she knew him, and when she told him, he took a slug of his pint and looked at the table thoughtfully.

Gerry got up to buy the next round. The man was still at the counter. Cushla watched him talk into Gerry's ear, a pint in one hand, the other turning in the air, a gesture of insouciance. Gerry was looking at the floor, arms folded across himself, a finger on his lip. The leg going like mad.

Your face, she said, when he came back. Are you all right?

Did you tell your man to talk to me?

No. I told him you worked in the same school as me. What did he want?

He asked if he could send a couple of boys round to cement sherry trifles into the wall of my garage.

Sherry trifles?

It's rhyming slang.

Rifles? Jesus. What did you say?

I said I don't have a garage.

Cushla went to the ladies'. Two of the bridesmaids were retouching their eyeshadow, giggling drunkenly.

Here, do you want a rub of this? one asked Cushla.

Aye, go on, she said, realizing she was quite drunk too. "Seasons in the Sun" came on and the girls shrieked and rushed out, leaving Cushla in front of the mirror. They had smeared her lids with a pearlescent tricolor.

Gerry said the sherry-trifle encounter had sobered him up, and he wasn't in the mood for dancing. They left just before eight. At the bottom of the road, Cushla turned to him. Can you drop me somewhere? she said.

Within reason, he said, glancing at her.

She told him the address and he went via the city center, a longer route, but safer than driving through the loyalist streets that bordered Michael's area. When they got to the corner of Michael's avenue, she said she wanted to get out. He protested, and turned left. He drove slowly, looking up at the tall houses.

My imagination's working overtime, Lavery, he said, as he pulled in.

She kissed him on the cheek. Thanks.

She got out of the car and skeetered across the gravel, shoes in hand. The light was on in the front room. She went up the steps and took the brass key from her bag. She unlocked the door and pushed it open, holding a hand up at Gerry in farewell.

She found herself walking straight to Michael's bedroom, an uneasiness on her that evaporated when she saw the bed was empty and he was not up on his elbow, mounting a woman. Yet she wondered what it would be like to watch him with someone else, going at her with his mouth and fingers like he did with her. The bed was straightened rather than made, an empty tumbler on the nightstand. The air in the room was cool and she took his Aran cardigan from the arm of the velvet chair and put it on over her dress.

On the dining table another tumbler, a swallow of whiskey glowing in the bottom of it, twists of tissue browned by tar from his pipe. Documents in stacks, a scrap of paper on top of each one with a name or word in inky capital letters. Beyond the window the night was still, the branches on the old trees barely trembling. She stepped away, afraid of seeing something horrible. The Ottilie Patterson record was still on the turntable. She lowered the needle. A boom, then, low and deep, that she felt in her lungs. It was nearby, huge; bombers had begun using hundreds of pounds of explosives. Fear came on her with terrible clarity, that something had happened to Michael. She drank the dregs from his glass, pouring more.

She sat at the table. The stack nearest to her was thick; the names Kelly, McAleavey, and Coyle written on the slip. She pulled it to her, tracing the curls of Michael's handwriting with her finger. There were copies of statements they had refused to sign, the paper reeking of cigarette smoke. Photographs, mug shots the police had taken, stark yet grainy. Their faces were unmarked, but all three were limp haired, hollowed out. Terrified. Polaroids of their naked bodies, torsos blotched with sprawling bruises, thighs slit with whip marks. One image was a close-up. She turned it upside down and sideways, unable to tell what she was looking at. Each boy had written an account of his arrest and custody. Doors battered down. The lineup, two policemen holding a gray blanket in front of a woman in crinkly leather boots, the surprising youth of her voice as she called out their positions: one, four, seven. Hoods. White noise. Electrical cables. She looked at the photograph again. It was a shriveled penis, the sac behind it sagging where a testicle had been kicked up toward a stomach. She laid the photo facedown on the table and slopped more whiskey into her glass. How could anyone deal with this every day?

Cushla arranged the materials as she had found them and went looking for cigarettes. There was a box on the mantelpiece. She went back to the table and stood by the window, smoking. Ottilie was singing "Shipwreck Blues," her voice heavy with portent. It was not yet dark, but the nearest working streetlamp was a few doors up and the dusk seemed impenetrable. Cushla drew the curtains, suddenly aware that looking at the illuminated window from outside was like watching television. The papers and books and whiskey, which had seemed like clutter, had taken on a menace. The record finished. She lit another cigarette and sat on his chair, sipping from his glass. The fridge shuddered, startling her, and she went to the turntable and lowered the needle again. His key turned in the lock. She rushed to him. There was a bomb, she said. Where were you?

A new play opened in the Lyric. *We Do It for Love*, it's called. It was great, from the little I saw of it. A car exploded outside the theater. He took the drink from her hand and threw it into himself. Look at you, he said.

Stop. I knew something had happened to you.

Nothing happened to me.

I passed hundreds of windows and yours is the only one with open curtains. You're careless. You've just been in a bomb and you're not even rattled.

Rattled? I'm fucking raging, he said; it was the first time she had heard him swear. I walked back from the theater thinking how terrible things are here. That nothing is sacred. That I was walking into an empty flat. But here you are. Playing Ottilie and looking wanton.

Tell me you'll be careful.

I went to see a play, Cushla. Not exactly living dangerously.

I've seen what you do for a living, she wanted to say, but she couldn't.

He sat at the table and pulled her onto his knee. You've got a bony arse, he said, dandling her like an infant until he found a position that was comfortable. How was the wedding?

The army raided the reception, she said, smoothing his hair. She

placed her hand under his chin and tilted his face to hers. As she prepared to kiss him he drew back.

Close your eyes, he said.

She lowered her lids, then remembered the eyeshadow and opened
them wide. Oh yeah, she said. I'm asserting my identity. Fidel and the
boys are going to love it.

She woke in half-light to the swell of his cock against her back. He
bent her into a comma and fucked her with long, slow strokes. She
was unsure if he was inside her or if she was dreaming, until he pulled
out and rolled her onto her back. He arranged her body—hands over
her head, legs barely parted—and pushed into her again. She was aware
of pajamas near her face then under her shoulder, as though they were
working their way around the bed of their own accord, reminding her
that another woman bought and laundered his clothes. In the beginning it had troubled her. Now it aroused her to think that in spite of his
wife's ministrations he did these things to her, and when the letter box
opened and the Sunday paper dropped on the mat, he had to cover her
mouth with his hand to spare the paperboy the sound of her yelps.

When they got up, he ran her a bath. She sat in the water and allowed him to wash her, soaping her neck and arms and breasts. Her
makeup left a patina of glitter on the flannel.

A woman I lodged with in Dublin told me the country girls were
called scaly backs.

Are you saying I'm bogging?

Filthy, he said.

He helped her out and dried her with a stiff towel. She felt abraded.
Clean. As if she'd shed a skin.

# 20

They stood on the curb, backdraught from a bus blowing briefly in their faces, and crossed the road in a lull in the traffic. As they passed the UDR barracks a voice said hello, startling them. Michael peered through the railings. There was a smell of cigar smoke, a man in uniform a foot or so away.

You should be in one of those Hamlet Cigar ads, said Michael.

The Wimbledon one? the man said.

The Venus de Milo one. You have a tortured look about you.

The man smiled morosely, revealing a line of small teeth beneath his ginger mustache. Are youse off out?

We're going to a party.

Well for some.

Cushla remembered Gerry at the checkpoint, saying he was going to a party. She turned and began walking.

Jim saw them from the dining room and opened the front door. His upper lip had tiny beads of sweat. Cushla wished him a happy birthday, kissing the cheek he offered. He asked Michael to help him move a table and she went through the hall to the kitchen. Cases of wine on the floor, corks removed then pushed back in the bottles again. China platters of raw vegetables, ramekins of creamy dips tucked among the carrot batons and cauliflower florets and wedges of cucumber. Toast piped with pâtés and spreads, curls of ham tied with chives.

Every time I see you you're in an apron, said Cushla, hugging Penny.

There was a petite woman at the sink, in a white blouse under a nylon tabard like the ones Betty wore. She was washing wineglasses, foam flying, then rinsing them under the cold tap.

Penny introduced her as Mrs. Coyle and said she could not live without her. On hearing Cushla's name the woman visibly unfurled.

Cushla lifted a linen tea towel and began to dry.

You've done this before, said Mrs. Coyle.

We've a bar.

Michael came into the kitchen, putting an arm around Penny's waist, telling her she looked beautiful. Charmer, she said. I haven't changed yet.

How's the other woman in my life? he said, coming to the sink. Cushla thought he was speaking to her, but he was planting a kiss on Mrs. Coyle's cheek. He told Cushla she was responsible for the hospital corners and shiny brasses in the flat. Mrs. Coyle's eyes flicked up then down and she wrung a cloth until it was as tight as her mouth, using it to mop up the pool of water Cushla had left on the worktop. Mrs. Coyle had cleaned around Cushla's toothbrush and pot of Astral cream, wiped her lip gloss from the second whiskey tumbler. She had stripped a bed grubby with her mascara, seen the dried-glue stains from semen that had drooled from her.

Cushla tucked the tea towel over the rail of the AGA and moved toward the table. There was an assortment of cutlery—bone-handled, King's pattern, angular designs from the fifties—that Penny was wrapping in napkins. Cushla took over, telling her to get ready before the others arrived.

Jim came in and poured Cushla a glass of wine, placing a bottle of Bushmills and a tumbler in front of Michael. A good Protestant whiskey, he said, and left the room with an armload of bottles.

Good Protestant whiskey. Good Ulster Prods. When something was clean and tidy, when it was as it should be, it was described as Protestant-looking. Even Catholics said it. Cushla looked at Mrs. Coyle's back, willing her to turn and give her a sign that said, yes, I heard it too, I know what they think of us. But she didn't. The only other Taig likely to darken the door of the house that night already despised her.

Michael poured himself a drink and stood with his back to the sink. Mrs. Coyle was speaking in a low, urgent voice, juking over her shoulder the odd time to check no one was listening. Cushla wondered if she was talking about her, but Michael began to reply. It was hardly above a whisper, but Cushla was used to the timbre of his voice when he lowered it and could make out what he was saying. *If he refuses to recognize the court he won't have a defense. A solicitor could ask for an appeal. I know one or two who might take him on.*

A long trill from the doorbell, a draft from the door. Laughs and hellos, the house filling with noise. Cushla looked at the clock on the wall. All the guests were arriving on the stroke of eight. Very Protestant of them. She and Michael had been there for half an hour. It occurred to her that he and their hosts had not wanted the other guests to see them arriving together. That no one cared what Mrs. Coyle thought mortified her.

Penny rushed into the kitchen asking for Jim. She had changed into a check dirndl skirt and a tight black jumper with three-quarter-length sleeves, her hair held off her face with a slide. Her arms were both slack and sinewy. Michael sat beside Cushla at the table and refilled his glass.

I want to be Penny when I grow up, said Cushla. That aging-beatnik look. General coolness.

He patted her knee. You'll do as you are.

It's kind of creepy, that. Feeling someone's leg under a table.

Are you all right? You're quiet.

That wee woman must think I'm a whore, she said. She had pronounced it *huir*, sounding like her granny, whose favorite term of abuse for a woman was "the ould haitch." The only time she had heard Michael use the word—playfully, after she asked him to do something to her, the thought of which was now making her ears hot—he had pronounced it correctly.

Penny came and went, putting cards and gifts and bottles wrapped in tissue paper on the dresser. Sometimes a guest stuck a head in and called out a hello at Michael, eyes sweeping the room to get a look at Cushla. You're in hiding, he said. Come on.

In the hall, in the drawing room, in the dining room, there were women in fitted dresses and heavy Victorian jewelry. Michael introduced her to a photographer—a press photographer, the man stressed—in a jerkin like Victor's. A playwright. An obstetrician who was drinking crème de menthe from a pint glass. Cushla spoke when she was spoken to, moving through the rooms in his shadow. Mrs. Coyle was moving too, her compact body lugging platters and stacks of plates.

She spotted Victor and Jane and tugged Michael's cuff in their direction. She regretted it almost as soon as they reached them, when Victor said he thought she was only allowed out on school nights. Cushla admired Jane's dress, bat-sleeved chiffon that faded from eau de Nil at the bodice to teal at the hem. Jane returned the compliment and Cushla thanked her. Manners were for shy people: without them, she and Jane would be looking at the floor. She asked Jane how she had been, expecting a wishy-washy answer, but her face seemed to collapse and she took off up the staircase, more scurry than grand exit. Cushla followed and found her in a bedroom with purple walls and a life-size poster of Rod Stewart pinned to the ceiling, sweating in an electric-blue body stocking. Jane was crying. Cushla fetched a clump of toilet paper from the bathroom. Will I get Victor? she said.

No, said Jane, mopping at her face. He's had quite enough of me. I had another miscarriage. My seventh.

So that was why she hadn't attended Penny's opening; it had not occurred to Cushla that there was something wrong.

I'm sorry, said Cushla.

I went eleven weeks this time, said Jane. You let yourself hope.

A shadow fell across the bed. It was Victor. He stood aside to let Cushla leave. She glanced back at them from the door. Jane was the youngest of the friends, but at least forty. Shoulders rounded, worrying at the tissue, she looked like a girl.

Michael was no longer in the hall. She sidled through the drawing room, searching for him. A hand caught her round the waist. There you are, he said. A woman with blond hair and brown eyes paused in front of them. Michael said her name was Marjorie. At the precise moment the woman pressed her lips to Michael's cheek, Cushla felt him withdraw his hand from her hip. A sudden, instinctive action. He had slept with the woman. It shouldn't have hurt, but it did.

They joined the queue for the buffet. Ahead of them, women were serving their men before they filled their own plates. It looked spectacular yet effortless, the mahogany table covered with white linen, short vases of rhododendrons here and there. Pieces of chicken in a creamy sauce that smelled of mustard, toasted slivers of almond scattered over it. Rice dyed bright yellow, flecked with butter and soft onion. A salad of watercress and croutons, all of it heaped rather than arranged. Michael filled her plate, ignoring her protests. The young lady is watching her figure, Agnew, said a man's voice behind them. It was the crème de menthe doctor.

Michael found her a seat on the arm of a couch in a poky room next to the kitchen with a television in the corner and went off to get a bottle of wine. Cushla unwrapped her cutlery, looking determinedly at it. She felt eyes on her and glanced up; she was the only woman in the room. She speared a piece of chicken and lifted it to her mouth, scratching her lip with the tines of the fork.

Crème de menthe man darkened the doorway then squashed himself on the seat cushion beside her, holding up a green pint. Bon appétit, he said.

Same to you.

How do you know Michael?

My family has a bar.

Ah yes, you're the barmaid. I did wonder. You're rather demure, actually, in a fecund sort of way.

Do you actually like that stuff or is it just an affectation you resort to because you have a shite personality? she said. She got up and stalked toward the kitchen. Mrs. Coyle was ahead of her with a column of dirty plates stacked against her middle. Michael was by the table, a bottle of wine in one hand and his plate in the other.

That doctor is a dick, said Cushla.

What did he say?

It doesn't matter what he said. I shouldn't have come.

I'm going to speak to him.

Then it'll look like I'm causing ructions.

Michael dumped the bottle and plate on the table and left the room. Mrs. Coyle half turned. You'd need a thick skin, she said.

Or a good Protestant one.

She laughed. You were well able for him.

Oh Jesus. You heard. You must think badly of me.

You wouldn't think much of me, love, if you knew my business.

Michael came back. So, did you beat him up, big lad? said Cushla.

I didn't have to. He was already chastened by whatever you said to him. How are you two getting along?

Great. Fenian Corner, we're calling it, said Cushla.

He picked up a wine bottle and, finding just a couple of inches in it, put it to his mouth and drained it. Imagine if I did that, said Cushla. Mrs. Coyle giggled.

They went back to the drawing room, leaving Mrs. Coyle at the sink. A man had begun to sing, crude words to an old air. Most of the other men joined in for the chorus, which ended in the line "and the hairs on her dickey dido hung down to her knees." Someone sang "Loch Lomond." Someone else sang an Irish drinking song, in an exaggerated brogue to show he was being ironic. One began to recite "Tam o' Shanter," but three verses in Jim told him to shut up. Cushla looked around her. The women were smiling indulgently, their gold glinting in the light. Please tell me you don't have a party piece, she said to Michael.

Someone called his name and he raised his hands apologetically, moving away from her, toward the piano. A glissando sounded that made everyone laugh. She moved a few feet aside, tucking herself into a corner by the door for a better view. He began to play, a slow, bluesy song she recognized from one of the Ottilie Patterson records.

*"I travel for Jesus, most of my life.*
*I've traveled o'er land and sea.*
*But I'm planning to take a last trip to the sky.*
*That will be the last move for me."*

A couple had moved in front of her and she could no longer see him. Without the distraction of his face, she heard something in his voice she hadn't noticed. A plaintive tone, both like and very unlike him.

*"When I move to the sky,*
*up to heaven up high,*
*what a wonderful time that will be.*
*I'm ready to go washed in Calvary's flow.*
*That will be the last move for me."*

He found her in the garden, smoking one of Mrs. Coyle's Embassy Regals.

You're full of surprises, she said, looking at the ground.

He turned her face to his. Why the fuck are you crying?

Your language has really deteriorated since you met me.

What is it?

I got a weird feeling again. When you were singing that song.

He took the cigarette from her hand and smoked the last drag. You Catholics are highly suggestible, he said. Come back inside.

I don't have one more word in me for those people.

All right. Let's go home.

The flat was home for neither of them, but she liked that he had called it that. He went in search of their jackets and Cushla stood at the back door and told Mrs. Coyle they were sneaking away.

I wouldn't have any of them ones looking down on me, said Mrs. Coyle. I clean for some of them. Dirtbirds.

I want to stay now, and hear every minging detail, said Cushla.

Michael came back and touched Mrs. Coyle's shoulder as they left. Cushla heard him say he would phone her when he had more information.

He swung her hand as they went up the road, pausing at the barracks, saying he wanted to have a chinwag with their friend from earlier. A security light came on and she pulled him away. A few steps farther on he lit a cigarette, the match briefly illuminating his face. It shocked her, how gaunt it was, but then he smiled and looked like himself. He began to sing the song again. She hushed him, tugging him past the tall terraces. The streetlight outside his house was broken, the sky above them the color of a bruise. He pushed her onto the bonnet of his car and parted her legs.

You are so pissed, she said.

Upstairs, he tossed his keys on the dining table and poured a drink.

What's going on with Mrs. Coyle? she said.

Her son is in trouble.

Cushla remembered now. His had been one of the names on the file she had read. What kind of trouble?

The kind of trouble in which unemployed youths from west Belfast tend to find themselves these days.

What did he do?

Nothing. He was identified in a lineup.

The case you were talking about before? Jesus. Can you help him?

I can if he'll accept the services of a solicitor, but he's been on remand with men who actually are involved and now he's refusing to recognize the court in solidarity with them. The fool.

That poor woman. Do the others know? Penny and all?

Hardly.

The folders had multiplied but were tidy, Irish books stacked by the decanter. She took the one from the top of the pile and began to flick through it. It was an epic love poem, "Caoineadh Airt Uí Laoghaire," that she had studied in school.

Read a bit, he said.

I am not reading poetry to you in Irish. Or English for that matter.

Read a random line.

No!

Please.

Fuck's sake, she said. She read a line in Irish.

Do you have any idea how sexy that sounds? he said, drawing her close and sliding his hand up her skirt.

You have a Fenian fetish, she said. Not that I blame you, when the alternative is shagging a woman who answers to the name Marjorie.

You don't miss much, he said, walking her backward toward the settee.

I miss loads. But that was pretty obvious, she said.

Shush, he said, pressing his finger to her lips.

Does Marjorie have a husband? she said, slapping his hand away.

Yes. She's married to your friend.

That pig of a man with the crème de menthe?

Yes.

Ugh. So what did Marjorie like you to do to her?

You really don't want to know.

She pulled the buckle of his belt tight then loosened it. I really do.

# 21

Two Catholic civilians were shot dead in a house in Mount Vernon in the north of the city. The Protestant Action Force has claimed responsibility.

Are they a new crowd?

It's a cover name for the UVF, said Jonathan.

A three-hundred-pound car bomb exploded beside the Lyric Theatre, causing extensive damage to the rear of the building. No one was injured.

Anything else? said Cushla.

I'm leaving next week, said Zoe. Me and my mum are going to stay with my nana.

It happened like this sometimes, with the soldiers' kids. They arrived as families and the women left early with the children, unable to stand a full tour of duty.

Cushla and Gerry were bringing their classes to the park for a picnic; next year they would have a proper school trip, a visit to the safari park on the north coast where the biggest attraction was a monkey that smoked Benson & Hedges. She checked that each child had a packed lunch. Davy came to her desk with his, peeling back the orange plastic lid. My mummy said I'm to make sure you see it, he said. It was crammed with expensive food marketed at children. Triangles of processed cheese. A Finger of Fudge. It was a message from Betty. I am coping, she was saying. And I don't trust you anymore.

Gerry's pupils were already in the corridor, sunlight slanting from the open door of his classroom, the terrazzo floor showering the walls with tiny spangles. Cushla's class filed out next. On the corner in front of the school they counted the children, instructing them to find a partner for the walk and hold their hand. The girls did as they were told. The boys winced in disgust, seven years old and muttering about looking like "pansies." There was an odd number of children in Cushla's class and an even number in Gerry's. She found Davy and asked him to carry her basket, a sinecure invented to spare him being left alone.

He walked between Cushla and Gerry, switching the basket from one arm to another. The boys were in T-shirts, bony arms milk white in the sunlight. The girls in summer frocks. Zoe in a pink jumpsuit and matching espadrilles. They set off toward the main street, hands clipping the school railings. On the corner, Paddy the caretaker was mowing the lawn of the parochial house into velvety stripes, Slattery standing on his doorstep, following the machine with his eyes.

He's like something out of a Hammer Horror picture, said Gerry. And please don't quote me on that, wee man.

Davy made a pincer of his hand and moved it across his mouth, as if he was zipping it closed.

Gerry went to the front of the line and led the children across the road, Cushla staying at the back with Davy. Without uniforms, there was a raggle-taggle look about them as they traipsed up High Street hand in hand. They wore their own clothes to protect them, but since all the other schools in town had regulation clothing, they were easily identifiable as Catholics. About ten feet ahead, Fidel stepped out of his shop. He lit a cigarette and watched the children process past him. How's about you, Miss Lavery, he said.

Great. We're going to the park for a picnic.

Fidel crouched in front of Davy, stroking his beard. Davy's head was down, and he began rearranging things in the basket, as if he was looking for something. Fidel straightened himself. He seemed put out. Cushla hadn't told the McGeowns where the Creme Eggs had come from and wondered now if Fidel expected the boy to thank him.

How are you fixed for sixty-odd ice creams in a couple of hours? said Cushla.

Sticking out. I'll get my mummy to help me.

Did Cushla fancy Michael because he was the only man she knew who didn't talk incessantly about his mummy?

Farther along the street, the butcher waved a cleaver at her. The baker put a basket of scones in the window and raised his floury hat.

All that's missing is the candlestick maker, said Gerry, who had hung back. He inclined his head at the giant tin cone. Friend of yours?

Customer. He's not the worst, she said.

A rubber ball bounced onto the road and Gerry roared at the children to stop, afraid its owner would charge into the path of an oncoming car to retrieve it. He hurried to the front of the line.

Near the end of the street there was a statue that had been erected in the fifties in memory of a local child who had been knocked down and killed. It was a skinny figure of a boy, naked except for a pair of wrinkled shorts, a concertina stretched between his hands, the pleats wide open. His knees were clinging to the plinth, his head inclined to the side as if he was listening.

Is that what he looked like? The boy who died? said Davy.

I don't know, said Cushla. I think the artist made something that would remind us of all wee boys. The impish look he has on his face, as if he shouldn't be up there.

Davy said he wanted to see what the boy could see. She took the basket from him and put her hand on his back as he clambered up the rock. He wrapped his legs around the bronze waist and leaned so they were at eye level. He told her he could see the footpath, low down where children walked, that maybe the woman wanted him to have company. Cushla had brought a camera. She asked Davy if she could take a picture. He said he didn't feel much like smiling but she could snap away. She took three and helped him down.

At the ruin of the priory, he stopped. Were the monks Catholics or Protestants? he said.

It was built a long time ago, before there was such a thing as Catholics or Protestants.

The good old days, he said. She laughed and he said it again.

The others were already scattered round the park when Cushla and Davy went through the gates. The roundabout had been replaced, and aside from a smashed bottle beneath the seesaw, the playground was free of hazards. Gerry called the children back and he and Cushla recited a list of rules, adding fresh perils as they thought of them. Don't go near the road. Don't walk in front of the swings. Don't walk behind the swings. Don't double up on the seesaw. No more than four children on the roundabout at a time. Don't go into the bushes. Don't pick the flowers. Don't come down the slide if another child is still on the end of it. Above all, said Gerry, do not, under any circumstances, enjoy yourselves. They stared at him for a moment and took off.

Davy chose a spot under a beech tree. Cushla laid out the blanket she had taken from her car. Sunlight was lying in broken pieces on the grass, a few wilted bluebells clouding the ground.

It's so late for them, she said. Dusty bluebells.

I know that song.

You know lots of songs, Davy McGeown. Most of which you shouldn't know.

He laughed. Why are we not allowed to pick them? said Davy, fingering one.

Because it's a public park and the flowers are here to be enjoyed by everybody. And because it's supposed to be unlucky to bring them into a house. He looked alarmed, as though trying to remember if he had ever done so and might be responsible for the misfortune that had befallen his family.

Don't look so worried. There are nice beliefs about them too. If you wear a wreath of bluebells you will be compelled to tell the truth. And if you turn a bluebell inside out without tearing it, you'll get the one you love. She didn't tell him that to walk in a bluebell patch would lead to a terrible enchantment. That a human who hears a bluebell ring will soon die.

Did your mummy tell you that? said Davy.

My mummy hates nature. My friend has a book about that kind of stuff.

Gerry was by the densest thicket of rhododendrons, the rest of the children surrounding him. Cushla and Davy left the blanket to see what they were looking at.

Jonathan was pointing at the remains of a fire. A couple of beer cans and a condom were strewn on the charred ground. Black magic, he said. They do that up the field at the back of our house. Devil worshipping and dirty stuff.

She hated when they talked like this. It had begun a couple years earlier, when the papers carried a story about the ritual killing of sheep on Copeland Island. Then the burned, dismembered body of a boy had been pulled from the Lagan, and there were whispers of witchcraft and satanism. There was even a rumor that blond, blue-eyed girls were at risk of being abducted and sacrificed. It was hard to convince the children the stories were nonsense when murder was so commonplace.

What's that white thing? said Lucia, pointing a toe at the condom.

Jesus, said Cushla, pulling her back.

Gerry clapped his hands. Picnic time, he said. He did another head count before joining Cushla and Davy on the blanket. Davy finished his lunch fast and ran to the swings, taking advantage of the fact that the others were still cross-legged on the grass, eating.

How's lover boy? said Gerry.

Shut you up.

We live here, Lavery. There are things we can't do.

That's intriguing, she said. What kind of stuff does Gerry Devlin want to do that he can't?

He laughed, a short sarcastic laugh that didn't sound like him. You'd be surprised.

She took more photographs. A class photo, all the children crowded on the roundabout, limbs thrown wide. Gerry sitting on the blanket. She showed Davy how to take a picture and he walked around the park snapping at the other children before replacing the camera in her basket.

They walked back up High Street and mobbed Fidel's ma's shop. Cones were doled out as they were ready, and Gerry whistled slowly when Cushla handed over the money. It was many times more than the price of a few Creme Eggs.

I hardly spend my salary, said Cushla, and I owe him.

Davy refused a lift home again—he had made his own way since the social worker visited—but lurked by his desk until the others had left. I hope the bluebell works out for you, miss, he said.

He had seen her pick a flower. She felt herself go red. Thanks, Davy, she said. So do I.

G ina hadn't dressed again. There was a sharp smell from her. Old urine and stomach acid. Eamonn was in, she said. He had Marian with him.

How is she?

Making a meal of it, complaining of a bad back.

Any wonder. Looking after the girls and doing all that cleaning when she's pregnant.

Are you saying it's my fault?

Cushla could almost taste the misery. It was repulsive. She took a cigarette from Gina's packet and went out to the back garden. She heard the squeak of a door, labored footsteps along a path. Mr. Reid's face appeared over the fence.

Isn't it glorious? he said.

She told him she had taken the children to the park and seen a couple of bluebells. He asked her to wait and disappeared for a moment, returning with a small tray of seedlings, cornflowers, since she liked blue. He asked after her mother and she told him without enthusiasm she was well. He had been in his garden the day Cushla had slung the bottles into the bin, had heard the glass shatter. When he wasn't in the garden he was at his front window. He had surely seen Cushla get out of Michael's car, looking as though she had been thoroughly handled. What must he have thought of them?

When she went inside, Gina had left the table. Cushla went upstairs to get ready and heard her moving around the bathroom, the gush of the tap. She changed quickly, putting on jeans—not the ones with a patch on the arse—and the cheesecloth shirt she had worn the first night. Freckles had come up on her nose and cheeks. She drew around her eyes with gray liner and rubbed it to soften it. Two coats of mascara and lip gloss and a rap at the door to tell Gina she was going to work.

What about your dinner? her mother said. There had been no dinner for days.

Four men were sitting on stools against the wall of the pub, pints in their hands. One lifted his hand to his eyes, as if he was gazing at the horizon from the deck of a ship. Here's my favorite barmaid, he said. It was the groper from before.

Inside, every seat was taken. Minty, Jimmy, Leslie. Fidel, who raised his vodka at Cushla, his preferred tipple when he was flush. How's my best customer? he said.

Skint, said Cushla.

Fidel laughed. She bought fifty-three pokes off me the day, he said.

You'd better spend it all on booze, said Eamonn. What are you doing here? he asked her.

Mummy said Marian's not feeling good.

Mummy's a murder picture, Cushla.

She's been on a bender for weeks. I tried to tell you.

I'm looking after this place. I thought you were looking after her, he said. When their father got sick, Eamonn had assumed the role of head of the family. But their father had been gentle and measured.

She went onto the floor with a damp cloth, gathering dirty glasses, wiping sticky rings from the teak tables. When she came back, Michael was there, slightly behind the other men. He already had a drink in his hand. She reached across him to put a fistful of empties on the counter.

You've been in the sun, he said.

You haven't.

He was pale, as if he hadn't seen daylight for weeks. There was something harried in how he looked along the bar, toward the door. She thought of Penny, saying they were worried about him. I'm all right, he said, as if he knew what she was thinking. Now please go behind that bar before I do something improper.

She washed glasses at the sink. A tankard was pushed at her and a man asked her for a refill. The sun was bright behind him and it wasn't until she put the drink up that she recognized him. It was the third RUC man from the school disco.

Oh, hiya, she said. I didn't know you without your uniform.

Oo-er, said Leslie, a few pints on him and therefore capable of speech. Disco Peeler chuckled. Michael, who was standing beside him, looked from her to him expectantly. She didn't think it appropriate to say the man was in the police, so she went back to washing the glasses.

The sun had moved, leaving the front of the pub in shade. The soldiers came indoors and took their usual table in the corner. Eamonn muttered an obscenity and went outside, clipping the door open. Chill air filled the room as he carried in their stools.

Minty took a tangle of gold from his pocket, stray charms, misshapen bangles, chains without clasps; lost property from the girls' changing rooms. He offered it to Cushla, told her to pick one.

Those belong to wee girls, she said.

They've been in my office all year.

Office? said Fidel. A gloryhole with a sink in it, more like.

You see them changing rooms, Minty began, and Cushla moved away so she couldn't hear him. Eamonn said Minty was a dirty bastard, that he watched the girls undress for PE and talked about their lovely wee diddies. Whatever he was saying now was enough to bring Fidel to his feet.

Fuck's sake, he said, I've a niece in that school.

All right, all right, boys, said Eamonn, behind the bar again.

Michael finished his drink and looked hard at Cushla, raising an eyebrow in the direction of the door. She took a dustpan and brush from under the sink and went outside, him a step behind her. The smell from the sea, the syrupy scent of seaweed. A crow picking at the contents of an overturned bin beside the flats.

Who was that man? he said.

One of the peelers who did the school disco.

I see.

What does that mean?

It's hard seeing you like this.

Like what? Flirting with alcoholics? Wise up.

I may not be able to contact you for a few days.

Incommunicado. Must be serious.

Disco Peeler came out of the pub. He tipped an imaginary hat and vanished into the tunnel. Cushla bent to sweep the fag ends, shredded Swan Vesta box, and scattered matches the soldiers had left. The glamour, she said as she stood up.

I love you, he said.

She left a kiss on his neck. You'd better, Agnew.

# 22

Roads over drumlins that made her stomach leap, the Mournes in the distance, lilac gray, looming larger the farther south they traveled. Lush fields, tidy farmyards. Handmade signs for gospel halls and Baptist churches, words of warning: THE END IS NIGH.

Miserable bastards, said Gina.

The hotel was in a seaside resort overhung by the mountains. They were ten minutes early and Cushla drove along the promenade on which she and Eamonn had gnawed at sticks of rock and sweetie cigarettes, past amusement arcades and chip shops with greasy windows. The shop fronts were hung with gimcracks: bucket-and-spade sets, rubber rings, plastic pinwheels. She doubled back and drove through the gates of the hotel. It had been built in the grand days of railway, between the station and the shore. As a child she had thought it was like a castle from a fairy tale.

She found a parking space close to the entrance. The archway and foyer still seemed magnificent to her, with chandeliers and decorative moldings. They went along a corridor to the dining room. It was stately, with wooden paneling and a red-and-gold-patterned carpet. Vast gilt mirrors and tables set with starched linen and heavy silver.

She gave their surname and they were led to a table set for ten. Cushla explained there must be some mistake. The manager checked and said two sets of Laverys had made reservations. He showed them to a small table by a window, a few feet away from the large one.

Gina ordered a gin and soda, Cushla a Coke that arrived with two pink, stripy straws.

Gina offered her a cigarette.

Why would you want me to smoke when it's bad for me?

You look stupid with that fizzy drink in front of you. It'll make you seem sophisticated.

I can't believe you're pushing fags on me, she said, but took one anyway.

The menus were handwritten in beautiful script but so full of mis-spellings it read like an offering from an *olde inn*. Cushla read the errors aloud. Chedder. Redcurrent. Parcelly: her favorite, she told her mother, because it looked as though they had made an adverb of the word *parcel*.

Nobody likes a show-off, said Gina.

As Cushla put down the menu, a child leaped into her lap. It was Emma, Eamonn's elder daughter. Eamonn was by the table for ten, looking around the room, and appeared momentarily confused when he saw his daughter with his mother and sister, as though something was out of place.

I didn't expect to see youse here, he said, when he came over. His hands were on his hips and there was a smudge of purple paint on one of his fingers.

Obviously, said Gina.

It's Marian's ma's birthday.

Marian was approaching, moving as if she had something balanced on her head, her feet in flat sandals. Her toenails were magenta col-ored, the shade that was on Eamonn's hands. When had her brother become a man who gave his wife pedicures?

This is the first time I've seen you out of heels since school, said Cushla, standing to kiss Marian.

I'm crippled with my back, she said, scratching at her swollen belly. Will youse come over and join us? They'll easily fit another two on our table.

You're all right, thanks, said Gina, knocking back the last of her drink.

Marian shrugged. OK, she said. Enjoy your lunch.

Smug bitch, said Gina, before they were back in their seats.

Mummy! Keep your bloody voice down. You wouldn't have come if they'd asked you.

Their food arrived. Gina ordered another drink. A double.

Cushla ate without appetite, her eyes wandering frequently to the next table. Emma and Nicola were clinging to their other grandmother. Eamonn's hand was on Marian's belly. When she laid her knife and fork on her plate—in the crisscross pattern that both delighted and repulsed Gina for its lack of breeding—Eamonn pulled it toward him and shoveled the last of her food into his mouth. She slapped his hand playfully and the girls clapped. Gina was watching them too.

They refused dessert. Gina ordered a third gin, looking into the glass between mouthfuls. When they stood to leave, the others got to their feet to see them off. Eamonn helped Gina into her coat, speaking quietly into her ear. She didn't reply to him, and his good-byes were more enthusiastic than his hellos had been.

They were almost out of the dining room when Gina stopped dead. Cushla took her elbow, afraid she had thought of terrible things to say to Eamonn, but her mother shook her off and swung to her right, saying, Ach, how are you! It came out like *har arr yah*.

Cushla turned in time to see Michael push his chair back and rise to take Gina's hands in his, just like he had done in the pub. Cushla felt her jaw go slack and stood gawping for a moment before forcing her lips together. Michael appeared unruffled, but when Gina took Cushla's hand and put it in his wife's, he winced. Joanna Agnew was sitting to Michael's left. Cushla had not noticed her; not because she was tiny or nervy or plain, as she had visualized her. She had, rather, a ghostly serenity. A heart-shaped face. Auburn hair, very straight, cut in a bob to her chin. A camel-colored dress, well cut, expensive. A bruise on the back of her left hand with a small hole at its center, from a cannula or injection. She was beautiful.

I haven't seen you since you were a little thing, the woman was saying, gazing into Cushla's eyes. You're like your daddy. Her grip was desperate, as though she was clinging on to steady herself. It was excruciating, feeling her touch, the struggle and sincerity in it.

Beside them, Gina had begun enthusing again. Cushla glanced, did a double take, trying to remember where she had seen the boy before. Then she remembered the rugby photo in the flat. It was like meeting Michael at eighteen.

Dermot, his mother said, finally releasing her, say hello to Cushla.

They had given him an Irish name and put him in a Protestant boarding school.

Cushla looked at Michael. There was an expression of such abject shame on him he appeared to have lost inches in height. He watched sidelong as his son shook her hand, smiled, blushed.

No need to introduce you to Michael, said Gina.

Hiya, said Cushla, digging her fists in her pockets. She could not bring herself to touch him.

When they got outside she thought for a moment she would vomit, and bent over the bonnet of the car. Gina lit a cigarette and wrapped an arm across herself. No harm to you, but I'm foundered, she said.

Cushla felt in her bag for her keys, pulled them out, but her hands were shaking and she dropped them. She knelt on the tarmac to retrieve them from behind the front wheel and, as she stood, she glimpsed the Agnews through the window. The boy was talking animatedly. Michael was smiling, his arm across the back of his wife's chair, the way he had done with Cushla in Penny's kitchen. It was as though the encounter had not happened.

They sat in the car. There was a fine film of sand on the windscreen that Cushla brushed away with the wipers. As she turned the key Gina elbowed her. What did you think of Joanna Agnew?

She seems nice.

She was wobbly, dear love her. She was a law student, you know, until he got her up the duff.

How do you know that? said Cushla. Her voice was hoarse.

Oh, it's no secret. Would you blame her? Sure he's gorgeous.

Cushla felt as though she had been thrown onto the road. At the gate she turned left, the wrong direction, toward the mountains. Along the promenade, children were licking ice creams, blowing on chips, mothers and fathers dandering behind them.

*Fond of the women.* Cushla knew he'd had other affairs. The dry way Penny said, *How do you know each other?* in the Lyric. The mild amusement with which his other friends accepted her, when they should have been scandalized. Marjorie. It seemed now he had been directing things. Showing her where he lived after one month, giving her his number after two, a key after three. Leaving her waiting for days on end then reappearing, reeling her back with a trip to Dublin, an afternoon in his flat. An hour in his car, fucking her until she couldn't think straight. She disliked that she was not the first, but the dawning knowledge that she wouldn't be the last was killing her. As for Joanna. How seldom the woman had entered her head. She'd been an irritant, that was all. It had suited Cushla to think of her as unattractive and slovenly, to believe Michael was stuck in a miserable marriage, unable to leave his fuckup of a wife.

The phone rang at seven. Gina pressed her hands to the arms of the chair but left her bum on the seat. Cushla got up to answer it, pulling the door closed before lifting the receiver.

How's Mummy? said Eamonn.

How do you think?

She can't stand Marian's family, so I never thought of asking youse. It doesn't matter.

It does. Daddy would be disgusted.

Daddy's gone, Eamonn.

You need to get away from her, he said. Join the circus. Leave the country. Get married.

Who do you suggest I marry?

I don't know. That teacher with the red neb? He was trying to make her laugh, but a sob had come up from her stomach. She waited for it to pass. Are you still there? he said.

Yeah. Look, it'll be OK. I'll talk to her.

When she went into the sitting room, Gina's eyes were glittering. Michael and Joanna will know we were at separate tables, she said.

Will you stop bloody talking about them? said Cushla. She left the room and went through the kitchen to the back garden. The baby plants Mr. Reid had given her were still on the windowsill. She carried them halfway down the lawn to where the daffodils were rotting back into the soil. She knelt and dug holes with her fingers, placing a seedling in each cavity, pressing the earth between them with her palms. Inside again, she stood at the sink and took a nail brush to her hands. She looked out the window. It was as though she hadn't planted anything at all.

# 23

A twenty-two-year-old man was shot dead in an ongoing feud between the INLA and the Official IRA.

The sixteen-year-old who was shot in the neck and chest on his way home from visiting a friend in the north of the city at the weekend has died from his wounds.

Zoe left on Saturday, said Lucia, looking dolefully at the empty seat beside her.

You could drop her a line, said Cushla. We have an hour to put in before Sports Day starts. I'll show you how to write a letter.

Can we write to Jimmy Savile? said Jonathan.

What in God's name would you be writing to him for? said Cushla.

Jonathan said Jimmy had a new program on television, where he made children's dreams come true.

OK, she said. I suppose it would be good practice.

She went to the board and wrote an address in the top right-hand corner.

Thirty-two Windsor Gardens, said Lucia. That's Paddington's address!

She told them how to begin a letter, with polite enquiries about the addressee. How to lay out the paragraphs, how to sign off. The children began writing; opening her journal, so did Cushla.

*Dear Jimmy*

*I hope you are keeping well. Things are fine here. The school
holidays begin in a few days and I will be off work for two
months. I had intended to spend the summer slinking round
Michael Agnew's flat, making myself irresistible to him so he'd
leave his wife. Only his wife is a lady, they appear to be happily
married, and he is a lying, cheating, philandering fucker.*

*Yours sincerely
Cushla Lavery (aged 24¾)*

Michael had phoned several times; at least she presumed it was him,
but on each occasion she had lifted the receiver and immediately replaced it, so she couldn't be sure. After three days she could bear it no
longer and, when the phone rang, she held it to her ear. He began speaking before she said a word, a rush of apologies. She had rehearsed what
she would say—that she hated him, hated herself, that she wouldn't see
him again—but was seduced by how distraught he sounded. He had
said he was around the corner and could pick her up, and it had taken all
her will not to walk out the door and stand on the curb. She had agreed
to go to the flat after school.

She walked around the room to see how the children were doing
with their own letters.

Lucia wanted to go to England to see Zoe. Grace wanted to sing
with ABBA. Jonathan wanted to read the news. Outlandish, yet there
was more chance of Fintan playing for Liverpool than of Cushla having a happy ever after with Michael Agnew.

Davy put his hands flat on his letter and said he'd show it to her
later.

She sent the children to the cloakroom to change into their gutties and carried the crate of milk outside, laying it in a shady place by the railings. It was a beautiful day, blue sky, big cauliflower clouds. Gerry was on the pitch, marking lanes for races.

You look wrecked, he said. Trouble in paradise?

Frig off, Gerry.

You need to be saved from yourself.

The contests began. Without Zoe there was an even number of children, and Cushla put Davy in a relay team. Jonathan rolled his eyes and drew the others around him for a prerace motivational talk. They were arguing about who should finish, and Cushla intervened and said Davy would do it. Words were forming on Jonathan's lips, but he saw the look on Cushla's face and they stayed there, unsaid.

Gerry roared Go! and the race began. They were neck and neck with a team from Gerry's class when the baton was passed to Davy. He seized it and took off. He ran without looking around him, leaning into the bends at the corners of the pitch. He was ungainly, legs flinging out in all directions. Come on, Davy, shouted Jonathan. The others had begun chanting his name. He picked up pace, running so hard his head was rolling from side to side, breaking through the tape at the finish with his eyes closed. He slowed to a trot, his rib cage heaving. Jonathan and the others were on him, then, hoisting him up and thumping him on the back. Cushla's camera was in her basket. She captured him in the midst of the boys, holding his medal. The cheap glint of it in the sunshine. The smile on his face.

He won the egg-and-spoon race. Cushla told him his center of gravity had been lowered by the bionic running. He almost won the sack race too, but lost his footing a yard from the finish, pitching sideways. He tried to stand, his face contorted in pain. Cushla helped him up, kneeling to lift his foot out of the pillowcase. The ankle was already beginning to swell. That's a pity, she said. I think you were in line for another medal.

I'm happy enough, miss, he said.

The bell rang. The dinner ladies had made a picnic. Cushla left Davy on the grass surrounded by the rest of the class, who were talking across him. His face hadn't completely lost its worried look. He knew how temporary their approval was.

She was sorry to see him in pain, but glad of the excuse to drive him home. He held his medals in his hand all the way up the road and through the estate. A man was scrubbing at last year's paint with a wire brush, dusting the tarmac with dull red, white, and blue confetti, in preparation for a fresh coat. On the McGeowns' wall, TAIGS OUT had been retouched. Another triumphal summer was beginning.

She helped Davy out of the car and linked his arm up the path.

Betty opened the door as they reached the step.

Do you want the good news or the bad news? said Davy.

Give me all of it at once, said Betty.

The bad news is I busted myself in the sack race. The good news is I won two medals. He shook them at her face and hopped into the hall.

Betty asked Cushla in. A draft was coming from an open window. Davy climbed onto the arm of the settee, leaning over his father, the brass in his open palm. I put my head down and ran like the clappers, he was saying. Cushla was so happy to be back in favor she did not mind standing in front of Seamie. The swelling had gone down and one side of his face had fallen, where the eye socket had been cracked. He reminded her of one of those Picassos, where a face had been disassembled and its features redistributed.

Davy played a blinder today, she said.

He's a good lad, said Seamie.

Cushla congratulated Davy again and said she should leave. At the door she asked Betty how everything was.

The younger two are all right. Our Tommy's another story. We hardly see him. When we do, he's swaggering about with a few bob in his pocket, acting the big fella.

Maybe it's just a phase.

I hope so, said Betty.


Michael's car was close to the steps, as if he'd pulled up in a hurry. She touched the bonnet. Heat, a smell of burned dust. She rang the bell, reluctant to use the key. He opened the door to let her in, leaning to kiss her, but she ducked past him and into the sitting room. The holdall was in the middle of the floor, bulging with fresh laundry. He toed it aside.

The room smelled of beeswax polish. The grate was empty, the hearth washed, brasses bright.

Mrs. Coyle was in, said Cushla.

She was.

How's her son?

A bloody disaster. He wasn't in the IRA when he was arrested, but he probably is now. Tea?

Yeah, she said, and followed him into the kitchen. He filled the kettle and began to unpack a bag of groceries. Glass jars of grapefruit juice, cans of Scotch broth and cock-a-leekie soup. Lime marmalade and ginger cake. An Ulster linen tea towel printed with rows of Grenadier guardsmen was hanging from the handle of a drawer.

He loaded a tray and brought it to the table. Thanks for coming, he said. He looked physically uncomfortable, like he did when his shoulder was acting up. She wished he would shift in his seat, re-arrange himself, but he didn't move.

I can't stay long, she said. Eamonn's expecting me by six.

Sunday was appalling, he said.

What was appalling? That I turned up? I didn't think about her much, you know, she said. Your wife. And when I did I pictured someone else. A wizened wee hag, or some rough-looking ould doll who needed her roots done.

I would prefer not to talk about her, he said.

She held my fucking hand, Michael. What are you at? You looked like a normal, happy family.

My wife has problems.

What's wrong with her?

He said his wife was an alcoholic. That she was being treated for depression. That he went home sometimes and found her curled on the floor. That she had been admitted to hospital over a month ago for an-other course of electric shocks. That sometimes she was well enough after treatment to do things. That their son had finished his A levels and he had brought them out for lunch.

Was that why you were able to see me so often? Because she was in hospital and your son was at school.

Yes.

Have you had lots of affairs?

Three.

Jesus. Including me?

Apart from you. I don't consider this an affair.

What the hell is it, then?

It's different.

A laugh came out of her, an ugly sound. Pull the other one, Michael, she said.

He poured himself a whiskey and knocked it back. You don't believe a word I say.

At this stage I don't believe a word I say. When you phone me or pick me up or come into the bar, I know you want me. The rest of the time I don't know what to think. Who were the others, out of interest? Marjorie, of course.

Please don't.

Am I the first Taig? I bet you I am. Does it make you feel better about yourself? That you're doing it for the sake of community relations. And why do your friends not care? How little they must think of your wife that they scarcely bat an eyelid when you parade me about.

Do you really want to have this conversation? he said, slamming his glass on the table.

Yeah. I do. She could feel her throat closing.

Are you sure? Because I would counter that this attack of conscience has been triggered by the realization that you are not the only woman I've been with outside of my marriage, rather than any concern for my wife's dignity.

Fuck off, she said, rising from the chair.

He passed a hand over his face. That was out of order, he said. I'm sorry. Please sit down.

She stayed on her feet. He seemed diminished, like he had in the hotel. It was true, what he'd said. She hadn't cared that he was married. If anything, it had begun to turn her on.

Do you want to stop seeing me? he said.

No, God help me. I don't.

It will be hell unless you can overlook my circumstances.

This is going to end really badly, isn't it?

It doesn't have to.

He poured the tea and told her she could stay more often, move in if she wanted. That there were lots of things they could do. There was a cottage in Donegal he took sometimes; they could go at the end of the summer, when you could see God in the skies. They could go to Amsterdam or Barcelona. She thought of all the things they wouldn't do. Remember this, she told herself. Remember that you made plans.

A t first she thought she was the butt of some joke and looked sharply along the counter, but the others were watching the television. Why are you smiling? she asked Eamonn.

I'm pleased to see you.

Aye, right. You're still feeling guilty about Sunday. What do you need done? said Cushla.

Just throw out a few pints and keep me company.

Minty was doing an impression of Frank Spencer. Fidel said he was actually doing an impression of Mike Yarwood doing an impression of Frank Spencer. Leslie, clearly on his fourth pint, was saying "very good" (it sounded like "farry" good).

I'm missing my daughters growing up because of these eejits, said Eamonn.

You love it.

They're a good laugh, he said.

Cushla remembered the camera was still in her basket. She gave it to Eamonn. Finish the film, she said.

Without looking up, she knew Michael had come in. Maybe it was the sound the door made, the pattern of his footsteps, but she felt it in her body. She lifted her eyes in time to see him put his hands on the counter. He squeezed his eyes in gratitude as she put a drink in front of him. Along the bar, Minty, Leslie, and Fidel were draping their arms around each other, posing for Eamonn. Jimmy was a little away from them.

Get over here, O'Kane, Fidel said, flinging an arm out.

Mind me egg, said Jimmy.

Eamonn turned up the volume on the television. Behind her, the jingle for the news was playing. She placed a beer mat under Michael's glass. She felt his fingertips on her wrist, just for a second.

Can you not keep away from me? she said. Like I'm only in the door.

It appears so. Are we all right?

We're doomed. Apart from that we're grand.

He smiled. Tomorrow?

Yeah.

Come as early as you can.

She was aware of him hovering in the doorway and looked up. A glimpse of his profile, and then he was gone.

# 24

She slept badly, afflicted by waking dreams from which she could not rouse herself. In the most vivid, she was driving Davy home, but instead of sitting in the front seat, the boy behind her leaning in the gap, she had been in the back seat beside him, unable to reach the pedals or steering wheel. She had left her room and gone downstairs to smoke one of Gina's cigarettes. The kitchen was white with moonlight and she had sat in its glow for a long time. Back in bed, she dozed off, but woke thinking she had opened Michael's door with the brass key and found the flat under rubble. She looked at her watch. It was five to eight. She got up and went into the bathroom. She filled the basin with cold water, plunging her face in it, holding her breath until she choked. The chill had shocked sense into her.

In the kitchen she took down a box of cereal, put it back. Her stomach was tender. She made a pot of tea and carried a mug upstairs to her mother.

No toast? said Gina.

You never eat it! There are pancakes in the bread bin. Buck one into the toaster when you get up.

Before she left the house, she threw a box of Ritz Crackers into her basket, in case she was fit to eat later.

The estate was like Nuremberg, with flags and bunting and painted pavements. She beeped her horn and Davy hobbled down the path on his mother's arm. His ankle was bulging, a tight bandage visible above his sock.

I'm like a human crutch, said Betty, as she tipped him into the back seat.

Cushla laughed. I'll bring him home later.

Is it very sore? she asked Davy as she took off.

I'll live, miss.

He entered the classroom with his head down, the way he always did, but the others treated him like a conquering hero, leading him across the floor. Jonathan pulled his chair out for him and chatted to him the way he did with the other boys. Cushla caught Davy's eye and winked.

Right, she said. The News.

No one put a hand up.

Jonathan? she said.

Nothing juicy.

There must be something.

The police closed off a road out our way, one of the boys said, a child who lived a few miles out of town.

There must have been an incident, said Jonathan. It'll be on a bulletin later.

At break time, the children helped Davy out to the playground, two of them carrying his chair. Cushla went to the staffroom. Gerry was sitting on the windowsill with tea for her.

How's the wee lad?

Limping, said Cushla. The others are being nice to him. He doesn't know what to make of all the attention.

What are you going to do for the summer?

Help in the bar. Take my ma to Killarney for a few days. What about you?

I'm going to France with some of the boys. You should think about it.

Gerry Devlin, you hardly want me away with you and your mates, she said.

You're decent craic, when you're not moping about with a face on you. And I need to get you away from lover boy, whoever the fuck he is.

That's all sorted out now.

You dumped him?

No. But it's going to be OK.


Cushla dropped Davy home, tooting her horn and telling Betty through the open window she was in a rush. She left them on the footpath, waving. On the way back to town, she parked across her driveway and ran inside to change her clothes. In the kitchen, the teapot was as she had left it that morning and nothing on the worktop hinted at dinner. She took the stairs two at a time and began pushing doors open, afraid of finding her mother bleeding or passed out in bed or bath, but the house was empty. Gina had been to the hairdresser's yesterday and usually did her gin run in the morning, when the off-license was quiet. Where could she be?

Cushla dialed the number for the pub. The line was engaged. She dialed Michael's number, knowing it was a little early for him to have made his way to the flat, but she wanted to hear his voice. It rang out. She went upstairs and ran a shallow bath, washing her hair as she crouched in the water. She put on the jeans she had worn the previous day, a clean black top; he seemed to like her any way she showed up, and so she did not feel compelled to ransack her wardrobe. The Aran cardigan she had taken from his flat after the wedding was on the back of a chair. It had been daft of him to suggest she could move in, but it seemed reasonable now to add some clothes to the cold cream and toothbrush already there.

Downstairs, she tried the pub again. Leonardo answered. Why are you working? she said.

We're full to the rafters, like.

Is my mummy there?

Hould on.

Eamonn's voice. Are you coming down?

I wasn't planning to.

You need to get her out of here, he said, and hung up.

The radio was on in the kitchen. Dead on arrival in hospital, the newsreader said, as she flicked the switch. What was Gina doing in the pub? Cushla had hoped to reach Belfast before rush hour, but if Gina put up any fight at all, Cushla was unlikely to arrive at the flat before six.

The car park was full. Inside, people who only came in occasionally were among the regulars. She went around the room, grabbing as many glasses as she could carry, bringing them behind the bar. Gina was on a stool, facing the television. She had a whiskey in her hand, her drink of choice for especially bad occasions. They were two deep at the counter, but the pub was strangely quiet. The air seemed to be trembling, as if they were all shaking their heads slowly.

What's going on? said Cushla.

Ach, love, her mother said, and fell on her.

Eamonn came toward her. What's wrong with her? she whispered to him.

Did you not hear?

Hear what?

Michael Agnew was shot dead this morning.

Cushla's hand began to pat against her mother's back, as if she was winding a baby, her body knowing what to do while her mind skittered. God be good to him, Gina was saying, he didn't deserve it. Cushla untangled herself and went to the sink, her movements stiff, like a mechanical toy that needed to be wound into motion again. She ran the cold tap at full flow to drown the platitudes and expressions of horror being muttered around the room. The voices became indistinct. She took a tankard, pumped it over the inverted bottle brush, placed it in the glasswasher, repeating the process until the tray was full. She was aware that someone was speaking to her and lifted her head, looking along the bar for the source of the words, but no one was paying her attention. She bent to the sink again, wringing a cloth and using it to blot away the sudsy water with which she had flooded the draining board. Eamonn touched her arm. She looked at his hand and walked away. In the doorway her legs stopped. She looked at her feet, willing them to carry her, but her hips were twisting to her right, as if Michael was beside her, close enough to graze her skin with his arm. She glanced back at the bar. Eamonn was at the end of the counter, watching her. She pushed open the door and stumbled across the car park. In the tunnel, a bleachy stench of urine, cans rolling in the draft, wisps of sweet wrappers flying up at her legs. On the esplanade, blue water, bluer hills across the lough.

Footsteps behind her.

What's going on? said Eamonn.

I was on my way to see him, she said.

To see who? said Eamonn, peering at her, looking at her eyes, her chin. When had she started crying?

Michael, she said, and a squall of grief left her, an inhuman sound.

Eamonn's face began to alter, as if a shadow had fallen across it. No, he said. No way.

How can he be dead? she wailed, and felt herself spiral downward.

Fuck, said Eamonn, jerking her upright and shoving her against the rail that overlooked the lough. You were seeing Michael Agnew? Was that why you were in here every other night?

A woman passed them with a Jack Russell on a lead. Eamonn let go of Cushla, his hands moving to his hips, and stood facing the water. Who else knows?

Cushla felt panic rise. Nobody, she said.

Are you sure?

Yeah.

They'd fucking better not. Now pull yourself together and get back behind that bar.

I want to go home.

Eamonn slammed his hands onto the railing and swung back. Are you fucking joking? he said. You are going to walk in there as if someone you hardly knew died.

When they reached the door, he told her to wait and went around the rear of the pub. He came back with six bottles of cordial and loaded them in her waiting arms.

If anyone asks, we were getting stock, he said.

I can't do this, she said.

You can. And you will.

Leonardo, unused to the exertion of manning the bar alone, had a spritz of sweat on his mustache. Gina was still seated, nursing a Paris goblet to her breast. Bad bastards doing a thing like that, she said. She was almost enjoying herself, like she had with the McGeowns, basking in the celebrity that being close to tragedy brought. It filled Cushla with fury.

Fidel ordered a pint from her. Eamonn had climbed on the stool to turn up the volume on the television. The room fell quiet, the Babycham fawn regarding it through heavy lashes.

A march on Stormont. The car-bomb footage they had begun to use the first night, when Michael watched her rub away the ashes. Mary Peters holding her medal.

Two RUC men on the road outside Michael's house, three on his driveway. A man in civilian clothes beside the rose bushes that were blooming now. His dark car parked behind the green Japanese one.

The man who was shot dead in his bed shortly before eight this morning has been named. Michael Agnew, a senior counsel, was killed in front of his wife, said the newsreader.

Footage from earlier today, of the stretcher being carried out. It was as though they'd thrown him on the gantry, his body jumbled under a white sheet, the awkward jut of his limbs. Something else was wrong, and at first she couldn't tell what it was. His shoulder, she said, unable to stop herself. Wouldn't you think they'd have been careful with his shoulder?

# When I Move to the Sky

# 25

She put her face in the revere of Michael's cardigan, inhaled. He was there, for a moment, but her nose became accustomed to the scent and he was gone. She was sticky with sweat, wearing only her underwear under the cardigan. She flung the covers off. Her bedroom door opened. Cushla seized the sheet, too slow, because Gina said, What if there's a fire? You'd have to stand outside on the street in your drawers. She was carrying the tray on which Cushla normally served Gina's breakfast.

Her mother was dressed in navy trousers and a Breton-style cotton jumper, her lips red. She pushed aside a pile of items Cushla did not recall assembling and laid the tray on Cushla's nightstand. There was tea, toast, an egg mashed in a Pyrex cup. Cushla felt a burn of sick at the back of her throat. She rolled away from her mother and staggered to the bathroom, thanking God the toilet lid was open. She put her hands on the cistern and vomited until she was bilious. When she lifted her face to the mirror, her cheek was embossed with a moss-stitch pattern from the cardigan. She cleaned her teeth and her tongue, retching as the brush reached the back molars, and sat on the toilet seat with her head in her hands, waiting to hear Gina's feet descending the stairs. She was still drunk. The window was north facing, the air chilly. She stayed until she could no longer bear the cold, and went back to her room, gripping the edges of the cardigan across her stomach.

Gina was at Cushla's dressing table, backcombing a tuft of hair. You'd better get your arse down that road to school, she said, smoothing the fuzz with a tail comb.

I'm dying, said Cushla, crawling across the mattress and under the blankets. Will you ring Bradley for me? Tell him I've a bug or something.

Disgraceful. Missing work because of drink, said her mother, her eyebrows and shoulders rising in a pretense of suppressing a giggle. When they got home the previous evening Gina had produced a bottle of Teacher's from her handbag that she had clearly stolen from the bar. They had sat at the kitchen table, guzzling, her mother telling stories about Michael. The time he and her uncle were lifted on an early civil rights march and Michael ridiculed the arresting officer so much he had the man in tears. The night his son was born, when he bought a drink for every single customer in the bar. It had made Cushla feel close to him. This morning it seemed mawkish. Indecent.

Her mother creaked her way across the floor and down the stairs. Cushla listened to her lie for her, in her telephone voice: gastric flu, she was saying, sure you couldn't have her going near the place with a dose like that. She forced down the now tepid tea and drew her body into a ball. The anesthetic effect of the alcohol was wearing off, her stomach juices fizzling, the scalded feeling returning to her chest cavity. She dozed off for a moment then jolted awake, sensing that something was very wrong, and sat upright, ready to run downstairs to the telephone to ask Michael what she should do. But Michael was dead. She closed her eyes and tried to summon his face, but the only image that came was of the stretcher, the untidy arrangement of his limbs. How he looked with the life gone out of him.

Gina came back with a bottle of Kali Water begged from Mr. Reid. Cushla's father had sworn by it for sick tummies. It seemed sordid to take it for a hangover, but she was parched and drank it by the neck, the mild quinine flavor reminding her of her mother's gin breath.

I need a lift down the road, said Gina.

Somebody might see me. I'm meant to be sick.

You can park at the bar.

No! You walk to the off-license every day, do it today.

A few minutes later the front door slammed. She got up and dressed in the clothes she had worn last night, putting the cardigan back on. Downstairs, she sat on the third step, cradling the phone. She had spent so much of the last few months here, circling the table, willing him to call. She lifted the receiver and dialed the number of the flat. With each ring, the anguish she always felt when he didn't answer grew until she could not bear it, because he never would. As she was about to replace the receiver, a man's voice said, Yes?

Michael? she said, knowing as she cried his name it couldn't be him.

Fingers snapping, low voices. It's a woman, someone said. Cushla hung up. Who was in the flat? His son? Jim or Victor? The police?

She took a packet of cigarettes from the carton Gina kept in the pantry and her keys from the kitchen table. Her car was on the driveway. She had no recollection of driving home. She could not, in fact, remember anything after exclaiming at Michael's shoulder. Eamonn must have ordered her out. She got behind the wheel and started the engine, letting the car roll backward, too fast; a horn blasted and a van swerved out of her path. When her breathing had settled, she checked her mirrors and inched out.

The day was bright and gusty. Before the entrance to the estate, a figure in a leather jacket, a sausage bag over his shoulder, was walking alone along the footpath. There was something in his gait—too purposeful for a young lad—that made her slow to look at him. It was Tommy McGeown. She held her hand up, and he stared at her as if he did not know her, and kept walking.

The barracks on the right, the trees lush with leaves, as if a net of camouflage had been thrown over the messes and family quarters. She drove on and turned left in the direction of the village. The gorse flowers were sparse and deepened to a yellow that was almost sulfurous. On a bend, she had to tug the wheel to avoid colliding with a motorbike that was lumbering up the hill, and dropped to third gear to gain some control over the car. Over herself.

Flags were fluttering from telegraph poles a mile from the village, festooning the place when she reached the crossroads. Along the verge leading to his house a gray Land Rover, a marked police car. A couple of cars so nondescript she wondered were they Special Branch vehicles. Three men in uniform by the front door, three in civilian clothes on the driveway, one with a camera round his neck, smoking a cigarette. Tape she had seen stretched between the gates on the news bulletin was lying on the ground. She was so distracted by the scene she almost knocked down the RUC man who had stepped on the road and was gesturing for her to wind down her window.

Are you a resident? he said.

I just came out for a drive, she said, afraid he would ask for her name.

There's nothing to see here. Keep going and turn left then left again, he said, tapping the roof to let her go. She held the wheel tight, checking the speedometer sometimes lest she draw further attention to herself. She almost missed the lay-by and had to brake so hard the car filled with the smell of hot rubber.

She sat on the bonnet, lighting a cigarette. The ditch had dried to a muddy trough.

The gully was wider than she'd realized, hard to cross without the pull of Michael's arm. Her right foot reached the far bank but began to slither down. She scurried back up, her hand grasping the barbed wire of the fence. She squeezed, felt the cold metal push through her skin. There was relief in the pain and she tightened her grip until she couldn't stand it. She opened her hand. The puncture was small and clean and bubbling blood. She saw him step across the gully, the shyness of him as he handed her the gorse. It was bad luck for the giver and receiver, he had said. Where was he now? On a cold table, someone in a mask picking fragments of shot from a brain that had, until yesterday, finished a crossword in minutes and argued in a court of law for a living. His body a piece of evidence now.

Gina had not come home from the shops. The Teacher's bottle they had emptied the previous night was on the kitchen windowsill. Cushla brought it outside and dropped it in the bin. She took a cigarette from the pack in her pocket, leaning against the back wall of the house to smoke it. Apart from the grass, the only color in the garden was from the brownish buds of roses. She heard a cough, a polite sound: Mr. Reid announcing himself. She wondered if he knew. Michael had been careful not to park outside the Laverys' house, and the old man would have had a clear view from his window seat. Cushla saw herself as he must have. Strutting past his window in high, tight boots and gauzy dresses, a man's cardigan over them. She tossed the butt in the grating and went inside.

She was dunking a tea bag in a mug when the doorbell rang. They had callers so seldom she placed her foot against the kickboard on the bottom and opened it an inch.

It was Gerry Devlin. She pulled the door just wide enough for him to slip in, closing it when he was barely on the mat. Any chance of a coffee? he said.

Yeah. He followed her to the kitchen. I missed the last day with the kids, she said, flicking on the kettle again. And poor wee Davy. How did he get to school with that limp?

Bradley told me you weren't coming in, so I took a quick spin up the road to get him.

Thanks, Gerry. Were the kids all right? I had promised them a party, she said.

They were grand. You're the best teacher ever, apparently. Even when you don't turn up. He hesitated. It was him, wasn't it?

She opened her mouth to deny it but felt exhausted at the prospect of more lying. Yes, she said.

Jesus. Go and sit down. I'll bring your tea.

She lit another cigarette. How did you know? she said, as he put the mug in front of her.

I wasn't sure, until you didn't turn up at school. When I heard his name on the radio. I remembered how he was with you in the Lyric. I felt awkward when I came back with the drinks at the interval, as if I was interrupting. You were standing so close to him. And that evening in the pub, before we went to the pictures. He wasn't one bit happy to see me. Did you love him?

Yeah, she tried to say, but nothing came out of her mouth. She took a drag of the cigarette.

How long were you seeing him?

A couple of weeks after that night in the theater he came into the bar and asked me to teach him and his friends Irish.

That was original, I'll say that for him.

I know how it sounds, but he wasn't like that, she said. Remember that night, when you said he was all right? He was.

I didn't mean you should start riding him, he said, raising his eyes to hers. Tears had begun rolling down her cheeks. She wiped them with the back of her hand. He reached to take it and stopped. Shit, he said. There was blood gathering in the webbing between her fingers and thumb. He opened her fist. Her palm was dented with the half-moon shapes of her fingernails and the puncture had split wide open. Go over to the sink and start rinsing that hand, he said. Where do you keep your plasters?

In the bathroom.

She watched the tomatoey juices swirl down the plughole. Gerry came back with a roll of Elastoplast and a tube of Germolene. Poor Lavery, he said softly.

After he left, she went upstairs and lay on her bed. She took the pile she had assembled last night. The Irish books, *Betsy Gray*. The copy of *The Black Prince* she'd been too giddy to read. A bar of soap wrapped in waxed paper printed with the name of the hotel in Dublin. A punt that had the metallic smell of a used note, Lady Lavery's long fingers on a beer-stained cheek. A single brass key. The novena she'd bought, that Michael had found silly. They were the mementos of a mooning teenager. Siobhán de Buitléar had got his life. His child. His death.

The bang of the front door, heels across the wood. Since she was a child, Cushla could read Gina's steps. Short and clipped when she was angry. Light when she was sneaking a drink. Erratic, now; she was drunk.

She got up and went downstairs to the kitchen.

I've all the details, Gina said, taking a bottle of Jameson from her bag and two tumblers from the cupboard. And this was poor Michael's tipple of choice.

Cushla went to the hall and lifted the phone, dialing Gerry's number. I can't stay here, she said.

. . .

Gerry lived on the outskirts of east Belfast, in a small semi-d in a cul-de-sac. He had bought it the previous August, he told her as he showed her in. Everything had been orange but he had managed to remove most of it. Except in here, he said, opening the door to the kitchen. The units were tangerine colored, the wall tiles brown with an orange geometric pattern. Brown lino on the floor had replaced an orange carpet.

In the living room a fawn Dralon couch, a cream shaggy rug. A white melamine coffee table topped with smoked glass. Shelves on either side of the fireplace, books to the left, music to the right, reel-to-reel tapes and long-playing records; a guitar and amp in the corner. Photographs in frames, one bigger than the rest, of a woman in a full skirt with a little boy by the hand: Gerry and his mother. He had her smile.

There was a western on the television. A man appeared in the doorway of a saloon and stood with his feet apart, fingers splayed at his hips. The room fell quiet as he crossed the floor. A barmaid approached him, a redhead with harsh makeup and a frilly black dress. She leaned over the counter and offered him a drink. As she poured it, she looked in the mirror to see if he was watching.

Gerry brought a bottle of rum and some Coke that he served in bubbly amber glasses Maxol had given out free with petrol the previous year. The man in the film was being pursued by a ruthless gang. He drank heavily and roughed the woman up, leaving her weeping and begging for more. Cushla lit a cigarette and turned from the television.

The film ended and a news bulletin came on. An incendiary

device had killed three soldiers. The police were following a definite line of inquiry in the murder of a prominent Belfast barrister.

They shot him in bed. In front of his wife, said Cushla.

I know, he said.

I shook her hand. Last Sunday. She was hardly there at all. And his son's. He's the image of him.

Easy, Gerry said softly.

They watched a game show. A man in a brown suit, smeared in blancmange, beaming. His son, an earnest boy in his teens, blushing for both of them.

The words began to tumble from her, things she had not known were true until she uttered them. That it had been as though something was stalking Michael. The drinking. How he had stayed by the window, watching the street, long after the strange car had left his driveway that afternoon. She talked until the room was purple with twilight. Gerry switched on a lamp and drew the curtains. She thanked him for listening and he put his hand on hers. The tenderness was so affecting she leaned to kiss him.

He pulled away gently from her mouth. It ain't me, babe, he said.

She apologized and began to cry. He gathered her back to him.

Beside Gerry Devlin's bed there was a copy of *The Black Prince*, a bookmark a few pages from the end. How little she knew him.

I'm sorry for taking a buck lep at you, she said, as she got in beside him. It's OK.

That night in your car. I thought you liked me.

I do like you. But I don't fancy you. I kissed you because I thought you were expecting it.

She lay on her side, Gerry's arm around her. He kept it there all through the night.

. . .

She called to the McGeowns' house on her way home. The net curtain flapped, then the front door opened. Davy came hopping
down the path as if he'd been waiting for her.

How's that ankle? she said.

Up like a bap and all the colors of the rainbow, he said.

He linked Cushla's arm and limped alongside her into the hall. She
told him she was sorry to have missed his last day, that she had been
sick. You still don't look a bit well, said Betty. Cushla said she wasn't
too bad and apologized for the messing around over lifts.

Not at all, said Betty. Mr. Devlin came to get him. He's nice. She had
a half smile on her face.

All the girls say that.

Not you?

Nah. He's my friend, she said.

Seamie's chair was empty. Betty said he had been taken away in a
minibus for physiotherapy that didn't seem to be doing him much
good.

It might be a long haul, said Cushla.

Mandy came out of the kitchen. I've the kettle on, she said. She had
plucked her eyebrows into fine arcs and flicked out her fringe. Cushla
told her she was gorgeous and Mandy looked as though she might cry.
Cushla cringed for her. She had hated being that age . . . both desperate
to be noticed and mortified. Mandy made them tea and put a plate of
buns on the table, insisting Cushla take one.

It was the first thing she had eaten for days. She said it was deli-
cious.

My wee homebird, said Betty. She made them herself.

I saw Tommy the other day, said Cushla. Walking up the road to here.

Betty's smile faded. He turned up out of the blue with a bag of washing, she said. Sat all weekend in the house with a bake on him, smoking fegs. Between him and Seamie we're choking. He's still here. Up in that bloody room.

Cushla finished her tea and put the mug in the sink. Well, Davy Mc-Geown, whoever has you next year will be a very lucky teacher, she said.

I wish I could be in your class again next year, miss, he said, running at her and throwing his arms round her knees.

I wish I could be your teacher again, she said, and, to her dismay, burst out crying. She tried to stop, but the tears were coursing down her face. Davy drew back and was looking up at her. Betty put her hand on Cushla's arm. Are you all right? she said. You really didn't look well when you came in.

Sorry, she said. I don't know where that came out of. Maybe I can call up sometime? To say hello?

Anytime. Isn't that right, Davy?

Cushla turned to leave. Tommy had come downstairs and was standing in the hallway.

I'll lock the door after her, he said.

His mother rolled her eyes and left them alone.

Tommy was wearing a dark blue T-shirt with a white collar. His face and arms were ruddy from working outside. Cushla avoided looking at his shoulders, aware that they had become strong. You were crying? he said.

I got a bit emotional about your wee brother. How are things with you, Tommy? No work today?

I've a couple of days off, he said. He swallowed. Maybe we can meet up. Since you're not our kid's teacher anymore.

The door to the sitting room was closed. His face was close to hers. Surely he wasn't asking her out. Or was he? There was a confidence in him that was almost oppressive.

Maybe, she said, wanting to leave.

OK. I have your number.

She tripped down the path, feeling unsteady in herself, and did not look back at the house until she was in the driver's seat. He was still on the doorstep.

# 26

Does anybody else know? said Eamonn, dropping his mug in the sink, splashing Cushla with suds.

No.

Bullshit. I know when you're lying.

I was teaching him and four of his friends Irish.

You're joking.

I'm not.

Where?

In one of their houses. On the Malone Road.

Fuck me. Is that it? Just them?

Yes!

It wasn't, though. All the people at the exhibition, the party, the neighbors who had seen her coming and going, people she couldn't even name. Mrs. Coyle. Maybe even Mr. Reid. How stupid she was. The police would be tracing Michael's movements, interviewing his friends. During Cushla's last year of teacher training, a classmate of hers was arrested for her part in a bombing campaign in London. The RUC went to the home of every student. The policeman who visited the Laverys drank in the bar sometimes and didn't search Cushla's room, saying it was just a formality. Her family had laughed about it afterward: *Imagine our Cushla making a bomb; she can't change a plug.* But this was different.

What are you looking at me like that for? she said.

Jimmy said something about you and Agnew being in cahoots. If that gormless eejit noticed, the whole lot of them did.

Jimmy keeps a raw egg in his breast pocket, she said. Nobody heeds a word that comes out of his mouth.

They heard Gina's footsteps on the stairs. Are youse right? she called. I hate being late for that lot.

I am warning you, Cushla, said Eamonn, his finger in her face. No tears. Not one fucking drop.

Outside, they got into his Capri. Gina made a show of dusting the passenger seat, tossing something over her shoulder. A legless Sindy doll. The news came on the radio.

A twenty-one-year-old man was shot dead by the British Army while attempting to booby-trap a bar in south Armagh.

A twenty-two-year-old man was shot dead in front of a mobile chip shop in the west of the city. It is believed the killing was part of an ongoing Republican feud.

The funeral of murdered Belfast barrister Michael Agnew is taking place this morning.

Eamonn flicked the radio off and briefly glared at Cushla in the rearview mirror. She turned away, resting her cheek against the window.

Jesus Christ, said Gina. Bloody mortifying, so it is, having to walk into a funeral when one of our ones did it.

*Our ones.* A Catholic.

It had said in the newspaper that the killing had all the hallmarks of an IRA assassination. Cushla thought of the documents on Michael's desk. She had only looked in one folder, the brutality case, but he'd told her he took on all kinds of work; who knew what was in the others.

They arrived ten minutes early, but the road leading to the church and the car park attached to it were packed. Gina was swearing softly.

Eamonn told them to get out while he found a space. Cushla helped her mother from the front seat—not that Gina needed it, but she was holding her arm out limply as if she required physical support. Cushla was glad of the fuss, terrified to turn and find she was being stared at by someone who recognized her. She needn't have worried; everyone else appeared to be inside.

Fidel, Minty, and Leslie were in the back pew. They had dressed for a funeral, toweling T-shirts and Glentoran jerseys swapped for out-of-fashion suits and kipper ties. They shoved along to make room for Gina and Cushla. Jimmy was two rows ahead. A choir began to sing a hymn. Cushla glanced over her shoulder. Eamonn was by the door. He looked hard at her and she twisted back around, drawing her hair across her face.

Beside her, Gina had begun a running commentary. Lovely flowers on the altar. Church of Ireland, not as bad as them Press Button Bs (Presbyterians). Cushla told her to shut up; Fidel, Minty, and Leslie were Press Button Bs. There were copies of the Book of Common Prayer lined on the ledge in front. Cushla picked one up and flipped through the pages. There was nothing in the proceedings she could connect to Michael. She had presumed he was not a churchgoer, but what did she really know about him? On Sunday mornings, she left his flat early so she could bring Gina to Mass; maybe he went home and brought his wife to Sunday service. Yet she could not picture him here, among this clear-eyed, good-living congregation, singing psalms and hymns.

But then the minister began to speak of Michael. The rugby he played as a youth, his selection for Ireland Schoolboys, a promising career cut short by injury. His academic record, his passion for the arts. His lifelong commitment to equality and justice. His pride in his son, Dermot. Cushla knew what was coming and could not prevent herself from raising her chin in time to see him turn slightly, to address his next line to the front pew: the great love he had for his wife, Joanna. Cushla was aware of someone at her back and glanced over her shoulder. Eamonn had stepped forward and was now directly behind her.

The final hymn ended. She was aware of movement at the front and, after what felt like an age, the coffin was carried down the aisle. A woman's voice began to sing, a cappella. Cushla focused her gaze on Jimmy O'Kane's old, shiny jacket, and looked up when she thought Michael had been borne past her, but they had paused for a moment to shift the weight of him. His son was just a couple feet away. He looked so very young, in his new suit, too young to be carrying his father's body. They began to move again. Oh dear God, Gina whispered. Joanna Agnew was slung between two women, her legs buckling like a wounded deer. Cushla lowered her head again, trying to keep out the words of the song, the soar of the woman's voice. She did not dare look up until Gina nudged her, indicating that it was their turn to file out.

A condolence book was open on a table just inside the door. Cushla joined the queue but, when Gina bent to sign her name, slipped outside and stood on the top step. The sun had come out. The crowd was encircling the hearse, Jim and Penny in the midst of it. She watched as the undertakers pushed a trolley bearing the coffin to the open door of the flower-filled vehicle. Dermot Agnew was slightly to the side, his mother clinging to him. You OK? said Eamonn.

Before Cushla could answer, Gina appeared and said, Right. We'll pay our respects.

No! said Eamonn and Cushla in unison.

The boys had come out and were standing solemnly in front of them. Awful sad, said Minty.

Aye. He was a gent, said Fidel, sparking a cigarette.

Leslie—sober—said nothing.

Jimmy was looking at Cushla as if he was about to say something.

She thought of the moment in *Ryan's Daughter* when the local half-wit made an exhibition of Rosy Ryan on the street, and it dawned on all the villagers that she'd been sleeping with the British soldier. Cushla linked her mother's arm and guided her down the steps toward the road. Eamonn had parked a couple hundred yards away. They were walking against the sun and she wished she had brought her sunglasses. The Capri was under a horse chestnut tree that was growing up through the pavement. When her eyes adjusted to the shade, she saw that Victor's MG was in front of Eamonn's. She looked back toward the church. Jane and Victor were approaching. Jane began speaking urgently to Victor, who raised his eyes to Cushla's. A look of contempt on his face. She took a step toward them, but felt Eamonn's hand on her arm. I need to talk to them, she said, trying to shrug him off.

The fuck you do, he said.

Let me go! she said, surprised at how loud she sounded.

He twisted her elbow and pushed her back toward his car.

Gina was standing very still by the passenger door as Eamonn shoved Cushla into the back seat. No one said a word on the way to the pub.


Cushla had forgotten how good Gina could be behind a bar, finding the right words, drawing the most dejected of drinkers around her. Poor Joanna was drugged to the eyeballs, she was saying, the young fella trying to keep her on her feet. A neighbor told the paper they didn't hear the shots but heard her screaming, three doors away.

The newspaper was on the counter, the print smudged from being passed hand to hand. Cushla picked it up. At the center of his obituary there was a photograph of Michael in his wig and gown, a little younger, his jaw defined, the jagged lines around his eyes shallow.

I'm glad not to have gone to the cremation, Gina went on. The big red curtains closing. The coffin disappearing into the floor. Like *Sunday Night at the London Palladium*, if you ask me. Lovely music, though. Someone sang a song as he was carried out. "When I Move to the Sky." There wasn't a dry eye.

Jimmy was blotting Guinness froth from the counter with the sleeve of his jacket. He licked his cuff and gave Cushla a sad wink. Eamonn was behind her, at the till. Look, you don't need to stay on, he said over his shoulder. Just get the chief mourner out of here. She's nearly drunk me out of Gordon's.

My car is at home.

Fuck, I forgot about that. Can you wait an hour or so for a lift?

She told him she would walk to the house and drive back down to collect Gina.

Eamonn handed Minty his change and frowned. What was that carry-on about with Victor McCusker? he said. How do you know him?

Cushla had forgotten Victor was well-known. He was at the Irish classes, she said.

Is there anything you're not telling me?

No.


I've no food in, said Gina from the larder. She emerged with a tin of tomato soup in her right hand and flicked on the radio with the other.

The Provisional IRA have claimed responsibility for the murder of Michael Agnew, alleging the barrister was a "willing agent of a most corrupt, rotten, and evil judicial system."

Our ones, I told you, said Gina. Bad bastards.

Mummy, please, said Cushla. She sat at the table, watching her mother totter between the cooker and the sink. When the bowl of soup was placed in front of her, her stomach lurched. There were pieces of bread suspended in it that had bloated into fleshy lumps.

Cushla forced in a spoonful and held it in her mouth until the nausea passed, before daring to swallow. She averted her eyes from it to keep it down.

You're gaunt getting, said Gina. A woman needs a bit of fat on her face.

Cushla lifted the spoon again, letting it hover an inch from her lips, then lowered it back into the bowl. I can't, she said. I'll try later.

Gina was staring at her. She didn't seem quite so drunk.

Cushla left the kitchen and went to her room. Michael's cardigan was on her pillow. She lay on top of the covers and put her face in it. For a few minutes he was beside her. Lemon soap, tobacco, whiskey. The toasty smell of him in the morning. It had not been so hard to keep herself together. Skulking at the back of a church during his funeral had just been a continuation of the lying and deceit of the past few months. And it wasn't as though she deserved better. Standing between her mother and the disheveled regulars had felt like her proper place. She didn't know what she had wanted to hear from Victor and Jane. Words of sympathy? An acknowledgment of her loss? That Michael had loved her?

She cried for a long time, not in whooping sobs as when her father died, some relief in the violence of them. The tears that were falling now were bubbling steadily, as if they might never stop. She lay without moving, watching the light outside fade.

Her mother was roaring for her. She must have fallen asleep. She pulled on the cardigan, wrapping it around herself, and went down the stairs. Gina passed her the receiver. It's that wee lad, she said.

Gerry? said Cushla into the receiver.

There was shouting in the background, jeering, a smashing sound.

Miss, it's Davy.

. . .

She could smell the smoke as she turned into the estate. The first few quadrants had a closed look, but as she neared the square the McGeowns lived in, all the front doors were open, as if their occupants had dropped what they were doing and walked out of their houses, drawn by some unseen force. She abandoned the car, unable to get past the crowd that had assembled on their street. There were people everywhere. The women who had stood in the garden scowling the day Seamie was attacked. The girl with the severe blusher with whom Gina'd had a stand-off. Trevor of the dirty rhymes.

Betty was on the path, holding Mandy by the sleeve, trying to pull her back, Seamie leaning against her, his face turned into her shoulder.

Where's Davy? said Cushla.

He was here a second ago, said Betty.

Cushla pushed through the crowd, calling his name. She looked at the house and saw him go through the open door. She ran up the path after him. In the sitting room, the smoke was thick, the room illuminated by the blazing foam of the settee. The net curtains were a molten drip across the windowsill and the wallpaper was rolling off the wall in sheets. She tried to call Davy's name, but her voice was choked with smoke and it came out like a scrawk. The staircase creaked heavily and she looked up to see him on the landing, his eyes squashed tight. He groped for the banister and stumbled down the stairs. She caught his hand on the fourth-last step and dragged him out the front door. A fireman pulled them away from the house and they fell on the raggy lawn, spluttering. A whooshing sound doused the crackling as the hose was pushed through the shattered window. A stench of wet soot wafted into the garden. The fire engine had arrived quickly, too quickly. She'd heard the fire brigade was sometimes called before a blaze was started, so as not to waste a good house by burning it to the ground. The police had arrived too, an officer making a pretense of clearing the crowd away. A halfhearted gesture; he knew some of them by name, and most of them stayed where they were.

Davy was gripping something in his arms, his chest heaving. Cushla gently unfolded his hands; he was holding his satchel. That was a brave and very stupid thing to do, she said. She was crying. She got to her feet and pulled him by the hand to his family. Is Tommy here? she asked Betty, who was clutching Davy to her.

That murdering wee bastard, a woman said behind them.

The crowd began to close in. Where was the policeman?

We need to get out of here, Cushla said, taking Davy's hand. Seamie's steps were slow. Betty was on one side of him, his arm over her shoulder. Mandy was on the other, her lips moving, as if she was praying. The crowd had begun to follow them, but another siren sounded, a momentary distraction, and Cushla managed to get them into her car.

Lock the doors, she said.

An RUC Land Rover pulled up alongside her as she started the engine. Two officers went toward the house, another came to her window and banged it, asking who they were, where they were going.

They're called McGeown, she said. They've just been burned out. Do you want them to stick about and watch or something?

He took her name and address and let them go. Mandy began weeping softly when they were out of the estate. Cushla looked in the rearview mirror, expecting to see Betty comforting her, but she was looking out the window, her face slightly to the side. Davy was rummaging in his satchel. He took something out and dangled it in front of his father, a paper bag that rattled.

I got your tablets, Daddy. You'll be able to sleep tonight.

.   .   .

Gina opened the front door as soon as Cushla pulled up. She led them to the kitchen, where she began buttering bread for sandwiches, making tea. Cushla got a bottle of Mr. Reid's orangeade from the larder and poured a glass each for Mandy and Davy, who were at the table. Seamie was sitting opposite them, his palms up, an oddly imploring gesture. Cushla pushed Gina's cigarettes and lighter at him and went to see if the tea was ready. Betty was by the kettle, describing the moment the window broke and the bottle smashed on the hearth, sending flames splashing across the carpet and up the side of the settee, where Davy and Mandy were sitting. The silence before the attack and the cheers after. They'd had to tip Seamie's chair back to haul him out of it and get him away from the fire. She said the police had come for Tommy at teatime.

Cushla remembered the woman lambasting them as they were trying to escape from the house. What about Tommy? she said.

He was lifted. They're saying he shot that barrister.

Gina glanced up at Cushla, eyebrows raised almost imperceptibly. Cushla turned her back to them and took a knife to the sandwiches, hacking them into misshapen triangles. How could Tommy have killed Michael? He could not even have known him. She put the plate on the table and took a cigarette from her mother's pack.

Why would they think Tommy had anything to do with it? said Gina.

I don't know. They near battered down the door when I was putting out the dinner. Three of them went upstairs and hauled him from his room by the hair.

Mandy and Davy were looking at the sandwiches, making no move to take one.

Maybe we should get everyone to bed, said Cushla.

Apart from Davy's schoolbag, they had brought no belongings. Seamie and Betty took Eamonn's old bed, and Cushla brought the kids into the spare room. The paraphernalia of her father's sickness was still there: a commode, boxes of pads, and disposable sheets. She worried that the beds would be dusty, but remembered Gina had changed them recently enough, on the last soup day. She switched on the bedside lamp and showed Davy and Mandy where she kept her old books, in a box in the wardrobe, in case they couldn't sleep. They were sitting on the edge of the bed in their clothes. She went to her room and found T-shirts for them to wear.

I know he didn't do it, Mandy was saying when Cushla returned. Our Tommy wouldn't kill anyone.

Downstairs, Gina poured tea. That she wasn't reaching for gin was a mark of the gravity of the situation they were now in. You know what people are going to think when they hear we took in that family? said Gina.

What was I supposed to do? I had no idea Tommy had been arrested. Do you think he did it?

How could he have? He was probably scooped.

Cushla cleared the table and began washing dishes. Dear God, she said in her head. If you can get us out of this I swear I will never look at a man again, never have a bad thought about anyone again, I will become a fucking nun if that'll keep you sweet, but please, please let this be a mistake.

When she lay down on her bed, her chest was pricklish. She could hear Davy was coughing too. She brought a glass of water to the spare room. He was sleeping nearest the window, and sat up when she put her hand on his shoulder.

Sip this, said Cushla.

Mandy turned to face them. I can't sleep, she said.

Any wonder. When I can't sleep I get up for a wee while, then have a second go at going to bed. Come downstairs. It might work.

They pulled their jeans on and followed her. She uncovered the tray of sandwiches and poured three glasses of milk. This time they ate.

Where are we going to live? said Davy suddenly.

I don't know, said Mandy. And all our stuff is there. Will we be able to get any of it back?

Something'll get sorted out really soon, said Cushla.

They went back to bed. Cushla stayed at the table and lit a cigarette. There had been a dreamlike quality to earlier. The baying mob, the smashing of glass, herself and Davy staggering from the burning house. It made no sense. How could Tommy possibly know Michael? She replayed every second she'd ever spent in the boy's company, frantic that she had mentioned Michael, that she had left an address somewhere, that he could have seen her with him. She began to fret that Davy was the link, but he was just a child, and on all the journeys to school she had never even said his name. Could Betty have gleaned something? But that was ridiculous. Even if she had, she was distraught about Tommy leaving school and hanging about with the cousins. Bad news, she had said. As for Seamie: he could hardly walk or talk, let alone mastermind an assassination. Yet Tommy had been arrested. Maybe there was a connection. And even if there wasn't, to the likes of Fidel and Leslie, the Laverys were harboring the family of a boy who had killed one of them. A customer in the bar. A Protestant.

On her way to bed, she put a foot on the bottom step, then turned to look at the phone. On Easter Sunday, Tommy had rung to thank her for the chocolate. She had said, Michael? And the evening he called to the house he had mentioned it, saying, That time I phoned you said "Michael?" She went upstairs, a feeling of dread growing in her stomach.

Could that have been enough information for Tommy? But she hadn't used his surname; "Michael" could be anybody. To distract herself, she tried to make a plan for the morning. Perhaps she could drive to the estate to see if any clothing or furniture could be salvaged, but she remembered the fury of the neighbors. Maybe she would call the school and the parochial house and try to get some emergency money for them; surely now they were homeless they were deserving of help. She would phone Gerry; he might know what to do. When the light came up, she went downstairs and outside to the garden. Wood pigeons were waking in Mr. Reid's apple tree, making a plaintive warble. She smoked a cigarette and told herself it would be all right. Tommy hadn't been charged, they would let him go. It was all just a mad coincidence. The McGeowns would be rehoused somewhere better.

The others came down at eight, entering the kitchen shyly. Gina busied herself with making tea and toast, scrambling eggs. Davy's face had been rubbed with a cloth but there was still a skiff of soot on his temple. Mandy ate a bowl of Rice Krispies, staring at each spoonful grimly before putting it in her mouth. Cushla stood at the worktop with a mug of tea and the Yellow Pages, looking for numbers that might be useful. The Housing Executive. The police. Social services, as a last resort. The front door opened, causing the kitchen door to swing. It was Eamonn, a clang that made Davy jump as Eamonn's keys hit the hall table.

You pair, Eamonn said, wagging two fingers between Cushla and Gina. A word.

They followed him to the hall.

They have to go, he said.

I'm going to try to get something sorted out for them this morning. They won't be here for long, just a few days.

Eamonn swung round at her, his hand open, as if he was going to hit her a slap. Gina's hand flew up and caught it.

They leave now, he said, looming into Cushla's face. You stupid cunt.

He took his keys from the console and made for the door, his fury so righteous he was almost graceful.

What do I do? said Cushla, as his car revved outside.

Do as he says, said Gina. And fast.

Cushla cleared the table, the breakfast things rattling in her hands, and went to the sink.

The ten o'clock news.

An eighteen-year-old man has been charged with the murder of Michael Agnew, the prominent Belfast barrister shot dead at his home last week.

A man, Betty said, and began to weep. Gina went to her, placing her hand on her shoulder and speaking into her ear. Betty looked around the table at her husband and children as she listened, then wiped the back of her hand across her face. Cushla met Davy's eyes for a moment. She turned her back to him and squirted Fairy liquid into the sink.

The gentle bustle of the town. Trays of bananas outside the greengrocer's, unripe to the point of Day-Glo. The giant cardboard ABBA in the window of the record shop, its Kodachrome bright faded to shades of blue and green. A trolley broken free from the chain outside the supermarket, spinning toward the road. The baker's fat, floury hand, placing a final meringue nest on top of a pyramid. Cushla was aware, as she drove, of the intensity with which the McGeowns were looking out the window. Faces pressed to the glass, as if for the last time.

The traffic on the bypass was light, schools closed for the summer, the morning rush hour over. At the roundabout she turned left and came along the road, past the boarding school where Michael had watched the hanged boy's body borne away on a stretcher, where his son, Dermot, had been when his mother was getting electric shocks and his father was fucking Cushla. The road narrowed and the terraces got tighter, the flags and bunting seeming to multiply. Cushla wondered if Betty had grown up in one of those houses, if she'd slept against a gable wall dabbed with a mural of the Somme or the Ulster Solemn League and Covenant. They passed the scrap of waste ground where Seamie had been left for dead. Beside her, he didn't flinch, but she glanced in the rearview mirror and saw Betty's face. A picture of utter despair.

They were at the perimeter of the Catholic enclave in which Seamie's brother lived. An RUC Land Rover was parked across the road, and the shipyard cranes towered over the rooftops. Betty got out and helped Seamie from the passenger seat, leading him across the pavement. He put his wounded hand against a wall and looked about him blankly.

Betty came back to the car and thanked her. Cushla began to apologize, but the woman held up her hand. Mandy murmured good-bye and slunk out, going to the wall where her father was waiting. Davy was still in the car, leaning between the gap.

Jesus, Davy, come here, she said. He clambered over the gearstick and onto the passenger seat.

I'll write you a letter, miss. I know your address off by heart.

Do you promise?

Swear to God.

You're such a great boy, Davy McGeown. It's been the joy of my life getting to know you.

He leaped across and put his arms around her neck. She held him so tight she was worried she was hurting him.

He got out of the car, and she pulled onto the road. She looked in the rearview mirror. Seamie, Betty, and Mandy had begun walking along the footpath. Davy was standing with his back to them, a hand held up, watching Cushla's car drive away.

T he house stank of smoke, not the usual cigarette smell that lin- gered in the carpets and curtains, but the oily, chemical fumes of burning nylon. She sniffed her top; it was coming from her. Upstairs, the bedspreads were neat, pillows fluffed and in their place. Cushla went around the bed in the spare room to open a window. Davy's satchel was on the floor, the leather smoky in places. She sat on the bed and picked it up. Something was jangling. She rooted around and found his Sports Day medals and the rosary beads she had bought him in Dublin. The Communion missal, his name written in joined-up writing she hadn't begun to teach them yet. His spelling notebook, a tables book, *Tommy McGeown Esq.* written on the inside page, crossed out, replaced by Mandy's name, then Davy's. She opened his English exercise book. On the last page was the letter.

*Dear Jim'll*

*Please can you fix it for my daddy to get better and for our Tommy to come home and for Miss Lavery to get the one she loves.*

*Yours sincerely*
*Davy McGeown*

*PS Jonathan says your hair is weird, but I think it's nice.*

# 27

They arrived on the third day. Two uniformed officers, the woman slight, her blond fringe flicked out at the sides; the man heavy, with skin tags on his eyelids and a liverish complexion. They asked her if she would accompany them to the station. Gina came out of the kitchen and stood a few feet back, by the hall table. Cushla looked at her mother, pleading with her eyes that she challenge them, insist on going with her, but Gina said nothing.

She sat in the back seat beside the female officer, who kneaded her cuticles the whole way down the road. The driver sucked a sweet and stopped opposite the parochial house to let them out. Cushla lowered her head, knowing there was a clear view from its bay windows to the police station.

The building was small, in direct correlation to the perceived security threat, further dwarfed by the battlements: high fence, barbed-wire Slinkies perched on top of it. A lone officer sat in a sentry box at the gate. Cushla used to know all the police in the town, but they moved the personnel around often now for safety, and they never stayed in one place for long.

A noticeboard on the wall, plastered with flyers and posters. How to check under your car for a bomb. The confidential telephone number. Cushla had been here before, getting permits signed for flag days or sponsored walks. Once, she had gone to make a complaint about a customer who'd come in with a gun and threatened her father. It turned out to be a toy, which gave the officer at the desk no end of amusement. But the incident had caused her father an angina attack and a fearfulness from which he never quite recovered.

The female officer pushed open a fire door and told her to walk to the end of the corridor. A man was waiting for her, half in, half out of a doorway. She was inches from him when she recognized him. It was Disco Peeler. She had only seen him in poor light, and he was fairer than she remembered, almost ginger at his sideburns and mustache. Handsome, in a dull, wholesome way, but something unappealing in his deliberate movements, his measured voice.

A Formica table, blue like the worktops at home, bolted to the floor. Two chairs one side, one on the other. Four walls, at the base of which were scuff marks, too high for heels, too low for knees. At kicking height.

He pulled out a chair for her. Cushla, he said, if I may.

She sat down, trying to stay still, but felt her shoulder go up. It must have looked like a shrug. There was a manila folder on the table, an ashtray. A tape machine that he didn't turn on. He caught her looking at it.

You haven't been arrested, he said.

Does that mean I can go?

He intertwined his fingers and smiled a smile that chilled her. We're hoping you can help us.

Who is we? There is just you and me.

Tell me about your relationship with Michael Agnew.

He came into the bar sometimes.

Did you ever meet him outside the bar?

He asked me to join an Irish-language conversation group.

He took a photograph from the folder and turned it over, pushing it toward her. She and Michael on the footpath on the perimeter of the barracks, lit by a streetlamp. He was swinging the bottle of brandy by the neck, his face lined with laughter.

To the home of James and Penelope Scott, he said. Cushla had put on a long-sleeved Rupert the Bear T-shirt under the cardigan and had not washed her face since the previous morning. He was looking at her with amusement, as if it was ludicrous that she could have been in the company of people like that.

Yes.

Did you meet him elsewhere?

No.

He laid another photograph on the table. Cushla talking, her mouth slightly open, a furrow between her eyebrows as if she was giving off. Michael's face turned to hers. The look on his face winded her. He had loved her.

She took a cigarette from the crushed pack in her pocket. Disco Peeler leaned forward and sparked a gold lighter under it. Who took these? she said, blowing the smoke through her nostrils.

Were you in a sexual relationship with Michael Agnew?

Why don't you just show me the picture? she said. I presume you have a really good one.

Did you visit him at his home?

The flat? You tell me. It was agonizing, how he was looking at her, watching the words form on her lips. She felt her left hand fold across herself to grip her right forearm, the other hand holding the cigarette close to her mouth.

He smiled and laid down another photograph. She and Michael were near the dining table. Her mouth wide like a yawn, his lips pushed out and almost touching hers. Her bare knee was clinging to his arse. It had been taken the day the car had reversed onto the gravel; from the light and angle, the photographer had been across the street, under one of the trees. Christ, she heard herself say softly.

Have you ever visited his family home?

She ground out the cigarette. Her mouth was dry. She tried to wash it with saliva, but it wouldn't muster. I suppose you have a photograph of that as well, she said. Even though I never visited his family home.

He was enjoying her discomfort, his fingers flexing playfully over the folder. Your car was seen outside the house on the night of May the twenty-fifth.

I was upset that I couldn't see him. I drove out the road to check if he'd gone home.

Michael Agnew was shot dead in his family home, he said, pulling the folder toward himself.

She had begun to cry, tears cooling on her chin, the salt itching her cheeks. She tugged a cuff down and held it in her fist, wiping the taut cotton across her face. How come youse didn't stop him getting shot, she said, when youse were following him all the time?

He didn't even blink. What was the nature of your relationship with Tommy McGeown? he said.

I don't have a relationship with Tommy McGeown. His wee brother was a pupil of mine.

You befriended the family, it seems.

Davy McGeown is a seven-year-old boy. His father was assaulted and I tried to help him.

You visited the house on numerous occasions.

Over Easter I sat with the kids while their mother was visiting their father in hospital. I gave Davy lifts to and from school.

Did you ever discuss your relationship with Michael Agnew with Tommy McGeown?

No! He's a teenager. He hardly talks. And he hasn't been around for the last while.

He opened the folder and took out a small black notebook; the one Tommy had kept in his back pocket. He opened it and held it up like a caroler. Did you give him your number?

Yeah. So he could ring me if they needed shopping done.

He's written something on the page opposite. Would you like me to read it to you?

No. I wouldn't.

Oh, it's quite flattering, he said, clearing his throat theatrically. "I actually talked to her today. Not the usual *how's yer da?* and *do you need any messages?* About books and stuff. I couldn't stop looking at her. She caught me once, and smiled at me. Until Mandy ruined it, calling me a kid. Jesus. Looking up the stairs at me with those eyes."

That's just daft, she said, it means nothing. So what if he was looking at me?

I'm sure I can find a better example, he said, bending the book, the pages flipping past as if he was a card sharp. He stopped abruptly. Here we are. There is an entry from Easter Sunday, an account of a phone call. "She called me Michael. Who the fuck is this Michael?" Oh, and after an encounter on the doorstep, he wrote this: "All she sees is a teenager, but there are things she doesn't know about me."

She had wondered if Tommy fancied her but had thought little of it. At that age she had been prone to brief, extravagant infatuations with boys she didn't dare speak to, Eamonn's mates, the sons of her father's friends. But "there are things she doesn't know about me"? What did that mean?

Michael phoned me sometimes in the evenings. I presumed it was him. I never gave his surname.

You spoke to Tommy McGeown two days ago, after the murder.

There's so much he needs to tell you, apparently. When you two go for a drink.

You're twisting everything, Cushla said. I told him I'd maybe go out with him, because I didn't want to hurt his feelings.

How did the McGeown family come to reside in your house?

They stayed for one night! Davy phoned me to tell me their house was on fire and I drove up and took them away. I didn't know Tommy had been lifted.

It's not looking great, he said, replacing the notebook in the folder.

You don't seriously believe I had anything to do with it?

You are the connection between the victim and his killer.

It's a fucking coincidence! she said, getting to her feet. His lip had curled in distaste at the sound of the curse. Don't swear, thingy, she thought.

Sit down, Miss Lavery, he said.

She lowered herself onto her hands to keep them from shaking. Look, I know I didn't do anything.

If there's a connection, I'll find it.

What happens now?

It's up to you.

What does that mean?

You could stand in the corner and take your clothes off.

What?

He laughed. I can keep you here for up to seven days.

She looked at the door. He had closed it when they came in. He had not taken a single note. There hadn't been a sound, not so much as a footstep on the corridor, as if he'd been left to do what he liked.

I haven't done anything.

He sat back. And then he smiled. Thanks for your cooperation, Miss Lavery.

Are you letting me go?

You were free to leave at any time.

He walked along the corridor behind her, soles slapping lightly off the floor. He reached in front of her to open the fire door, making her dip under his arm to avoid touching him. His shirt smelled of mown grass. She walked out of the station and into the sunlight. As she crossed High Street, she fancied that a curtain twitched at Slattery's window. Along the school railings, left at the corner, past the chipper. No basket, no keys, no car, as if she'd been divested of who she was.

Why had they been following Michael? Standing outside his flat, taking photographs. Noting the cars that passed his house. Was it because of her, or had they been shadowing him before she came along? There was something harried about him, in the final weeks, that she had put down to the strain of moving between two homes, two women. She had spoken to Michael about Tommy but, aside from stupidly saying his name on the phone, was sure she had never mentioned Michael to the boy, or to any of the McGeowns. It had seemed that her affair with Michael and her befriending of Davy had been running concurrently, but separately. Now she could see that they were twisted together, each informing the course of the other. One by one, she undid each event, each decision, each choice. If Davy had remembered to put on a coat. If Seamie McGeown had stayed on the dole for another month and not found himself alone on a dark street, a few pints of stout in his bladder. If Michael Agnew had not walked through the door of the pub on a quiet night in February in his white shirt. If Betty had persuaded Tommy to stay in school. What if she was the conditional clause? What if Michael Agnew would still be alive if he had not met Cushla Lavery?

She had reached the house. She pressed the doorbell. Gina let her in and stood twisting her hands. Eamonn had phoned. Twice. Half the town saw her going into the RUC station and the other half saw her coming out, the hair hanging round her. She was to stay out of the bar. Her voice petered out and she was looking beyond Cushla. There's somebody outside, she said.

Cushla turned the handle and opened the front door. Slattery and Bradley were on the step.

It didn't take you pair long to mobilize, said Cushla. She walked into the sitting room. The men followed her.

I presume I need to be sitting down for this, she said, flopping onto the settee.

Slattery was looking around the room as if he was casing it. See, we have a color TV as well, Cushla said, pointing at the set in the corner, although it's probably not as snazzy as the one you swindled out of my father when he was dying.

Bradley fingered his collar, his bald head turning pink. We have serious concerns, he said.

I'm all ears, said Cushla.

She had befriended a family of ne'er-do-wells, despite being advised against it; in fact, she had harbored the family even after one of them had been arrested for murder. Community relations in the town were delicate and her position on the school staff was not, at present, tenable. There would be an emergency meeting of the board of governors later and Cushla should expect the worst.

You're sacking me?

We feel it would be best if you took a year off.

Are you not going to say anything? Gina said, stepping toward Slattery. He looked at her coldly and turned away.

# 28

Gina laid the tray on the bed. There's post for you, love, she said.

It felt strange to be mothered, especially now, when Cushla had never felt less like a child. She rummaged among the blankets for her cigarettes and lighter. The first drag sickened her, but she held it in her lungs until the nicotine began to flicker through her limbs. Gina had tugged the curtains apart and was lifting the sash window. The sun cast long shadows across the room. The summer was ending. Cushla had hardly noticed it pass.

Gina left the door ajar and began running the vacuum cleaner around the landing. Cushla lurched from the bed and drew the curtains again, standing at the edge of the window frame and moving with the panels of fabric. Even as she held the material she knew the act was absurd. When they came back for her they would not scale the front of the house, SAS-style. They would ring the bell and Cushla would walk obediently to their car.

It had been twenty-seven days since they had questioned her; thirty since she dumped the McGeowns at the edge of Short Strand; thirty-five since Tommy McGeown emptied a gun into Michael's body. There was no word of Tommy's trial, although she had played it out in her head, in a physical space she had made months ago, in daydreams of Michael; a room bright with television lights and tiered with ma-hogany benches, lifted from *Rumpole* and *Crown Court*. Tommy in the dock. On bad days, she is there too, beside him. Mostly she is tak-ing the stand, turning to face the terraces of spectators. They are all there. Joanna Agnew, held up by Dermot. Jim and Penny, Jane. Victor, sometimes with them, more often among the press. Betty McGeown, alone. All except Michael, who has been reduced to photographs, bal-listic analysis, autopsy reports. Plastic pouches of punctured, bloodied clothing.

She licked her index finger and lifted a piece of ash from his cardi-gan. His smell was long gone, but she liked to wake with its stitches printed on her skin. Blackberry, honeycomb, diamond. Sometimes the turning row where the cable crossed over itself. She reached for the ash-tray. Beside it, Davy's missal and medals had joined *The Black Prince* and the key and the bar of soap. The novena Michael had read in jest, that didn't stop him from getting killed. A Havishamesque assemblage. She understood, now, her mother's grief. The heaviness that pulled her down into the center of the bed, that made the smallest task or move-ment feel like an Olympian feat. Washing. Eating. Standing up.

She had seen no one but Gina and Eamonn since Gerry left, al-though she kept out of Eamonn's way when he called round with the children—there was a third one now, another cherubic girl. Cushla stood at her bedroom door to listen to her mother and brother speak. The business was trickling down the tubes. Leslie drank in the bar the soldiers drank in. Minty no longer had a wave for Gina in the town. Fidel still came in the odd time, with the hoods he used to meet in pri-vate above the shop. They sat at a table like the soldiers, and after they left Eamonn found cigarettes ground into the carpet, black molten holes on the upholstery. The Catholics had drifted away too, not want-ing to be seen to condone their sheltering of the McGeowns. Only

Jimmy still came in every evening. Because he wasn't right in the head, Gina said.

There was a postcard on the tray, an image of a straight, red, metal bridge straddling a river, a cathedral rising on the bend beyond. Gerry and his friends had left France and driven to Girona. He had written, *Bridge designed by Gustave Eiffel, a dry-run for the tower.* There was a letter too, in a blue Basildon Bond envelope. Her address was printed in a hand she didn't recognize, but as she opened the folded page, her heart leaped. It was from Davy. Before Gerry left, she had asked him to find out where the boy was, but short of knocking on doors in Short Strand, he didn't know where to look. Once, Cushla had driven toward the east and made it within sight of the spot at which she had dumped them. But the flags and bunting on one side were too florid, the walls on the other too oppressive, and she drove away, the panic on her again, afraid she was being followed. Davy had laid out the letter the way she had shown them in school. *Dear Miss Lavery, I hope you are keeping well.* She smiled to herself, but as she read on her joy faded. They hadn't found a new house. Davy had been placed with a foster family. Mandy was somewhere else.

Who's the letter from? Gina said, coming into the room and lifting the tray.

Cushla handed it to her. Gina replaced the tray and sat on the bed to read it. Jesus, Mary, and Joseph, she said.

I did that, said Cushla.

What do you mean?

I asked Bradley to help them and he reported Betty to social services.

That's not your fault.

It's all my fault.

I think you should see Dr. O'Hehir, said Gina.

So he can drug me to the eyeballs with whatever pills he gives you?

You don't eat. You haven't left the house in weeks. Maybe you could do with a wee prescription.

I'm not actually mad, you know. I've lost my job. I'm barred from our pub. The whole town thinks I'm a Republican sympathizer. There's a limited number of places I can go.

This carry-on, said Gina, has to stop.

OK, said Cushla. Maybe I'll go for a dander down High Street. I might call into the police and ask if they've found any evidence against me. Then I'm going to buy a Ninety-Nine and have a chinwag with Fidel and his ma.

Gina put the letter on the nightstand. It's not your fault. And Michael wasn't your fault either.

You knew?

I saw you getting into his car.

Why did you not say anything?

Because I was hoping to God it would play itself out. And Gerry's a nice wee fella, but I didn't fall for that, she said, sitting on the edge of the bed.

Cushla was filled with a strange euphoria. We were being followed, she said. The RUC have photographs. Of me in his car. Of us in his flat. I was interviewed by a peeler who spun records at a disco in the school. He told me if I didn't take my clothes off he'd hold me for seven days.

Dear God. I should have gone with you, Gina said quietly, her eyes downcast. There was a faint scent of gin.

What am I going to do about Davy?

There's nothing you can do about any of it. But you can't take to the bed for the rest of your life. I'm going to run you a bath and you're going to dress in something other than that bloody cardigan. It's practically walking about by itself.

Gina left the room. Cushla read the letter again and put it back in the envelope, placing it on the nightstand with the other things. In the bathroom, she stripped and climbed into the tub. The water was deep. She shampooed her hair and bent her knees, lying back, hair and suds floating like seaweed and spume. She reclined against the cold enamel. Her body had changed, bones jutting at her hips, stomach concave. She liked how it looked: pale and empty, the outside reflecting the inside.

When she went downstairs, Gina was mopping the floor. There was a wheaten loaf on the table, a slice of butter in its Pyrex dish. Shelled boiled eggs, slices of cooked ham from the butcher. Two custard tarts and two gravy rings. Gina left the mop protruding unsteadily from the bucket and crossed the kitchen to the table. She sat heavily. Eat, she said.

They were like a tag team, taking turns to fall apart.

Cushla spooned the filling from a custard tart and sipped at a cup of tea. She pulled her basket toward her. The camera was still there. She removed the film and held it between her thumb and finger, looking at it for a moment before leaving the house.

She turned the key in the ignition and nothing happened. On the third attempt it seemed to start then puttered to silence. She tried once more, worried she had flooded the engine, but it shuddered to life. She drove down the road, parking by the parochial house. She found herself half running along the footpath, her head down. There were BACK TO SCHOOL stickers in the draper's window, mannequin children wearing the uniforms of the Protestant schools. Someone had dressed Johnny the Jig in a blue anorak. In the chemist's, she left the film to be developed, and was aware of the assistant hesitating, registering her name as she spelled it.

Past the slip road that led to the pub, the ruined priory, onto the dual carriageway and eventually left, down a tree-shaded road. To her right and left, grand merchants' houses shaded by sycamore and mountain ash. The car park by the beach was almost full. A dog barking, thin nervy yaps, in the car beside hers. The tide was rising. She crossed the bank; the marram grasses were paling already, bleached by the summer she had missed. The sand sucked her feet down as she walked to the edge of the shore. The water was coming in fast. A wave rushed over her shoes, filling them with the brutal cold of the lough.

She went back toward the car park into a wind from the north that seasoned her lips with salt. Behind the beach, a wood. At its edge, a couple of teenagers lying in the grass. The boy's coat was spread beneath them, his mouth at the girl's ear. Her face was turned up to the sun, his hand working under her jumper. As Cushla passed, the girl's eyes rolled upward. It filled her with longing.

She took the path through the trees to the old viaduct, ivy snaking up its stone arches, following the pattering sound of the waterfall. It was only a few feet high, a gentle flood. She turned back. A man was walking toward her. She knew his face, perhaps from the bar, perhaps she taught one of his kids. Maybe he was following her. What if he was? They might as well come for her.

# 29

A beer delivery had been left in front of the anchor, five kegs. A couple of months earlier there would have been twenty. The front door was propped open with a stool.

Come in and talk to him. It's killing me that youse aren't speaking, said Gina.

No, said Cushla.

He's not as angry as he was, Gina said. As she prepared to leave the car, Eamonn came out. He glowered at Cushla and turned a keg on its side, rolling it across the tarmac with his toe.

He looks pretty furious to me, to be honest, said Cushla.

Gina sighed and got out, a housecoat and bundle of orange dusters and a chamois cloth tucked under her arm.

Cushla stopped at the chemist's to collect the film, though she was unable to meet the eye of the assistant. She drove a mile out of town to a filling station on the Bangor Road. She sat in her car looking through the window of the shop, waiting until it was empty before going in. She bought cigarettes and a newspaper, dropping the change the boy behind the counter handed her. A car had pulled up at the pumps outside. A man got out and opened the cover of his petrol tank. He was tall, with sandy hair. She began to panic and rushed from the shop, leaving coins scattered across the floor. When she was behind the wheel, the doors locked, she looked up. It wasn't Disco Peeler.

She went back the way she had come, bypassing the town, and along the dual carriageway. At the roundabout, she turned left, following the perimeter fence of the barracks and then making the series of turns that took her onto the hill road. The summer had been warm. There was a rancid lushness about the hedgerows, the gorse past flowering, its foliage almost black. She pulled into the lay-by and opened the paper. There was a small mention of Tommy's trial on the front page, a note directing the reader to a double-page spread. The feature included an opinion column on the peril of working in the judiciary, as a couple of judges had been shot the previous year; an article noting that most of those appearing in court on terror charges were under twenty, and condemning the men who recruited teenagers to avoid getting their own hands dirty; and an account of the trial in the center. Tommy's image was a mug shot, almost pixilated, like the ones she had seen in Michael's folder. He had the lean, bold look he'd worn the last time she saw him, but his eyes gave him away. They were bright with fear. Tommy had refused to recognize the court, offered no defense, answered no questions. He was convicted on the basis of evidence described as forensic, circumstantial, and damning. He had been working on a house opposite Michael's, repairing a path. It began to rain and, knowing the family was out, Michael asked the boy in for a cup of tea. Cushla pictured him moving between the kettle and the sink, taking down cups, hunting for biscuits. The kindly way he would have spoken to an awkward boy like Tommy, trying to put him at ease. What must Tommy have thought as he sat there? Had he warmed to the man who had asked him in, had he answered his questions, laughed at his attempts at jokes? Had Michael asked him about school, told him he had a son his age? How long had Tommy sat there before his eyes came to rest on a photograph on the dresser of Michael in his wig and gown, wrongly deducing that the man who was making him a cup of tea was a judge? Had he seen the opportunity then or had it come to him later, when he was telling his cousin about his working day? Tommy McGeown with all his rage. Desperate to belong. The thrill he must have felt when he was handed a gun and told to go back and kill him.

She got out of the car and sat on the bonnet to smoke a cigarette, leaving the package of photographs on the passenger seat. The lambs she and Michael had seen skittering in the field were waddling now, fat on the grass. There had been no connection after all. It was just bad luck, the sort of thing that happened here all the time.

# 30

An eighteen-year-old has been sentenced to life imprisonment for the murder of Michael Agnew, the prominent Belfast barrister. Thomas Ronald McGeown, of Hollyburn Estate, showed no reaction as he was led away from the dock.

An incendiary device exploded in a public house in County Down, causing extensive damage. No one has claimed responsibility.

Gina was by the fence, on which Mr. Reid was resting his bony elbows. He had knocked on the front door the previous night, offering help he couldn't give, reducing Gina to tears. Gerry had called later, carrying sugared almonds and a half brick of lavender soap, gifts from his summer abroad. No one else had come near them.

Cushla went to the table and took the wallet of photographs from her basket, tucking it into the pocket of Michael's cardigan. She grabbed her keys from the hall table as she left the house.

The radio came on when she started the car. The news bulletin had finished. They were in for an Indian summer; typical, the presenter said, a hot spell on the way after the school holidays. At the bottom of the road she glanced to the left, in the direction of St. Dallan's; she had been replaced by a girl from Ballyclare called Bride, according to Gerry, who claimed to have the gift of tongues.

Cushla turned the dial to another station. "Superstar" by the

Carpenters was playing. She sang along, but as it built to the chorus realized it had been written from the point of view of a despondent groupie.

Fuck up, Karen, she said, switching it off.

The pub car park was empty; Eamonn's Capri had taken much of the impact of the explosion and was on its way to a breaker's yard. To the right of the door—shattered windows aside—it was almost as if nothing had happened. To the left it was a different story. Part of the gable wall was gone, and the upstairs lounge resembled a squalid doll's house. Cushla took in a deep breath and went inside.

The carpet squelching beneath her feet, the high stools at the counter tossed aside, as if there had been a brawl. Shards of plasterboard dangling from the ceiling. The jade-green upholstery brackish from the firehoses, pieces of colored glass scattered on the tables like boiled sweets. Behind the counter, bottles fizzling on the lino, oozing beer and ginger ale and stout. The shelves had collapsed. She began to lift pieces of debris, moving them aside with her hands and feet. She found the small plinth on which the whiskey dogs had sat; the Scottish border terrier was intact, a pair of chalky paws all that remained of the Westie. The bottle of green chartreuse. The Babycham fawn, which had under-eye circles of smoke.

Eamonn came in from the back, carrying a refuse sack. Have you managed to save anything? he said.

A few bits. She forced her chin up to look at him. I'm so sorry, Eamonn.

You might have done us a favor, he said. We were losing money.

People could have been killed.

They weren't.

The bomb had been left in an empty beer keg to the left of the building. The police received an anonymous phone call fifteen minutes before it detonated and the bar had been evacuated. Eamonn had stood in the tunnel between two RUC men and watched it explode. Somebody's looking after you, one remarked. Nobody gets that much notice. Fidel had not been seen in over a week and the Laverys were inclined to think he was behind the leniency, for that's what it was; in a place like this, no deaths was a gift.

Do you have a plan? she asked him.

Aye. I'm going to put the place on the market and move the fuck away from here. Down south, maybe.

We'll miss you.

Oh, you're coming too, so I can keep an eye on you. Fucking head case.

The door opened. A figure entered and paused for a moment, surveying the damage. The power had been turned off and it was hard to see. That'll be the insurance assessor, said Eamonn, narrowing his eyes. I'll deal with him, but be sure to exaggerate if he asks you any questions.

Cushla crouched and began to pick over the debris again.

Quite a mess for such a small quantity of explosives, a man's voice said. She looked up to see who had spoken. Victor was standing over her, in his war-reporter jerkin with all the pockets. It had looked silly in Penny's kitchen, but was appropriate attire for a bomb site. She got to her feet. Eamonn was behind him. I'll be outside, he said.

Are you looking for the inside story? said Cushla, wiping her hands on the back of her jeans.

No death or mutilation. It wouldn't be much of a scoop, he said. There was a bottle of Jameson on the counter. He inclined his head at it. Any chance of a drink?

She found two unbroken glasses and poured. Why are you here, Victor?

Can we sit down?

OK, she said. If there's a stick of furniture that's not ruined. She followed him, bringing the bottle too. They sat in the banquette in the corner that the soldiers had favored.

He lit a cigar. I gave you a hard time, he said.

I didn't give a great account of myself. Hanging out of somebody's husband.

That's not what bothered me. I thought Michael was drawing too much attention to himself.

They questioned me. The police. They'd been following him, taking pictures. She thought of the one taken in the flat and lowered her eyes. Perhaps Victor had seen them.

I heard.

God. Is there anything you don't know, Victor?

He let out a sigh. I know more than I want to know, he said. They were leaning on him to drop a police brutality case. I tried to warn him.

With all that going on he could have done without me.

I thought that. But he was happy, the last few months. You made him happy.

I loved him. But I couldn't tell him. And I don't know why the hell I'm telling you.

I'd say he had a fair idea, he said, smiling.

How's Jane?

Pregnant, he said. Early days.

I hope it works out.

So do I. What will you do? he said.

Leave.

He clinked his drink against hers. Wherever you end up, think of the rest of us poor bastards, stuck in this hellhole.

After he left, she stayed at the table and took the paper wallet from her pocket. It had been in her basket for weeks, but each time she looked at it she remembered Disco Peeler laying Polaroids on blue Formica. Images taken without her knowledge, each more shameful than the last. She took a slug of whiskey and peeled back the sticker from the pouch.

Davy, his arms around Johnny the Jig's neck. He had said he didn't feel much like smiling that day, but the eyes in the serious little face were bright. The photographs Cushla had taken in the park were overexposed, making it hard to distinguish who was who. The ones Davy took were magic. Cushla and Gerry on the blanket, a shaft of light falling across them. Images of the other children as they played, full of verve and motion. Next, the photographs Eamonn had taken. Fidel drinking vodka and bitter lemon, still flush with the money Cushla had paid for the ice creams; Fidel, Leslie, and Minty with their thumbs up; the three of them with Jimmy, the elliptical bump of an egg discernible in his pocket.

And the last one. Michael standing at the counter. He was smiling, although the quarrel they'd had was still on him, in the stooped, defeated set of him. Cushla's hands were just in the frame, slipping a beer mat under his whiskey, his outstretched fingers almost touching her wrist. She looked at the doorway. For a moment Michael Agnew was there, his broad body turning away from her. And then he was gone.

# 2015

All the times Cushla pictured this moment she had seen herself bending to a small boy, but a middle-aged man is standing in front of her. Beneath the glasses his eyes are very blue, not the violet shade of Tommy's, but the icy color of his mother's. He is dressed carefully: navy peacoat, a denim shirt beneath a maroon sweater that reminds her of the day she soaked him. The skittishness is gone, she thinks, until he takes her hand and swings it.

I looked for you, Davy, she says, a mortifying old-lady quiver in her voice.

She had looked for him on the street, in every classroom. She made Gerry trawl each new edition of the telephone directory for their name. She taped Tommy's funeral, pausing and replaying it again and again, searching for Davy among the mourners but, in the press of police and news crews as shots were fired over the coffin, could not find him.

This is the man our Tommy killed, he says, pointing at the sculpture.

I know.

What are the chances?

Cushla knows that it is merely happenstance that has placed them, in this moment, beside Penny's gauzy monument to Michael Agnew, that there is no more reason to it than there was to the ghastly fortuity that placed Tommy in Michael's kitchen one wet morning. And yet.

Are you still Miss Lavery? he says.

I've been Mrs. McTiernan for a long time, she says. And call me Cushla, for God's sake.

I'll try, he says. I thought you'd marry Mr. Devlin.

Mr. Devlin is in a civil partnership with a Mr. Mulgrew. He's still my best friend.

Do you have kids?

Three. And four grandchildren. What about you?

A daughter. She's angry with me. I wasn't up to it at the time.

Remorse, so natural to her it is like breathing, swells in her chest. Is it my fault, she almost blurts, that you were sent away and didn't learn how to be a father? He sees her anguish, lets it take. For a moment she is afraid he will turn on her, but he squeezes her hand. She doesn't know whether to apologize or thank him.

We see each other a bit now. It's a start, he says.

Voices rising at the far end of the room. The guide in the moss-green dress has broken away from the group and is walking toward them. Davy lets go of Cushla gently, placing his hand on the girl's arm, around the gorse tattoo. Ellen, he says. This is Miss Lavery.

Davy told me about you, she says, picking a fleck of lint from his sleeve, straightening his collar. He accepts her attentions shyly.

Are you rushing off, miss? he says.

I will if you call me "miss" one more time.

Ellen's laugh echoes around the room. She says she has one more tour to give before she's finished and will meet them in the café in an hour.

She's lovely, says Cushla when she's gone.

She's young. You probably think I'm a dirtbird.

No, says Cushla. I don't.

She looks at the shrouded figure one last time. The tight, precise weft of the old linen is visible through the resin, its folds voluptuous, as if it has been starched. She reaches for it, expecting it to yield to her touch, but it is hard and cold. The cast is hollow. It conveys a sense of emptiness, as if a body has stepped out of it. Cushla moves her hand to the shoulder, expecting, for a mad moment, to feel a bump at the collarbone, but it is not there. She runs her fingers down along the right arm and covers the hand with hers.

I was going to check out the John Lavery stuff, says Davy. Would you like that?

I would love that, Davy McGeown.

# ACKNOWLEDGMENTS

I appear to have written a novel. Very many people helped me.

I am grateful for the ACES Award I received from Arts Council of Northern Ireland in 2019, which gave me both vital financial assistance and a shot of self-belief. Thanks to the Achill Heinrich Böll Association for a residency in their cottage on beautiful Achill in November 2019. Thanks to Paul Maddern of the magical River Mill Writing Retreat, where I spent way more time than I am willing to admit; delightfully, no matter how hard I worked, the calorie count always exceeded the word count.

Thanks to director Glenn Patterson and all my friends at the Seamus Heaney Centre, Queen's University Belfast, for support and understanding. In 2021, I was one of the inaugural Ciaran Carson Writing and the City Fellows there, and it is particularly humbling to have been allowed to quote from "The Irish for No" in *Trespasses*; thanks to the Estate of Ciaran Carson and Peter Fallon of Gallery Press for their generosity in this regard.

The writing of this book began in earnest in March 2019. Una Mannion was with me from early scratchings on the page to literally typing responses to the copyedits for me when I was too sick to do it myself. Without her, there simply wouldn't be a book. I inflicted the final draft of *Trespasses* on Michael Nolan; his consideration and good opinion meant the world to me. Susan McKay's nordie female gaze and attention to detail were invaluable in the last stages of writing. (She is also some craic.) Thanks to Réaltán Ní Leannáin for putting manners on my mediocre Gaeilge at very short notice and for not making me feel thick.

*Trespasses* opens and closes with an imaginary sculpture inspired by the work of Sligo-based artist Bettina Seitz. I am indebted to Bettina for inspiration, and for describing how she makes her beautiful ghosts.

Thanks to Margaret Halton, John Ash, Rebecca Sandell, and Patrick Walsh of PEW Literary. Very special thanks to my unbelievably brilliant and lovely agent, Eleanor Birne; what a completely insane three years we've had.

To Sarah-Jane Forder: not only are you an exceptional copy editor, but your patience and kindness are boundless.

Thanks to Rebecca Saletan, my wonderful editor at Riverhead, for a massive injection of clarity and energy in the last stretch, and to Catalina Trigo.

So many people at Bloomsbury helped me with this book. I am grateful to you all, but thanks especially to the unbelievably amazing Ros Ellis; there is no one I would rather get on the next train with. Huge thanks also to Stephanie Rathbone for being great at everything, Lauren Whybrow for keeping all the balls in the air with such humor, and Cormac Kinsella for seeing no problems where I see many. Thanks to Greg Heinimann for yet another staggeringly beautiful cover . . . it made me fall in love with the title. As for you, Alexis Kirschbaum, my brilliant editor, thank you for having a vision of what this book could be when I could not always see it myself, and for making me want to do my very best. You are something else.

Lastly, thanks to my family and friends for everything. I would name you all, but somehow there are more of you than ever. Which, considering I have hardly left the house in two years, is a bit mad.